All or Nothing at All

All or Nothing at All

Patricia Abbott

Five Star • Waterville, Maine

First Edition
First Printing: July 2004

Set in 11 pt. Plantin by Ramona Watson.

Printed in the United States on permanent paper.

Library of Congress Cataloging-in-Publication Data

Abbott, Patricia.
    All or nothing at all / by Patricia Abbott.—1st ed.
       p. cm.
    ISBN 1-59414-231-9 (hc : alk. paper)
    1. Women college students—Fiction. 2. World War, 1939–1945—United States—Fiction. 3. Female friendship—Fiction. 4. Young women—Fiction. I. Title.
PS3601.B39A79 2004
813'.6—dc22   2004049289

I dedicate this to the DFW Writers' Workshop, to my children whose constant encouragement has meant a great deal to me, to Larry Names who began it all, and to my fellow writers in the Thursday Group.

"With memories of dances left undone
And wasted songs, their melodies unsung—
A stardust melody . . ."

Chapter 1

"Liz, telephone." The dorm monitor stuck her head around the door of 306. "Sounds Hubba! Hubba! A real cool cat."

Liz Chase whooped. "Hubba! Hubba!" could only mean Alan Bannerman. She uncurled her legs from where she sat propped against the pillows of her bed and dashed for the hall.

The monitor stepped back from the onslaught. "Divvies!"

"Hands off. He's mine!" Ordinarily the phone was three steps from her crowded freshman room on the third floor of BG's Kohl Hall. She made it in two and snatched the dangling earpiece, holding it tightly, wishing she were holding him.

In the calmest tone she could muster, not too adoring, although adore him she did, she said, "Hello, Alan?" She really wanted to purr, but with her here at Bowling Green, him at Georgetown, surrounded by all those rich, probably gorgeous girls, it might be smart to play it cool. Her heart wouldn't let her, though. She gave in on all fronts. "Oh, Alan, it's so good to hear your voice. I miss you so much."

"I did tell you to come here, didn't I?"

"You could always come here." She knew that wouldn't happen. A senior there, Georgetown was one of the best schools for a would-be diplomat. Tiny Bowling Green State University had only recently grown from a normal school for teachers into a state school of Ohio.

"Mm. I could major in shoe shine, I guess." His voice

7

softened. "I love you. I do miss you. How are you doing?"

She gave him a quick rundown on the stupid beanies and the words to the school song they all were in danger of being stopped to recite. But, not tonight. The mixer would be time-out.

"We're more sophisticated here. We make you recite the preamble to the Constitution."

"I guess that lets me out for sure. Oh, Alan, I miss you. I do like it here, though. I guess I'm just a hick at heart. We've got lots of space, lots of trees. I think small colleges are cozier. Besides, I'd feel guilty asking Dad to pay those Georgetown fees."

Her dad owned a drugstore in Chillicothe, Ohio, which gave them a nice living, but she never figured they were rich. Not like Alan's family. "I hate being separated from you."

The monitor had said it. Alan was about as Hubba! Hubba! as they came, with a hefty load of blond wavy hair, hazel eyes, nice firm chin and teeth that turned his smile on like a 300-watt lightbulb. Alan was definitely nifty.

"I'm glad you like your BG. All that frosh stuff brings back a lot of memories I'd just as soon forget, I think." He sounded amused. "I didn't hear you mention all those vets the school had to crowd in, even delay the term for."

"Crowded in's about right." The war had only ended in August, but already, newly returned vets flooded the campus under the GI Bill. BG had put the starting date back to October.

"Well, there aren't any apple trees to sit under." She had one at home and he kidded her about the old Andrews sisters' song. "There is a cute guy in French." She didn't know his name even but he had somehow curiously gentle blue eyes with a lot of dark curly hair, one of those guys any girl would notice.

"You're mine and don't forget it." Did she detect a slightly aggrieved tone? She hoped so, then guiltily remembered the mixer tonight. Dare she ask him if he minded? Her roommate, Dottie, would never let up on her unless she did. "What would you think if I went to a mixer tonight? I'm not really dying to, but everyone's been trying to talk me into it all day. It would be something to do."

He laughed again.

She loved that laugh, full of self-confidence and easy humor. Mellow came to mind. Melodious, pleasing, resonant. The words fit.

He said softly, "Go ahead. You can't sit in your room all the time." Then the laugh came back. "If that fellow from your French class is there, you can't dance with him!"

"I couldn't be rude." Feeling guilty about teasing him, she relented. "I've never even talked to him."

"You can't dance to 'Stardust.' "

Their song. "I wish you were here and we could." She pictured herself in his arms, her face against his, gliding around the floor. She touched her cheek. "I miss you. What are you doing tonight?"

"The frat's having a party for dumb blonds only."

"Seriously?"

"Well, they are having a bash but I'm headed for a movie. My roommate's engaged, so we shall combine our forces and keep each other out of trouble."

Alan was a nice guy. She didn't really worry, but Georgetown had to be filled with them—the debs in *Life* magazine, beautiful, important, old-money girls. Before she could question him, he said, "The guys here are mumbling threats. I've got to get off the phone. I'll call you to-

morrow." He lowered his voice. "I love you."
The whisper made it sound lonely. She sighed and
clenched the phone. "Me, too. You hang up. I don't want
to."

At the soft click, she clenched the earpiece harder, as
though it still contained the sound of him. Finally she
handed it to the girl pressed against the wall, waiting
without a smile.

Dottie Cook, one of her two roommates, barely waited
until she got in the door to say, "You have to come tonight."

Liz hesitated again. Alan had said okay, but . . . "I know
it's only a mixer but I don't see any point in going. If I met
someone cute, I'd have to explain I'm going steady and
then in the unlikely event someone like Clark Gable showed
up, well, what could I do about it? I don't know."

Dottie stopped sorting through her clothes and parked
herself beside Liz. "Why did you pick BG? If I had a guy,
I'd stick to him."

Liz repeated the same reasons she'd given Alan then
asked, "Why'd you come here?"

"They've got a great drama department."

Liz smiled at that. Dottie's thin oval face and long
straight hair made Liz think of a Siamese cat even though
her green eyes were maybe too round. She wasn't exactly
pretty. Cute was a better word. And she bubbled so that
you couldn't resist laughing with her. Already half the dorm
dubbed Dottie "Tallulah," for her imitation of the stage
star's deep voice, the distinctive trademark drawl, "Dah-
ling."

"Well, I'm going no matter what. I wish you'd change
your mind." Dottie hopped off the bed and began again to
rifle through the closet she shared with Liz. "I don't know

what to wear! Wish I had Sarah's clothes."

The cramped room had never been designed for three but with all of the returning vets, students were stuffed into every cranny like jelly beans in a druggist's jar. The third roommate had a closet to herself. Dottie opened it and smacked her lips over the crush of clothing. "I wonder if she likes Shakespeare."

Liz laughed. "What has he to do with anything?"

"Neither a lender nor a borrower be." She sighed and went back to her own clothes and pulled out a black crepe. "Too dressy, isn't it? I really think you should come. Alan or not. It's not like it's a date. Just getting acquainted. Besides, I hate going alone."

Liz drew her knees to her chin. "Sarah's going, isn't she? Where is she?"

Dottie checked her watch. "Library. Do you suppose she'd lend me that green sweater of hers? Think she cares?"

"Maybe not." Sarah Johnson didn't mind much of anything. Temperamentally, she was velvety smooth, never frayed at the edges. Liz worried Sarah might be too even-tempered.

Dottie stopped moving hangers long enough to say, "You're the one who ought to wear green with that hair of yours. Gorgeous stuff."

"Alan's always after me to wear it." She stopped herself from touching her hair. Why was there a compulsion to smooth the sometimes untamed mane any time someone mentioned it? Truth was, although she'd never admit it for fear of seeming conceited, she liked her hair. The red got as much attention as blonds did without having to put up with the "dumb" business.

But when it came to gorgeous, well, Sarah was the one, with her perfect, classic oval face, high cheekbones and long blond hair that shouted "Nordic." The prettiest girl she'd ever met.

"You've got to come tonight. You just can't sit here in the room every weekend. You said you're not engaged. He trusts you, doesn't he?"

"The question never came up. We were together. But he said he didn't mind." Going might be better than sitting here. Weakening, she rose and went to stand beside Dottie at the closet.

"Oh swell. You are going then? Here, wear this." She pulled out a green wool from the tight bunch of Liz's clothes now pushed to the end of the rod.

"I'll save that for Alan. Maybe he'll come down soon. Or up. I guess Bowling Green is up from Georgetown."

"Excuse me!" To make herself small as she tried to squeeze past, Sarah held in a stomach that under almost any circumstance would be hard to find.

Dottie yelped, then bubbled at her. "Boy! Am I glad to see you! You're going tonight aren't you? I've almost talked Liz into it. For a while I thought I'd have to go alone. That always makes me feel sort of out of things."

Sarah dropped her books on the bed, took off her jacket and tossed it on them. She stepped out of her shoes and left them in the middle of the room. "To tell the truth, I rather dread it. I'm never at ease. But I'm going. I guess I need to. I wish you would too, Liz."

Pointing at the shoes, Dottie grinned. "Who was your maid this time last year? One of these days you're gonna trip on those things."

"My mother, I guess." Sarah smiled back weakly. "Sorry. I really will reform. Just takes time when you're an only child."

Liz was an only child too, but her mother never waited

on her. Pleased that at least her two roommates hadn't fought over it, her thoughts went back to the mixer. She could always leave if a problem came up. "You guys talked me into it."

Dottie jumped at that. "Yeah, you said Alan wasn't upset."

"Wish I had someone to upset." Sarah picked up her towel. "I'm for the shower."

Dottie raised an eyebrow at her. "Well, can I have dibs on the last three guys in your line?"

"Sure. The long one. That's a joke. When guys talk about dumb blonds, it's wishful thinking. According to them, the words are not only synonymous, they're ideal!"

Liz had always envied beautiful women. How could being gorgeous be anything but a blessing? Problem was, Sarah was brilliant and being a major genius was a big drawback with a lot of guys. She said sympathetically, "I imagine a lot of them are scared to ask you. But you know, the vets here are older, more grown-up. They might be different."

Sarah didn't look convinced. "They are either scared off or they ask for the wrong reasons."

Liz nodded. She could see Jimmy Cagney in his gangster movies: pin-striped suit, spats and an empty-headed blonde on each arm. It couldn't be fun to always wonder if it was you or your looks someone liked.

"But you've got to go."

"As I said, I guess I need to." Sarah got her shampoo and soap and left the room.

They all finally settled on which dress to wear, had their showers and dressed. They were just about to leave when the hall monitor put her head through the doorway again.

13

"Hubba! Hubba's back, Liz. If you haven't time to talk, I'll be glad to oblige!"

Liz flew to the phone. "Alan. Are you okay?"

"Of course." After a pause when she could almost see his lips turn up at the corners, his voice turned mellow again. "I miss you. Wish I had my arms around you right now." He kissed the air. "That will have to do."

She reddened as though Dottie and Sarah, who waited now in the doorway, could see. She covered the mouthpiece and told them, "It's okay. I'll meet you there!"

She frowned at the phone. "Are you sure you're okay? I love your calling again, but . . ."

"I just wanted to remind you whom you love."

Ah. "Whom I love?" She laughed. "Whom, hmm? You are proper, aren't you?" She could see him now with every thread, every hair in place.

"Proper? Me? The guy who wants to run off to a cabin with you and cover you with kisses?"

A warm flush started at the back of her neck even though she knew that though he might want to, he never would.

His laughter dared her. "Ah, but you wouldn't, would you?"

"Would you?" She knew the dimple would be getting deeper, but they were both too proper to go running off.

Changing the subject back to whom, he said quickly, "As for who and whom, as ambassador, I'll be around a lot of people who learn English by the book. Don't want to throw them with bad grammar, do I?" His voice lowered. "Just don't forget, I am he whom you love."

"Ambassador, hmm? Sure of yourself, aren't you?" His self-confidence was one of the things that made him so easy to be with. Not conceit as she'd teased. He didn't sound as though he doubted her. She hoped not. She admitted, "Yes,

14

you know you're 'he whom I love.' "

He sighed in satisfaction then said soulfully again, "I wish you'd move here."

"You know I can't. And as long as I am here, I might as well like it. I like my roommates too."

"Oh?"

"Yeah. Dottie's cute and Sarah is gorgeous."

"Think I'll have to come up and meet them."

Liz sniffed, "They'll be out of town." Then, quickly, lest he get away before she had him pinned down, "Come up? Will you really? When?"

"That's really why I called back. Got to thinking and was trying to figure it out. Something special up there?"

"You don't have to wait for something special, do you? The only thing I can think of is homecoming and that's not for three weeks."

The laughter came back into his voice. "Class Z football, I suppose?"

"Well, they aren't exactly in the Big Ten. They're really good at basketball." She said more hopefully, "There is a homecoming dance." She could almost feel his cheek against hers.

"Okay. And wear green. Makes your hair flame." His voice grew faint and she could hear the sound of a tussle. "Got to go before these guys get surly."

"You mean you're coming? Really?" She said it loudly, hoping he could hear, then looked to see who else might. The hall was still empty.

He managed to get out, "Yeah." Then louder but from a distance, "I'm coming!"

After a moment, he came back to say quietly, "I'll let you know when I'll get there."

Wondering for the hundredth time that day, how one

could hear a smile or feel the touch of love over a phone line, she sighed and agreed. "Okay. But, Alan?"

"Mm?"

"Do you love me?" She wanted him to say it again.

"Of course, Goose. I keep looking around." His voice was cocky. "I guess I'm partial to redheads. I just can't find anyone to compare, so I'm stuck. Or you are! Besides, redheads are famous for their tempers. I wouldn't dare not!"

"No. You'd better not, dare not!" Second thought told her that hadn't come out right, but she didn't care as long as they were on the line together. "I love you too."

"Mmmmm. Well, have a good time. Remember, don't dance to 'Stardust.' I'll see you in three weeks." She felt their longing weigh on the line. Why did it not snap?

He said, "I hung up last time. Your turn."

Liz kissed the air and pressed the button. She wanted to sing. Three weeks. Three weeks. She hurried toward the gym where the mixer would be. Perhaps they'd already played "Stardust." She did like to dance.

Chapter 2

With guilt, yet anticipation, Liz hurried to the gym for the mixer. Dottie and Sarah waited just inside. The look in Dottie's eye said she might explode if she had to wait much longer. Sarah immediately tugged at Liz and motioned toward the walls. "C'mon, let's go back there."

Blocking the way, Dottie pronounced, "Oh, no! Front and center!"

"Let's go sit." Liz sympathized with Sarah on this one. "I feel like a parakeet surrounded by cats out here." Great grinning cats licking their chops. Tomcats. She wondered how many other girls here felt the same way. "What's the opposite of Big Man on Campus?"

Dottie gave her a blank look. "Huh?"

"Freshmen, maybe? Looks like we're not very high in the pecking order. No decorations."

"It's exciting to finally be in college, though, isn't it?"

Liz murmured, "I've dreamed of this for as long as I can remember." But she hadn't dreamed of being alone.

"It's all those old Andy Hardy movies." Dottie stopped her humming, maybe purring, just long enough to say it.

Still, Liz couldn't help but be a little disappointed by the bareness of it. Only the dim lighting that shadowed the cream-colored block walls saved the scene from the dreary feel and memories of phys ed classes and the hollow echo of a gymnasium with the bleachers down.

If Alan were here now, she wouldn't have noticed. It would be a corner of heaven. The magic lay not in the place but in the person who held you in his arms.

There was color. The wines and browns in the girls' skirts swirled past like autumn leaves. Here and there, a dash of bright red interjected a touch of bravado to this rite of passage from the old and secure to the new and intimidating.

Dottie at least seemed to have no concerns at all, other than her intense study of the males. She was definitely one of the cats, not a bird. She pointed and hissed, "Wow! Look at that Marine!"

Liz blushed and whispered, "Don't point. He'll see us. And it's ex-Marine. War's over, you know."

This time, Sarah tugged at Dottie's sleeve. "I feel so obvious standing here, let's go sit."

Much too interested in the dishes of cream in front of her to chance melting into the background, Dottie never moved. "Obvious is all to the good. Double hubba!"

Liz tugged at her too, saying, "Come on. What makes you think he's a Marine, anyway?"

"Well, look at him! He's no kid. Has to be one of the vets on the Bill." She did a little quiet lip smacking. "And honey, with a build like that, he ain't nothin' but a Marine!"

The Marine came toward them. He looked not so much a cat, Liz thought, as a cat-eating tiger.

Dottie took a deep breath and purred, "This one's mine."

How she said it without her lips seeming to move, Liz didn't quite figure.

He gave the three of them a quick smile and parked his frame in front of Dottie. "Hi, babe. How about it?"

She looked over her shoulder, then turned back. Two dimples appeared in her cheeks and flirted with him for a second in a show of "yes/no" before she answered. "Well, I sort of promised Jim but I don't see him. Yes, I'd love to."

Before he gets away! Liz said silently and almost choked. Jim indeed! Dottie hasn't even spoken to a boy till now. And "Hi, babe" yet! She couldn't imagine the words in Alan's mouth.

Dottie held out her hand. "Dottie Cook."

"Bob." The Marine took the offered hand and led her onto the floor.

Before Liz could nudge Sarah into retreating, a tall kid with a baby face, one that looked almost never shaved, crossed the dance floor, his gaze on Sarah. His head and shoulders moved well above the sea of bobbing heads, steady as the mast of a ship. As he passed, most of the couples hailed him, and he waved without taking his eyes from Sarah.

"That's Rick," she whispered, trying not to let the movement show.

"Rick?"

She turned slightly away from the oncoming figure. "Rick Jason. You know. Basketball. He hasn't played here yet, but everyone knows him. All State and stuff."

Liz laughed. "Not me."

"Yeah, well, you're not in line."

He came up and tapped Sarah on the shoulder. "May I?"

When she smiled, he placed his hand on her waist and led her onto the floor. Liz told herself she only imagined that in spite of the baby face he had authority in the way he claimed her, and a look of proprietorship in his eyes. She also told herself she had no grounds for such assumptions and it wasn't her business. Still, with Sarah so vulnerable . . .

Curious about her perhaps rash reaction to him, Liz

watched them. The grace of the athlete showed in his dancing, and perhaps as lead man on the court, he was used to command. He did lead and Sarah did follow.

Of course she'd heard about the basketball center BG had signed but hadn't seen him until now. According to the talk, because of him BG might have a good chance of winning the national championship. Over DePaul even. Rick wouldn't be a bad catch for Sarah if he had brains. On the other hand, such assertiveness made Liz uneasy. Sarah might just let the gentle side of her be swamped by him.

Again she told herself it wasn't her business and looked about for a corner that might offer comfort. She might watch for a moment then leave. As she turned, a tap on her shoulder stopped her. A nice-looking guy who seemed to shout "country club" asked, "May I?"

She hesitated, but he didn't seem to notice.

"I'm Dave." The inflection suggested she should know.

Actually she did, of him, that is. His dad had been a famous quarterback. Her own dad talked about Will Keller constantly. She didn't want to admit she knew that, though. "Liz. Liz Chase."

He grinned at her as he led her into the dance. "That's too easy."

She waited for the rest of it.

"It's a game I play with names. I'd love to chase Liz."

She couldn't stop the groan.

"Well, mine always comes out Killer. Lady Killer."

Telling herself it wasn't fair to dislike him already, she decided to be polite.

He drew her close. She tried to put space between them. He held her firmly there. "Actually I knew your name. I made it a point to find out. You and that Sarah you're with, are the two prettiest girls in the room." He smiled again.

She saw not warmth but two neat white rows of perfectly formed teeth.

She managed to draw away. "Got your own private eye or do you use your father's?" He probably thought she should be flattered.

"Looks and wit, too! I like that. Actually, they'd probably follow him. Me, I like to spend my money on pretty girls."

Once more, he drew her close and this time, put his cheek against hers. He even sang a few bars of "Dancing Cheek to Cheek."

She tilted her head away from him. "I go steady."

"Not smart. You miss too many opportunities."

She bit her tongue to keep from telling him he was the one who wasn't smart. Thankfully, the music stopped and she turned to leave the floor.

He grabbed her hand. "You can't go yet. I get the next one, too."

It wasn't even a question. She stiffened. "Look, I told you, I go steady. I only came to pass the time."

"But he's not here, is he?"

She used her loftiest tone. "Georgetown."

"Better him than me. Those schools make you work too hard. I'm only looking for that little piece of lambskin." The band went into "I'll Never Love Again" and he took her by the arm.

"Look. I don't want to dance." She didn't move.

"Because of him?"

She raised her chin.

"He's there and I'm here." He held up her left hand and transparently looked for a ring. "Might as well enjoy yourself. Don't believe in going steady."

"I happen to love him."

21

"Why are we even arguing about this? You're here. Let's dance." His eyes glinted as though that were an acceptable challenge. "You're too good a dancer not to want to dance."

A pleasant male voice said, "She promised me this next one." Liz looked up into the gentle blue eyes of the guy in her French class.

Any girl in her right mind would find it hard to say no to him under any circumstances. As a knight riding to the rescue, she had no intention of refusing now. She smiled her thanks and took his hand.

"Too bad, chump. She's going steady. Aren't you, babe?" Dave sneered and walked off.

Her knight said, "I'm Tom. You looked as though you were having trouble. Anyway, I've been trying to get to you to ask, 'May I really have this dance?' " His smile, too, showed perfectly formed teeth. These sparkled. On that Dave Keller they had announced, The better to eat you with, my dear! Tom's eyes and the innocence of his smile denied any such intention.

Realizing she was taking an inordinately long time over a simple question, and feeling a bit foolish, she said, "I'm Liz. Thanks for rescuing me."

"Think nothing of it. My degree's in Rescue."

"Ah. So, Lanceloting's your major then?"

Laughing, he put his arm on her waist. She'd been so annoyed and then relieved, it wasn't until then she noticed the song was "Stardust." She stopped dead. The melancholy wail held her rooted to the spot. Not that! She'd promised. She said, "Uh," not quite sure what to say. If she was going to dance, she'd like to dance with him, but . . .

A young boy at the mike took up the lyrics and she heard

Alan singing the words that came soft and low, ". . . remain my stardust melody . . ."

Tom looked at her with a raised eyebrow and a half-smile. "Change your mind?"

She shook her head. "It's the song. I promised not to dance that one. I'm sorry. I probably shouldn't have come. I go with a guy at Georgetown. I promised . . . that's our song."

He led her off the floor. She thought he would leave but he didn't. "But you're not engaged?"

"Not officially." She found herself saying, "He's coming up in three weeks."

"That's nice." The tone was equivocal. When the band began "My Dreams Are Getting Better All the Time," he placed a gentle pressure on her back. He was a good dancer. Almost as good as Alan.

He said, "I've noticed you in French. You like to sit in front. I like to sit in the back. Until now, that is." His grin grew bigger. "Don't look around much, do you?"

She took the easy way out, denying implicitly that she had paid attention. "My friends all tell me I'm hopeless about noticing things. Everyone I know can tell you every make of car on the road. I can hardly tell a Model T Ford when I see one."

"Not many around to practice on. Anyway, I figured you were the thinker type. I think I like that. What do you think?"

Liz groaned but secretly she loved puns and words.

He held on to her hand as the last notes of the song floated off. "I've enjoyed dancing with you. How about the next one?"

She withdrew her hand but hadn't the heart to say no. "Okay. One more." It didn't help that he danced like a dream.

23

Until intermission she danced with him off and on. Each time she looked around, he seemed to be watching her.

Every once in a while she saw Dottie still with the Marine and Sarah still with Rick. They looked as though they were having a good time.

When the band put the instruments down for intermission, Tom asked if she'd like something to eat. She shook her head. "Thanks. I think maybe I'll go back to the dorm. I've really enjoyed dancing, but I think I ought to go." Truth was, she had enjoyed it too much. The sax, the wail of the horn, floating in the half-light to the sound of romance . . . If only Alan . . .

It was too much. Her conscience pricked. All she wanted was a hasty retreat.

He took her by the arm without arguing. "I'll walk you back."

On the way he told her he wanted to be an architect, that he had six sisters and lived in Springfield, Ohio.

For a while they sat on the steps of Kohl. The evening was cool, but not cold. Indian summer. The air smelled of late autumn leaves. The stars, with their brittle glitter, spoke of winter.

"You have to be a vet," she ventured, picturing him in a cockpit, flying a fighter plane. Something like Errol Flynn in *Dawn Patrol*, only updated.

He told her he'd been a Navy man in the Signal Corps, had been on a cruiser in the last battles in the Marianas and Okinawa. From the thin line of his mouth, she decided he would rather not talk about it and for a while they sat silently.

He asked her dreams, and she said, "Psychologist, I think. I like to know why people do the things they do. And I'd like to write too." She found it hard to stop talking.

Finally, when she wound down, he took her hand and helped her up. "I have to assume you'd say no if I tried to kiss you, but keep it in mind."

He watched until she was inside.

As she signed in, she decided letters would be a good defense against nice smiles. All that talk had made her feel lonely too. Good thing she had lots of letters due.

She had sealed the last envelope when Sarah came quietly into the room and stepped out of her shoes. She draped her dress across the bed. Always quiet, she tended to become even more so when things went wrong.

Liz wanted to get up and hug her, but decided a cheery voice might do as much. "How did you get along with Rick? Any grey cells in that lofty crow's nest?"

"He didn't say 'youse guys.' That's a good start. What happened to you?"

Liz skipped the new question. "Rick's a nice-looking guy. Quite a catch, according to the looks you two got." She felt guilty praising him. She didn't understand why she didn't like him. She wanted Sarah to be happy.

"Yeah. Well, he is nice and a really good dancer." The thought seemed to perk her up a bit. "I don't have to marry him!"

Liz laughed. "You know my grandmother once told me, 'Never date a man you wouldn't want to marry.' Only I never could figure out how you'd know about most of them if you didn't date them."

Sarah gave her a small smile. "I'll know when I meet him. Maybe not always, but there's something in the way they look at you the first time. It's like they're an adding machine going into action. When I meet a guy whose motor doesn't spin, that's the one I want."

Liz laughed, but on second thought it wasn't funny. She

knew the look but it wasn't always so for her. Maybe her red hair brought out the mischief and humor in the guys. It was something like being a red devil's food to Sarah's wedding cake. As for the spinning motor, "Well, he does have to have one, you know."

"Ummm. Your grandmother wasn't the only one who handed out advice. Mine was forever saying, 'Still waters run deepest.' But you never did answer my question. What happened to you?"

"Tom? He's in my French class. Much too nice for me to hang around with. I ducked out in self-defense." Liz held up her stack of letters.

As she did, Dottie burst through the door. "Wow. How come you left? Bob's a great dancer. I think I'm in love." She stepped on one of Sarah's shoes, still in the middle of the floor. She put them in the closet. "Ah! Ah! Messy, messy."

Sarah groaned and switched the subject back to Dottie. "Yeah. Well, just don't be in such a hurry to fall in love. You do want to be a movie star, right?"

"Li'l ole me a movie star?" Dottie twirled. Her two oversized dimples with an extra set of small ones, appeared at the corners of her mouth. "Yeah. Well, he's just a high-steppin', passin' fancy. There'll be no one stopping me, dah-ling."

"Okay, Tallulah."

Dottie took off her dress, got a hanger and flourished it at Sarah. "See? This is what you're supposed to do." She grinned and put it in the closet, then turned to Liz. "When do we get to meet this Alan of yours?"

Liz glowed inside and out at the thought of Alan coming down. "He'll be here for homecoming if he can."

Dottie said, "That's swell," and walked out of the room with towel and soap in hand.

Liz shook her head but the grin betrayed her. "I think

26

Dottie talks to make space in her brain for something just as unimportant." She stopped then added, "Well, I mean the words pour out and other nonsense pours in, I guess." Thinking perhaps that sounded unkind, she added, "That rather frenetic quality of a Betty Hutton, maybe tamped down just a little, is fun to be around."

Obediently hanging her dress in the closet, Sarah draped her slip on the back of a chair. "I danced with that Bob. I don't like him. I can see why Dottie does, though. She's right about him being a good dancer. Trouble is, he's got all the homing instincts of a barracuda. I don't trust him."

She grabbed a towel and went across the hall. Thankfully, Dottie was already in the shower stall. Sarah stood and stared at her own face in the mirror, wishing her hair was red like Liz's. Maybe only a cute face like Dottie's. She liked being pretty but wanted a flaw. She touched her chin. If there were a big fat pimple there, would Rick still date her? She piled her hair on top of her head. Maybe if she cut it short and got a curly permanent, it would look awful. Dispirited, she let it down.

Why couldn't she find a man who looked beyond her face? But was that fair? Rick had been perfectly respectful. It was only that he had acted all evening as though he owned her. Except for Bob, and Rick could hardly refuse him with Dottie there. He'd shut out anyone who even looked like they wanted to ask her.

Liz had sort of introduced Tom to him as they danced by. That is, they'd spoken quickly. She bit her lip. Tom had smiled but his motor hadn't spun. Nice smile.

The last thought made her feel guilty. She liked nice things too, didn't she? She told herself, it really wouldn't matter if the one wasn't handsome, though. Just nice.

Tom was handsome and nice.

Chapter 3

Friday night again! Friday and Saturday were the worst. Loneliness settled in then, like a drab weekend uniform. Maybe Alan would call. Since they were going steady, she could call him, but girls weren't supposed to call boys and she was never comfortable doing it. She'd hate to have his frat brothers remark about "the girl who called all the time." It was early. Only a few minutes after seven, maybe he would.

She tried to bury her troubles and her nose in her psych book, hoping the complexities of people's psyches would make her forget for a while.

A smiling Sarah came in and threw her books on her bed, stepped out of her shoes, went to her closet and rifled through her clothes.

Liz eyed the shoes with a mixture of amusement and wonder. At such close quarters, a stray flea in the room, let alone discards in the middle of the floor, could trip you up. The Miss-Fix-It in her leaned from her bunk to shove them under the bed, then stopped. Wanting to fix things could get to be a bad habit. She asked instead, "Going someplace?"

"A bunch of us are going bowling. I wish you'd come along." Sarah tossed her skirt and sweater on the bed and took out a pair of grey wool slacks.

Curious at all this exertion, Liz queried, "You have to dress for bowling?"

"We're walking. These are warmer. You need to come.

You're a real stick-in-the-mud, up here all the time." She slipped into a long pink angora and adjusted the pearls she'd not removed with the other sweater.

Liz plucked at her BG sweatshirt and squirmed. She wasn't even in the same league with her roommate. No matter what Sarah wore, she looked elegant. For a moment Liz had a vision of Sarah in a sweatshirt with pearls. She probably wore a strand the day her mother brought her home from the hospital.

Stepping over the shoes, Sarah went to the mirror and combed through her hair, letting it stream softly down her back, not like the tied-back ballerina look she usually wore.

Liz touched her own hair with an unfamiliar pang of envy. She wouldn't change her own red for anything, but just looking at Sarah's cool white-blond was enough to make anyone wish.

For a moment, Liz watched then rose and gently shoved the stray shoes under the bed. She picked up the skirt, grinned and handed it to Sarah. "Good thing Dottie's not here!"

"Oops. Sorry. She's always after me, isn't she? Oh well, gives her something concrete to put in her head." She chuckled. "Mom never made me pick up after myself. At least in my own room." She hung the skirt. "I do wish you'd come with us."

Liz went back to her psych but put it down and picked up the biology, then discarded it too. A textbook made poor company on a Friday evening. It couldn't dance, take you to a movie or kiss good night. Oh, Alan! She closed her eyes and tried to summon his kiss but his arms couldn't reach from Georgetown. She might as well get used to being dateless and dull.

Sarah slipped into a pair of saddle shoes and stuffed her

mad money and a lipstick into her pocket.

Liz sat forward, unable to resist the thought of something, or someone, better than a book to communicate with. There must be plenty of other kids who didn't have dates. Probably a lot of them at the alley. She weakened. "Who's going?"

"Rick says just a bunch. He's been after me to bring you along. No real couples, okay?"

"Well, if it's not dates, maybe I will." She squirmed, embarrassed to admit the truth. "Trouble is, I've never bowled in my life. Do you think anyone will mind?" She had a picture of ten kids chasing her down Main Street for ruining their game. How many were on a team? She didn't even know that.

"Don't know why they'd be mad. You can be on my side, so they won't have to worry about a score page full of gutter balls."

"I think I should be insulted by that, but I'm not sure what it's about."

Sarah didn't give her time to worry about it. She picked up her discarded sweater still on the bed, dangled it in front of Liz, then stuffed it in her overloaded drawer. "See? Just for you. Now you owe me."

"We'll get you trained yet."

Sarah chuckled, "Don't count on it. I've been spoiled for seventeen years. Are you ready? We'll meet the kids there."

"Sure they won't mind?"

"It's not a tournament. Don't worry."

"You look so nice. Do I have to change?"

Sarah looked surprised and shook her head. "You look fine. You always do. I wish I was a redhead. Ready?"

Bowling Green was a typical small midwestern town with a turn-of-the-century look. Students could drive, but it was easy to walk almost anywhere they needed or wanted to go. A grey stone bank building anchored the drugstore, the movie theater and a string of two-story, redbrick buildings with glass-windowed shops on the Main Street crossroad. On the next block a nineteenth-century grey stone courthouse hid from the crossroad. It wasn't easy to hide anything that large, but grassy space and plenty of trees did a good job.

The bowling alley, all ten lanes of it, was in a little hole-in-the-wall near an alley just past the intersection. Inside, it looked to Liz like a polished barn. Hollow sounds as the balls clicked against wood, or just rolled heavily down gutters, reverberated from bare wall to bare ceiling and back again. Like a gym.

For the moment at least, "the kids" turned out to be only Rick and Tom Butler, the owner of the gentle blue eyes and easy-gliding feet. The one who, these days, gave her a big smile whenever they met in the French class. He still sat in back and never tried to say more than a few words to her. Just smiled a lot.

Now, she managed to tear her gaze from him to look beyond and around, then give Sarah a puzzled look. "Big crowd? I thought you said there'd be a bunch of kids."

Sarah raised her eyebrows, and mimed, "Uh . . . I don't know."

Rick came up and put his arm around her, claiming her as though she were the ball at center court. "You're beautiful tonight."

Liz thought that, for herself, "You're beautiful" anytime, would be a compliment, but she knew Sarah desperately wanted to be a person, not a pretty face. She watched her friend's shoulder stiffen and a tiny frown gather between her brows.

Liz had to remind herself such good looks caused as many problems as they cured. Still, feeling outclassed again, she put her hand to the neck of her sweatshirt. There were plenty of other BG sweatshirts in sight, though, along with the ever-present hip-length sweaters like Sarah's.

She breathed a sigh of relief when Tom came over and distracted her. It evaporated when he said, "I'm glad you came. I wasn't sure you would." That sounded awfully like he thought she came for him. She looked past him at the door. "Are there others coming?"

"Just us. Why? Expecting someone?"

Yeah. A crowd. Liz tried to explain, "Sarah said—." Anger and embarrassment made the words sound sharper than she meant. She backpedaled, "Uh, well, never mind. It's not important." As far as she could tell, Tom seemed a nice guy, not the type to pull something like this. It had to be a setup. She wanted to snarl at someone but didn't know who. Sarah had acted as though she didn't know it would turn into a couples thing. Had Tom set this up or Rick?

She looked again toward the door, hoping by some miracle kids would still appear. She guessed this was what her mother had in mind when she tried to tell her, "You're so young to go steady. You'll miss all the fun."

Liz had to admit having an absent boyfriend, who she was sure was true to her, did promise to put her in some iffy spots. "Maybe I shouldn't stay. I need to go to the library."

"You're here now. Stay. Besides, if you're as good at everything as you are in French, I doubt if you really do have to study on a Friday night."

"Well, I . . ." Her embarrassment grew by the minute. She couldn't stay and just be with Tom. But she didn't want to hurt his feelings, either. Maybe Alan wouldn't mind this once, if she explained. She sighed and gave in, not knowing what else to do, short of being mean. "Okay. Might as well as long as I'm here."

"That's not exactly the most flattering 'yes' I've ever had." The trace of laughter in his expression belied any hurt.

Her anger eased and she looked at those blue-blue eyes, thinking again he would be a hard one to dislike. "It's just that, well, Alan . . ."

"I remember. Georgetown, isn't it?" He scratched his dark hair that looked as though it couldn't make up its mind whether it wanted to be a Navy butch or grow. She wondered idly how long it took a guy's hair to become civilian. Even if he meant it to look that way, it didn't hurt his looks. Definitely a dreamboat. When he flashed those white teeth at her as he did now . . . But polygamy wasn't in her schedule.

He rubbed his forehead as though to erase embarrassment. "I asked Rick to ask Sarah to bring you. Didn't they tell you?"

Flushing, she shook her head. "Sarah said it would be a crowd." Maybe she hadn't known, either.

Tom frowned and shot a quick look at Rick's back. "Oh. I'm sorry. I never told . . ."

So, Rick planned the ruse. Rat. But she couldn't be mad at Tom. She even felt a bit sorry for him.

"It's okay. Don't worry about it." Then she remembered. "You'll be sorry, though. I don't bowl!"

He drew back and threw up his hands as if to ward off a blow. "Horrors. My doom is sealed!" He paused and the grin came back, "You mean, never never?"

"Never. Still want me to stay?"

"Hey, you two," Rick interrupted, "do you have your own shoes?"

Liz looked at her feet. Saddles. "Shoes? Won't these do?"

Sarah said, "They don't allow those. Rick has his own, but we have to rent some with rubber soles. Ones that haven't been out in the grime."

"You mean, someone else's? Ugh!" Liz turned up her nose. Her toes curled in protest.

Tom laughed at her. "They put foot powder in them. What size?"

When she told him, the clerk handed her a pair of five-and-a-half's. They looked like dead rats. She flinched, hoping they didn't smell as bad as they looked. Nothing quite like sweaty feet to turn your stomach.

Tom took them from her and led the way to the seats by their assigned alleys. "They don't bite. See? Germ powder with a deodorant. Come on."

She sat in one of the hard curved benches and forced herself to put the shoes on. She had to concentrate to keep her toes from curling. In the end, the fear proved worse than the fact. She tentatively stood.

Tom laughed at her expression then went to look over the bowling balls. "You need to get one that's comfortable." He rolled them around and picked one. "This one's not too heavy." He showed her how to hold it, then turned the holes toward her.

His hand brushed hers and her skin grew warm. She flicked the thought from her mind and tried to grip the ball. It slipped from her fingers and dropped with a crash. Certain that the whole building had rocked, she cringed, then inspected the floor expecting to see a jagged hole with splintered boards. Almost to her disappointment, the waxed boards lay before her whole and undisturbed. She had hoped to disappear through that hole.

She put her hands up to her red face, afraid to look at all those grins she knew were out there. "Oh, gosh. I'm sorry. I had no idea those things were so heavy." How could she know the dumb ball weighed a ton?

"Better be careful. They'll make you pay for the floor!"

"They wouldn't!"

He laughed and patted her on the shoulder, then retrieved the ball and showed her the basics.

Rick chided, "Okay, guys. That's enough. We'll take it easy on you. We'll just go for spares instead of strikes. Go ahead, Sarah."

Tom retorted, "Sure you will. I've seen you trip those guys on the basketball floor."

"Never happened." He grinned, then as Sarah stepped up and rolled the ball, he added, "I meant Sarah would take it easy on you."

Sarah's pins all fell except for the one in the left corner. That wobbled precariously but stood. Her second ball hit it with a crack loud and hard enough to instruct further stubborn pins on proper behavior.

Rick looked surprised, then grinned and patted her on the back. "Good girl." He gave Churchill's V sign and sniggered at Tom. "See? Spares."

"It's your funeral," Tom said.

Under the circumstances Liz thought that a gallant thing to say. With her on his side, he hadn't a prayer. She muttered, "Praise the Lord and pass the ammunition," hoping maybe that would be acceptable enough to keep the ball in the alley. She picked it up, carefully positioned her thumb, made three steps and took a practice swing.

"Looks good, just not quite so high."

She drew in her breath, paced again and let the ball go. It thundered to the floor and rolled into the gutter. She winced. How awful! She never should have come. "I have to go to the library."

"Don't worry. Try again. Not so high. Follow through with your arm. Like this." He turned her thumb slightly. "Line it up like that."

She closed her eyes for a second, took another deeper breath and rolled. This time the ball went straight for the head pin. Two stood. She gave a little jump and clapped. "It didn't go into the gutter!"

"Great. That's what you call a split but you don't get another chance to knock them down this time."

"I'd need a big fat ball to do that."

Tom grinned. "It can be done, but it ain't easy." He rolled and made a strike.

Rick made the same split Liz had and didn't pick up the rest of the pins. "Shoot, it slipped."

Liz's ball rolled into the gutter again. She groaned.

When Tom's neighbors grinned, he told them, "Well, at least it's our gutter." He tried not to laugh but the sparkle of his eyes betrayed him.

"You might, please, keep a straight face, thank you."

He sucked in his cheeks but couldn't help himself. He laughed aloud. "Here, too high. Do it like this," he took her arm and moved with her, "and follow through like this."

She bit her lip. He smelled like Old Spice. To distract herself, she said it out loud this time, "Praise the Lord and pass the ammunition," then took a practice swing.

"Amen and hallelujah," he intoned gravely, then took her hand and turned it. "No. Watch what your thumb does." The ball rolled straight. Seven down.

"Good. You've got it." His eyes glinted. "Almost."

He made another strike.

Sarah made a strike and Rick patted her on the back and

gave her his "Good girl," again.

His smile turned to a frown when he left three standing again on the first roll. He glowered and waited. The ball didn't return. Rick yelled, "Set 'em up."

The boy looked up from setting the downed pins in the next alley and kept on. Rick yelled again. "Hey, slowpoke. Set 'em up."

Embarrassed, Liz looked away. Others near did the same. Sarah kept her gaze on the score sheet.

The boy took his time and just as slowly cleared Rick's pins and returned the ball. It hadn't enough momentum and Rick shouted an exasperated "Hey," before the boy sent it back again. Too angry for good control, Rick rolled and it went into the gutter.

"Well, you did spare the pins," Tom chided.

Rick ignored that with a pout on his face which turned to relief when he made a strike on his next turn. By the time they finished, Sarah had rolled a respectable 190 to Rick's 155. He glared at the pin boy. "Dumb kid distracted me."

Liz scribbled over her score so no one could read it and Tom winked at her and scribbled over his too, although she'd already seen that it matched Sarah's. He laughed and told Rick, "We didn't get any score. You guys won that one, but we're going to do better next game."

If it hadn't been for Alan, Liz would have kissed Tom, on the cheek at least. Nice guy. Her conscience whispered, "And much too cute to hang around with."

Rick patted Sarah but he didn't smile. "Okay. That was practice. Now let's get serious." He rolled first and made the strike.

Sarah seemed to flag and left pins standing.

Tom gave Liz the V sign. "C'mon, champ. See if you can beat me this time."

"Oh, sure. You and Sarah with your one-nineties. Your turn anyway."

Rick scowled at the mention of the score.

As Rick stepped up to the line, Tom moved his arm into the swing, then let go. The ball landed with a loud thump in the middle of Rick's alley and rolled into the gutter. Rick dropped his and it went into the gutter too. Rick glared at him and Tom said, "Sorry" and turned away with a straight face. The pin boy gave him a thumbs-up sign.

For a moment, Liz thought Rick would go down the alley after the kid but instead he turned and marched back to the desk. She couldn't hear what he said, but the man behind the counter shook his head. Rick came back red-faced, picked up his ball and rolled without a word. The anger didn't help his game this time, either, and he ended with 145. His shoulders straightened again when Sarah's total only came to 135.

Tom took his and Liz's score sheet, tore off a strip and wrote something she couldn't see. He folded the scores out of sight, then took a paper clip from his pocket and fastened the torn strip to the neck of her sweatshirt. "On behalf of freshman bowlers of the world, I hereby solemnly award you, Liz Chase, this BG Open Badge of Merit." He gravely shook her hand. "Ma'am, you're a born golfer, never cracked a hundred!"

She admitted, "Pretty bad, wasn't it?" then took off the clip. The words said, "Bowling Green International Open." She folded it and put it in her pocket. "I'll frame it. But do you always carry paper clips?"

He reached into his pocket and pulled out half a dozen along with a string and a pencil-tip eraser. "Always, ma'am. I'm a dedicated scholar and a Boy Scout."

As they left, she said, "I did have fun. I'd really like to

learn but I can't . . . Well, you know, Alan . . ."

Tom considered her words. His blue-blue eyes lightened for a moment, then he leaned down and kissed her forehead. "I enjoyed it too. Thanks for not going back to the dorm and leaving me standing. If you change your mind about things, let me know."

She couldn't help it if her steps were light as she ran up two flights to her room.

Sarah barely made the curfew. She seemed awfully quiet as they undressed for bed.

"Did you have fun?" Liz asked. For herself, she was pleased with a fun evening with a nice guy. Yes, her guilt did nag and hang about, ruining a perfectly good glow even though she never meant to let anything come of it.

Sarah put her shoes in the closet. "It was okay but I did get embarrassed about the fuss Rick made." She hesitated then tried to explain it away. "He's not like that most of the time. He's usually nice."

That wasn't a word Liz would use. Still, she didn't really know him. Know him well, that is. She did know she didn't like being set up by him. "I didn't think he was nice when he tricked me into this thing with Tom."

Sarah tried to soften the accusation. "They both belong to Sigma Chi. He said Tom asked him to ask you. I didn't know they'd arranged anything." After a moment of silence she added, "Don't you like him? I think he's swell."

"Yeah, he definitely is a real hep cat. Only I can't. There's Alan." She studied Sarah who had turned away. "Tell you what. You can have him."

Sarah's voice fell an octave. "Well, Rick . . ." She stopped, obviously unable to explain or maybe tired of trying to. "He's really nice most of the time."

Liz shrugged. Maybe. She thought Rick cared most for

his ego. A bad sport on top of that. Trading Tom for Rick would solve a lot of problems for Sarah.

She couldn't say such things, so she asked, "You're a pretty good bowler. You did one-ninety on that first game. What do you usually do?"

"I was off tonight."

"Rick did 155. You're better than that, aren't you?"

"Yeah. Well, on a really good night, about maybe two-twenty."

"Oh. That's good, isn't it?" Certain now that Sarah had held back, Liz wanted to scold her.

Sarah look as though she wanted to cry. "You don't understand."

"It can't be fun when you're so smart you don't know how to be stupid." Liz reached out and hugged her. "I hate to say it, throwing that game tonight was stupid, though."

Sarah retreated a little and insisted again, "He is real nice most of the time and he can be funny when he wants to. Anyway, it's something to do. At least he's not afraid to ask me out." She took her towel to the showers.

Liz tapped herself on the side of her head. Talk about stupid, Stupid. You should keep your mouth shut and mind your own business. How could she know how much Sarah hurt? That stupid Rick too. When she was a psychologist, she'd make a study on why boys had to be so darn insecure. Except of course, girls were insecure too. Maybe she'd just figure out what made everyone tick and write a big book. She did like to write. She saw herself in flowing black robes on a podium. "May I introduce tonight's guest, Dr. Elizabeth Ellen Chase, best-selling author and expert on human relations." Not bad.

When Sarah came back, Liz didn't say anything more

about the evening. Instead she started to worry about Dottie. Lights out in two minutes.

Sarah said it first. "Dottie's not here."

"Maybe she's in the common room."

"I looked."

"Oh." As Liz said it, she could hear the proctor coming down the hall.

"Jimminy, Sarah! Dottie's gonna be in trouble. Where is she anyway?"

"If I know Bob, I'd guess in the backseat of a car about now."

They could hear the proctor opening doors, shutting them, counting noses. She opened their door. "Everyone in? Only two? Where's the third?"

Sarah stood in front of the closet. "Uh, in here."

The proctor stepped into the room.

The closet door stood open a crack and Sarah opened it a tiny bit wider and peeked in, then pushed it too hastily. "Don't, she's not dressed and she's really bashful. Country kid."

Liz, sitting at the head of her bed next to the closet, leaned back as far as she could, thumped the wall with her elbow and dropped a book down the wall.

The girl looked at them for a moment, then said to the air, "You in there?"

Liz squirmed back again and gave a muffled, "Yeah."

The proctor, a junior, grinned. "Used to be like that myself. Around here she'll grow out of it. 'Night." She went on down the hall.

Liz let out her breath. "That was close. Pretty quick, you are. But where the heck is she?"

"Like I said, with Bob," Sarah answered grimly as she nodded at the now-empty hall. "At least she's not a stickler. Do you think she knew?"

"Maybe not. She'd not want to get herself in trouble."

For the next half-hour, they alternated between whispering and staring at the empty bed until they fell asleep.

Chapter 4

Dottie eagerly ran her fingers along the cold steel frame of the maroon '42 Plymouth as she waited for Bob to open the door for her. She knew he had plans for tonight that should have made her blush, good churchgoer that she was. She expected him to try to finish the business he'd started last night. Should she? Shouldn't she?

Aloud, she said, "I do love this car, only I think we ought to put the top up. I'll freeze." She got in and hunched her shoulders against the November wind and pulled her jacket tight around her neck.

Bob brushed the frame with his handkerchief where his hand had been. His hand lingered on the door handle.

Dottie eyed the fingers jealously. She wanted his hand to linger on her, not the car.

He murmured as he said, "Yeah. This little beauty was one of the last to roll off the line before the war. My dad drove it to the grocery store once a week while I was gone."

He might have been talking about a woman. She wanted to reach out and take that hand.

He let her in then reached into the glove compartment and pulled out a heavy scarf and draped it across her head. "Here, I keep this just in case I'm out with a sissy like you."

She tied it on, acknowledging to herself, And now I know where I stand, second to a Plymouth. Aloud she said, "Well, it's better than nothing, I guess. Thanks." She probably ought to be annoyed, but the truth was, she figured she liked buzzing around town in this little job almost as much as he did. It was worth a bit of freezing. A convertible with the top up was just another car.

Her parents, good Bible Belt Baptists misplaced in Northeast Ohio, always had things like Ford sedans. It seemed the Lord didn't approve of gaudy people and things.

Being in this thing with the top down was like being let out of jail. Not that she'd ever been in jail, but she'd seen enough of Pat O'Brien and Cagney to know what it must feel like. Then too, when her mom and dad robed themselves in their Sunday-go-to-meetin' posture, well, there were definite similarities between that and jail.

She snuggled farther down in the seat, determined to endure the bitterest wind and cold for this privilege. Her mother did keep telling her suffering was good for the soul, didn't she?

But then no one would see her clear down here, would they? She sat up a little and rolled the window higher. "Compromise." She pulled the coat tighter around her neck.

Bob opened his door and climbed in beside her. He rolled his window up a little too. "That's what I like, compromise my way."

"I like your way." She snuggled near him. "Especially last night." Their necking had reached a fever pitch.

He squeezed her thigh.

She gulped and asked, "Where are we going now?"

"How about the Center Line for a little warm-up? Frank's bringing Veronica. I think she's from your dorm."

"Veronica? Oh, you mean Ronnie Meyers?" There was a quiet, homely girl down on the first floor of Kohl Hall by that name.

"Could be. Let's go." He drove carefully enough

through town, but the minute he got out onto the divided SR 25, he put the needle on eighty.

The wind wrapped her in an ice pack. She slid down in the seat. Even though her soul might need it, she didn't like suffering much. Or spending the evening at the police station with a traffic fine. "Jimminy, Bob. You'll have the cops on you!"

When he ignored her and kept going, she sat up and watched him breeze past the few cars on the road. This was certainly better than a prayer meeting. "What church do you go to?"

"Huh?"

"Well, you can't be a Baptist. At least not my kind."

"Cripes. What brought that on?"

She got a bit embarrassed. What had? "Oh, nothing. It's the car."

He looked down and pushed her away. a little and laughed into her face. "That's what I like about you. You're nuts."

"Yeah. Well," she adopted a mobster voice, "it's youse guys that make a dame go bad. But ya better slow down, Buster."

Bob did slow down, but only because the bar was in view.

He pulled into the almost-vacant lot, and parked. "Them flatfoots'll never take me alive, doll. Know where they hide." He laughed at her and jingled the keys in front of her nose. "I live down the road. Pass here all the time. Got them spotted."

Dottie knew he had an apartment in nearby Perrysburg but she hadn't seen it yet.

The Center Line bar wasn't exactly the Ritz, but it was better than nothing. Dottie couldn't see what the fuss was about, why the place was off-limits to students. Just ordinary working guys and gals having a little fun.

Liz and Sarah kept telling her she'd get kicked out of school if they caught her, but she'd never seen anyone except beer drinkers in here, certainly not campus cops or whoever it was that prowled for the college. She supposed deans had better things to do than come in here for beer.

The inside was as plain as the outside, with its dim lights, dark wood booths, beer ads and a Petty Girl calendar on the white walls. The only interesting thing about the bar was the idea that it was off-limits. That turned the nothing special, whitewashed block building into Rick's Casablanca Bar.

Frank and Veronica were already in a booth but hadn't ordered.

Dottie waited for Bob to get in first, he waited for her and they did a little dance. Finally he laughed and stood aside. "Beauty first."

Frank preened and turned to Ronnie who sat on the inside. "Guess I ought to change places, huh?" He gave her a shove on the shoulder.

She blinked as though she'd been struck in the face but gave a small smile that tried to say she believed he was kidding.

Dottie glared at him. They'd been out with Frank before, but he'd been with other girls. She didn't like him much. Under the circumstances, his remark was cruel. Ronnie was painfully plain until she smiled. It was a gentle smile that her eyes seemed to absorb and heighten. Dottie decided she liked her.

Bob said, "You two gals know each other, don't you?"

She gave Ronnie her warmest smile. "I've seen you. You have a room on one, don't you?"

"One-oh-eight. Frank says you're going to be in a play."

"Yeah, well, I get to cry. A starring role for a freshman, I guess. That Eva Marie Saint is really good. You've got to see her."

"Beer, everyone?" Bob motioned for the waiter. He ordered for them, adding, "A boilermaker for me. And we'll have a hamburger with everything, make mine rare—no onions." He winked at Dottie. "Right?"

"Good idea. Us too. Boilermakers." Frank waved toward Ronnie.

Dottie looked doubtfully at Bob. She'd never had one of those, wasn't even sure what it was. Still, she meant to be game for anything. She sat up straight and said, "Me too. I want one too."

The waitress pushed her pencil in the hair over her ear and snapped her gum. "You twenty-one?"

"Yeah."

"No, you ain't."

Bob waved her off with, "Okay. She'll have water and I'll have two boilermakers."

The waitress shrugged. "Nothing to me as long as it's yours."

When she'd gone, Dottie complained to Ronnie, "She didn't even ask you."

"I kind of leaned back so she wouldn't see my face. I think when she saw Frank, she just thought I'd be older."

Bob put up his hands and shrugged at Dottie. "I can't help it if I have a baby face."

"Sure you do." Actually, he didn't but Dottie liked the creases across his forehead and at the corners of his eyes. He looked as though he'd been around. A refreshing change from the straitlaced look of home.

But part of it was sad too. How many of those creases

had the war put there? It must have been pretty bad for him. He never talked about that part of it. He did brag a bit, sergeant stuff, but she guessed maybe it was a way of making the best of a bad thing. Some of his tales were hilarious. Like the time when he was still a corporal and he'd been out without a pass. He'd sat up in a tree for an hour, with only a bottle of whiskey for company, while MPs ate lunch below. Thank God it was all over. She shook off the momentary melancholy.

Just being with him made her feel older. Her mother would probably call him a wolf, but then her mother didn't like men much, including, Dottie thought, sometimes her own husband. He ruled the roost like a little Hitler.

Bob did take over. Part of it, she figured, was the noncom in him, part of it rooster. But he wasn't mean. At least he asked her opinion sometimes and paid attention to what she wanted.

Looking at him now, something stirred in her belly. He had shoulders and a chest like John Wayne. She turned away quickly to stop the blush that heated the back of her neck.

Ronnie interrupted the meditation on Bob's virtues by asking her, "Has anyone rushed you yet?"

"One of the girls in the theater department asked me to her rush party. I was thinking about joining her sorority, but I kinda hate to leave my roommates. I like them."

Bob said, "That Greek stuff is silly. Bunch of rich kids playing games. Children."

Dottie shrugged. It wasn't something an ex-Marine would understand. It meant you were accepted. Part of the good crowd. She thought maybe no one would rush Ronnie. Perhaps she could help. "Have you been asked?"

Ronnie studied her glass as though she expected to find

an answer to her problems in it. "I really don't know very many people."

"Come around to rehearsal Thursday night. I'll introduce you to the girl who asked me." She figured Ronnie would be too scared so she added, "Just smile. You'll be okay. You've got a sweet smile. Your face lights up when you do." Sweet was one of those words she didn't like much but she didn't quite know what else to say.

It worked because Ronnie's face became animated again. "That would be swell. Frank?" She tugged at his sleeve but they were interrupted by delivery of their orders. Four beers and four shots, and a glass of water.

Dottie surveyed the array. "Where's the boilermaker?"

"This is it, babe. Like this." He dropped the shot glass of whiskey into the beer and handed it to her.

She stared at it. "What do I do with that? Will it stay there?"

Bob laughed, picked up his own and downed a good part of it. "Like that."

Sure that the shot glass would hit her in the nose when she tipped the drink, she sipped hers gingerly. She didn't like beer much. Should have ordered a seven and seven.

"Drink up."

"Mmm. I will, in a minute." If he could do it, she could, but she'd eat a bit first and watch to see what he did with the glass.

Bob took a small sip then checked the doneness of his burger. "Nice and red." He groaned when he tasted it. "After all those Marine rations, this is like dying and going to heaven." He wore the same look on his face as when he'd stroked the car.

Dottie turned away from the sight of the pink. She liked her meat well-done. That red turned her stomach to look at it. Still, in her present mood there was something sexy in the way he relished that raw meat, turning the sandwich slowly in his hand, drooling over it, chewing it slowly. She watched the muscles in his face work. She imagined his mouth churning against her lips.

Her stomach mimicked the motion. She took a deep breath. She'd never known that the act of eating could actually provoke such visceral responses. She made a mental note to use those feelings on stage when she got a good role.

Frank interrupted her musing. "One of these days, I'm going to have a used-car business."

She didn't want to hear about cars, she wanted to mull over Bob, watch him eat. She put down her burger.

But Frank had no intention of stopping. "One day I'm going to have a dealership." He straightened up as though he already did.

She wanted to glower at him. He hadn't the brains to begin with. He'd even dropped out of school, hadn't he? She wasn't sure, but she thought Bob had said that.

He went on, "I'm on my way. With all these old cars around, I can make me a pile. The other day some guy brought in a Packard. Big thing . . ." He told at length about the ways he could make a small job into a big one.

To Dottie's annoyance, Bob forgot his pleasure in the burger to talk about the engine, the cams, the pistons and stuff like rpms on the convertible.

Sighing, she settled back to endure their car talk, wondering if they had any idea how dull they were when they got on one of these kicks. But that was one of the things a girl had to put up with.

In spite of the car talk, or maybe because of it, Bob finished his food and drink quickly. He ordered another boilermaker for himself and one for her even though she hadn't finished her first. The waitress snapped her gum at him. He changed the order to one beer, two shots and a 7-Up. "The 7-Up for her."

Dottie tried to drink up and make room for the expected seven and seven. It wasn't easy with that shot glass in there, threatening her. She screwed up her courage and downed it quickly. Surprisingly, she finished with her nose dry.

Her glass was empty and beside Bob when the waitress returned. She sniffed, said, "Hmpf," and put the 7-Up in front of Dottie. She placed the rest in front of Bob.

When she walked off, Bob laughed and laid a couple of dollars on the table. "C'mon, Frank, pony up. She's a good waitress." He drained half his glass. "Drink up. Time to go."

"Where we going?" Frank asked.

"For a ride. Get some fresh air in our lungs. Bottoms up." He pushed the shot glass of whiskey toward her.

Dottie looked at her watch. Nine o'clock already. She took a gulp of straight whiskey and choked.

Bob laughed and pushed the glass again. "It gets easier."

She made a face and downed it in two more tries then took a big gulp of soda. "Time's a-wastin'. Gotta be back by eleven-thirty."

Bob stood and eased out of the booth. He asked Frank, "You got a car?"

Frank shook his head. "Got a lift. Figured we'd be together."

Bob nodded. "Let's go."

They piled into the car. He didn't hit eighty this time. He settled for sixty till they got near Perrysburg when he slowed.

The scarf stayed in the glove compartment and Dottie, still

warm from the whiskey, let the wind whip her hair about her face. November at BG wasn't exactly midwinter, but the cold reminded her of winters in Rocky River when the winds crossed Lake Erie and dumped their mounting load of snow over everything east. Her house along the River Road had to be the magnetic east. The snowflakes settled there like white iron filings. She loved it.

Now, in the open car, she curled as close to Bob as she could without pinning his driving arm. Her head spun a little but she felt cocooned in a comforting warmth, whether from Bob's nearness or the alcohol, she wasn't sure. She knew she liked the feeling. "Mmmm. It's gonna be a hot time in the cold town tonight."

He put his arm around her and massaged her shoulder. If she could have moved closer, she would have.

"Where we going?" Frank asked again.

Ronnie spoke up from the backseat. "Don't forget. We've got to be in. They'll lock us out."

Frank kissed her and said, "Yeah. Yeah." Between kisses he repeated, "Where we going?"

"Down by the river. Know a good spot. Fort Meigs. Eighteen-twelve stuff. Old Chief Tecumseh was there. Mad Anthony Wayne, whoever he was. There's an Anthony Wayne Trail around here somewhere. Must have been some big Indian fighter."

Dottie remembered her first sight of the river when she'd come to BG. They'd driven over the bridge past the place where the old Fort Meigs would have sat on the hill. Now it was only a park, if a place crowned by trees gloriously cloaked in autumn could be said to be only anything. Along the foot of the park, the tree-lined Maumee River wound its way, flaunting spectacular crimson, golds and rust. Splotches of the brilliant red sumac puddled in the October blue of the water.

For a city girl, the scene had been like a Technicolor movie setting.

She pictured herself on the silver screen as Maureen O'Hara kissing John Wayne good-bye at the old fort. She'd have to change her name from Dottie Cook. A ton of jokes could be made out of that. Caroline. But not Cook. No, Cara, Cara D'Talia. Properly romantic. One day.

The car swerved a little going around the corner but luckily they had the road to themselves. He turned on to the small road just before the bridge, parked at the top of the hill in a small circle and put the top up.

The trees were almost bare now but a thousand of the fall leaves swirled and churned deep in her stomach. She wiped the last trace of lipstick from her mouth and waited.

He climbed into the car on her side and took a bottle of Seven Roses from the glove compartment. He took a healthy swig and gave it to her.

She closed her eyes and gulped. Heat engulfed her as he pulled her to him and breathed, "Now, baby."

A wolf calling her to slaughter. Charles Boyer with that deep voice and French accent, leaning over Irene Dunne.

She shivered and closed her eyes. Oh, Charles! Yes!

She had no idea nor did she care what Frank and Ronnie did in the backseat. She didn't care either about the warning from her mother about petting and going all the way. All the way to heaven, she sighed.

As his hands slid beneath her sweater and explored her skin, slipped beneath her skirt, along her legs, she pictured the hungry way he'd turned the sandwich in his hands, the look of gluttony in his eyes. She felt the heat of his body on hers and moaned with pleasure.

In his passionate embrace, it seemed as though the minutes were hours and hours were minutes, that a lifetime, more or less, passed.

From the backseat, Ronnie gasped and pushed Frank away. "Do you know what time it is? It's eleven-thirty. The doors will be locked if we don't hurry."

Panicked, Dottie shoved at Bob and tried to sit up. Oh boy! If she got suspended her mom and dad would have a real down-home, Bible Belt Baptist fit. "Jimminy, let's go."

Frank pulled Ronnie down. "We'll go stay at Bob's."

Bob straightened. "Oh, no, we won't. Bob has a nosy landlady."

"And I've got a mother," Frank groaned.

Ronnie giggled. "We can sneak in the window if we have to. Betsy'll let me in."

"Well then, there's no hurry, is there?" Bob settled down again.

Dottie pushed him away. "C'mon. We'd better go." Even if Betsy could let them in, she'd have to get past the proctor with her room at the head of the stairs, then she'd have to face Liz and Sarah. They were sure to give her a hard time. She felt a bit like a hypocrite when she prayed, "Dear Lord, don't let us be late." She added, "For Mom's sake?"

Bob reached for her. "Not yet."

"Now." She pushed him hard and rearranged her clothes.

"Oohhkay. If we must." He tried to continue his kisses.

"No!" She pulled away and smoothed her hair.

He frowned and growled, "Nuts," but he squirmed and wiggled his way across her to his side of the car.

As he did, a spotlight lit up the car. A police car slowed and stopped. The face of an officer appeared in Bob's window.

Dottie covered her eyes and held her breath, wishing she could disappear under the floorboards. What next? She had a vision of herself in a police lineup. Did they arrest kids for necking?

Bob held up the keys. "Just leaving, officer!"

Dottie cringed there for what seemed at least an hour. Finally the cop grunted and said, "College kids, are you?" He shined a light on Bob's then Frank's faces. "How old are you girls?"

Both of them squeaked at once. "Nineteen."

Silence.

Geez. She hoped he wouldn't ask for IDs. She was almost nineteen. In ten months anyway.

He didn't, but then he didn't say anything else right away, either, just stood and let them sweat it out. Finally he said, "Okay. But this isn't very smart, being out here. You never know who's around."

Bob said, "Yes, sir. We haven't been here very long. We were just going."

"We were, officer. We have to get back," Dottie squeaked, hoping he'd take the hint and let them go. She didn't dare look at her watch.

He said, "Yeah," like, sure you were. "Get going." He got back into his car. The spotlight went out but he waited.

Bob put the car in gear. "Let's get out of here."

Dottie got the nervous giggles. Between fits, she managed to say to Bob, "For a big tough Marine, you sure were awfully meek."

"Even a Marine knows when to salute." She could have sworn he blushed.

This time he didn't speed and Dottie fidgeted, staring at her watch, willing it to slow down. "Can't you hurry?"

"Can't get stopped again."

It was well after twelve-thirty when he finally parked on the street not too near the dorm. They piled out and tiptoed across the grass to the back of the building.

Ronnie threw small sticks at the window while the rest of them darted anxious looks over their shoulders.

Dottie held her breath and counted the seconds. They dragged by on a rusty minute hand. She started at every dry leaf the wind dropped at her feet.

Something landed in front of her with a soft thump. She jumped and squealed then bit her lip. Bob snickered quietly.

The window slid open.

"Betsy, it's me, Ronnie. Let me in."

The figure in the dark room paused for a moment then opened the window wider and stepped back.

Frank made a cup with his hands. "Okay, Ronnie. Up you go."

She stepped up and grabbed for the sill and slipped. She fell but managed to catch his arm, landing on one knee. She cried, "Ouch," then put her hand over her mouth and giggled. She rose, took a testing step and brushed herself off.

"Shhhhh," Dottie whispered. They were making enough noise to wake not only the dead, but the proctor too.

"C'mon, Dottie." Bob stepped up to the window and gave her a boost. She grasped the sill. He boosted higher and she swung her leg over, then tumbled in. "Thank you, Lord. So far. It's for Mom, remember?"

Dottie whispered, "Thanks, Betsy," and rushed past the other form sitting up in the third bed. The form hissed at her, "You'll get us in trouble."

Betsy turned back to the open window.

Cracking the door open, Dottie peered into the hall. Only a faint light showed from beneath the shower room door. All clear. She took off her shoes and tiptoed as fast as she could, hugging the wall up the two flights of stairs. Her last obstacle, the proctor's door, was at the top, dead ahead. Again, the only light came from the showers. Holding her breath, she crept past, feeling like a thousand-legged bug with football cleats.

At her own door, she took a deep breath, and slowly turned the knob. The shower room door creaked and light spilled out.

She slid into her room and pushed the door shut, then stood there, panting and leaning against it, her eyes closed tight against the vision she didn't want to have.

The door shoved against her. A voice whispered, "Let me in!"

Liz! Dottie, sure she was going to faint, tried to steady her trembling knees.

Liz shoved harder at the door and Dottie managed to move.

"It's almost one," Liz rasped. "We were worried sick about you. Where've you been?" She climbed onto her bed and sat there scowling.

Dottie giggled in relief then kept on giggling until she doubled over. She laughed alone.

Finally she straightened. "We went for a . . . uh . . . Bob, uh, a ride in Bob's convertible. We, uh, had a flat tire."

Frosted flakes would have made an appropriate lunch when Dottie joined Liz and Sarah. Most of the dorm must have opted for the Nest. They had plenty of space to themselves.

Dottie had tried ever since they got out of bed to change the subject but they kept going on about her getting into trouble. Actually, now that she was safe, she did have to admit to herself, only to herself, that maybe there'd better not be a next time. But it had been a great evening . . . She tuned out their scolding to think about Bob, his kiss, his touch . . .

Sarah, always the quiet one, raised her voice. "Dottie, aren't you listening? Do you have any idea . . ."

Dottie blushed. "I hear you. I hear you. Have heard you for hours." She wished there were more kids in the dining hall. Maybe then they'd be quiet.

Both Sarah and Liz gave a disgusted sigh and picked up their forks. A girl with red eyes and a puffy, scarlet face, bore down upon them. From the surprised looks of both her roommates, Dottie figured they didn't know the kid, either.

The girl evidently knew her, though. She sat then hissed at Dottie, "It's all your fault."

Dottie drew back. "What's my fault?" She had a sinking feeling she knew.

"They caught Ronnie last night. She didn't make it."

For a moment, Dottie's heart stopped. "How? Did they get the guys?" She felt sorry for Ronnie, but she was worried about Bob.

Liz interrupted. "What happened?"

The girl turned to glare at Liz and whirled back around to Dottie. She gave her a look of contempt and said between her teeth, "Don't worry, they only got Ronnie. Her and that Frank. She didn't squeal. Worst luck. They had her on the carpet this morning. Too bad that guy's not in school. I'd love to see him get kicked out. And too bad they didn't get you."

Now that she knew Bob had gotten away, Dottie allowed herself to feel bad about Ronnie. And guilty. But it wasn't really her fault. It was Ronnie who suggested using the window. And she had gone first. Only she'd fallen. They all took their chances.

Liz and Sarah both leaned over and asked at once, "What happened? Did they suspend her?"

Tears ran down the girl's face and she said through clenched teeth, "Ronnie's expelled. Betsy's on detention and she doesn't deserve it. She didn't do anything." She glared again at Dottie.

Sarah got up and went around to sit by her. She put her arms around her. "I'm sorry."

"Ronnie said it was her own doing." The girl took Sarah's napkin and blew her nose. The sympathy seemed to calm her a little. "She didn't want to be seen talking to you so she said to tell you it's okay and she was glad they didn't get Bob or you. After he helped you in, he'd already gone back to the car. She stopped to kiss that stupid Frank good night. The watchman found them just when Betsy was helping her in. They thought she'd just climbed out at first but when they smelled the liquor . . ." The girl stopped to wipe her eyes. "If she'd not been drinking, they might have just suspended her."

The girl muttered at Dottie, "I ought to tell," then rose and stumbled off.

They all pushed their food away.

Chapter 5

Homecoming. Finally. The three weeks had crawled, but now, he was here. Alan was here!

Liz ignored her banana split to devour him with her eyes. Emily Post, the doyenne of manners, would never approve of the urge she had right now. No. It would never do to muss that blond hair in public. Or kiss him hard. Right now.

He grinned as though he could read her mind. She saw the lines gather at the corners of his eyes and watched as the hazel picked up that laughter to lighten and turn green.

Miss Post won the argument. Instead Liz fidgeted, picked up her spoon and put it down, then picked it up again, and sank it into the ice cream which again she didn't eat. She finally gave it a rest and said, "There's a bonfire tonight. Or we could go to a movie. *State Fair* at the Cla-zel. Jeanne Crane, Dana Andrews."

They had elbowed their way through the crowd and snared the last empty table at BG's student union. The chatter of students released from a week of brain drain, mixed with the sounds of "Juke Box Saturday Night," to make the place sound like a jar of bees next to an amplifier.

Alan wasn't far from the mark when he asked, "You said you called this place 'The Bee Hive'?"

"Falcon's Nest. For the Bowling Green Falcons."

"I must say it's, ah, quaint."

Liz wrinkled her nose. "You're the only one I know who could make a log building sound Victorian." The woody look of pine and logs gave it a warm feeling despite the long center space, the cafeteria-style order service, and the ordinary booths that lined the walls. Any place filled with as many kids and as much noise as the Nest at this moment, became automatically cozy, if only because you found yourself elbow to elbow.

Alan countered her accusation with, "Hmm. Do I detect a note of reproach in that statement?"

She tilted her head and thought about it. "No. Maybe you're just a teensy stuffy, but very, very cute."

Alan leaned forward and frowned. "Am I really?"

"Stuffy or cute?" She wasn't quite ready to let him off the hook for making fun of the Nest.

"Oh, I do want to be cute!"

Figuring he'd suffered enough for such a small sin, she gave him a quick version of the kiss she'd thought about a moment ago, then, throwing Emily to the wolves, kissed him again. While it was still short of what she meant, a red wave rose from his neck.

"See, you're embarrassed, aren't you?" she teased, then relented. "How about stuffy and 'Hubba! Hubba!' instead of cute?"

For a second she thought a shadow darkened his eyes. She hastened to take any sting from her teasing. "It's a nice stuffy. Compared to some of these GIs, especially like that Bob, well, you're so polite and everything. I somehow expect you to turn up in morning greys."

He leaned forward, lowered his voice, and put a straw between his teeth. From the corner of his mouth, he muttered, "Well, doll. I can fix that. Just got me a new set of pinstripes. How's about you and me going to the Cla-zel and doing a little neckin' in the balcony?"

"Maybe there isn't one." She giggled then stopped in

mid-"hee" as Dottie showed up with a hamburger in hand. "Bob's back there. Do you mind if we join you? Everything's full."

Liz slid over. "Sure. Sit. I rather hoped we'd run into you. Wanted you two to meet." She gave Alan a sidelong glance then said with a straight face, "Dottie, this is George Raft."

Dottie held out her hand. "Oh, gee whiz, Mr. Raft, I saw you in *Body and Soul*. You were swell!"

Alan gave Liz a laughing look that said, "I'll get you for that. Wait till we're alone!" He took Dottie's hand in his and rose slightly. "Alan. Alan Bannerman."

"Dottie Cook," she said, then drawled, in Tallulah's deep voice, "Just dot your i's and cross your t's, dah-ling."

"Surely it's Miss Bankhead, incognito!"

Dottie giggled and slid into the booth. Her face was the color of the catsup on her burger. She couldn't get her dishes arranged fast enough. The bun slid from the plate and the pickle spilled out. The half with mustard and catsup flipped, bun down, onto the table. She shook her head, "So much for glamour."

They were laughing when Bob came up. "Is this a private joke or can anyone join?" He set his Coke on the table, looked Alan up and down and held out his hand, "Sergeant Bob Arnold, late of the finest, the U.S. Marine Corps. You look like a Navy man." His words held the smug tone that got the land arm of the Navy into fights.

Alan's eyebrow dipped as he moved over to make room. He raised his glass and took a long drink. "I'm wearing my best barnacles today." His glass could have frosted over and manufactured ice cubes from the tone of the rebuff.

Bob persisted. "What ship were you on? South Pacific? You Navy types had it easy. Y'shoulda been on Tinian and

Okinawa. A real hell. All the while you guys sat around on your big cans eating ice cream."

Liz couldn't resist asking how, if the Navy sat eating ice cream, he thought the Marines got on the islands. She got as far as, "How do you . . ."

Alan interrupted. "One does what one can."

Liz knew he seldom bothered to explain that the draft board turned him down for flat feet and asthma. Since he didn't go in for track, he never cared that his feet were less than perfect. The asthma he claimed he had outgrown. Sometimes when questions were asked in arrogance, he got very British about it. He wasn't British but his grandmother spoke with an accent that sounded as though she'd endowed Oxford personally.

Bob didn't let it go. "Where were you, Atlantic or Pacific?"

Alan said, "Both."

"What ship?"

Liz had never seen Alan lose his temper, but he could and did turn the temperature near him to minus zero.

Now, without batting an eye, he said, "*Enterprise,*" and gave Liz a poke under the table when she gasped.

She bit her lip to keep from laughing. He was telling the truth, but not the whole truth, and who cared? His dad was a distant cousin or something of Admiral Halsey and Alan had actually visited on the flagship.

Bob raised a brow, impressed in spite of himself. He went into a long bragging session about his struggles and then quizzed Alan again. "What did you do in the Atlantic?"

"I transferred to a sub. Admirals aren't my style." He had been treated by another cousin to a sub visit at Norfolk.

Such cool, Liz thought to herself, and wondered if it

occurred to Bob to question how a full-time student at Georgetown, a senior, managed all of that. But then, Bob wasn't really interested in anything but playing the hero, which Liz thought sad. He probably was a hero. Too bad he couldn't accept that and let it go.

Still, she almost felt sorry for Alan in spite of his lack of need for sympathy. It must be annoying trying to explain something that shouldn't have to be explained. Truth to tell, she was secretly glad he'd not been over there somewhere getting shot at. She liked him home and in one piece. She instinctively reached out and touched his sleeve.

Liz's reflections were interrupted by Sarah with Rick in tow. She leaned her tray on the edge of the table. "I don't suppose we could squeeze in here, could we? Nothing's empty."

Liz felt rather than heard Alan's quick intake of breath as he got his first glance at Sarah. Liz might have turned Nile green if she hadn't liked her friend so much. Sarah wore her hair back in that ballerina look again. Her long-waisted cashmere, a Nordic ice, matched the clear blue of her eyes.

Liz took a deep breath and smiled. If she turned green in envy, she'd only clash with Sarah's blue and come off looking terrible.

In Alan's honor Liz had foresworn her sweatshirt but next to Sarah, she felt like a poor cousin: the wool of her sweater was almost as soft, the color almost as blue, and her pearls almost as long. She reached up and touched her hair. It must look like she'd been out in a high wind compared to Sarah's cool, sleek look.

Alan rose slightly and smiled at Sarah but the smile was, after the first shock, friendly rather than ogling and Liz relaxed a bit. She said, "Sarah, this is Alan, as you might have guessed."

Alan reached out to her. "Hi, Sarah. At last. I've been waiting to meet this math genius Liz keeps telling me about. My worst subject. Now if you three ladies would all move to Georgetown, my problems would be solved."

Sarah beamed and Liz wanted to kiss him. Again, but this time for Sarah.

Rick, standing just behind Sarah, bristled. "What's this genius bit? And she's not going anywhere."

Most people, when they first saw Rick, started at his clavicle, which was on a level with their eyes, went to the top of his head then worked their way down the long thin frame.

Alan didn't even blink. He just smiled pleasantly.

Dottie saw his glance and quipped, "Quite a feat to reach his feet."

If Rick heard, he didn't acknowledge the humor.

While they all shuffled plates and glasses to make room, Dottie said, "We're going to the bonfire tonight, Liz. Anyone else going?"

Bob said, "Yeah. Come with us. We're going to do the snake through town afterwards."

Liz frowned and looked up at her. "The kids got in trouble last time. The town police were really mad."

Dottie winced.

"We're going to the movie." Alan spoke the words at the top of the ex-Marine's crew cut.

All the distraction had improved Liz's appetite and she scraped her almost-empty ice cream dish. She didn't dare look at Alan. She was irritated with Bob, but Dottie was her friend. She asked her, "Why don't you come with us?"

Bob snorted. "*State Fair*? You've got to be kidding. How about going out to the Center Line?"

Liz glared at him. How dare he! She forgot Dottie and

snapped, "I'd think you'd learn, but then you weren't ex-pelled, were you?"

As soon as the words left her mouth, she was sorry. Dottie pushed her dish away and looked as though she were going to cry. Liz reached over and took her hand. "I'm sorry. It wasn't your fault." But wasn't it, at least partly? Still, who was she to appoint blame? She just wished Dottie would say no sometimes. As for Bob, well, she'd rather not even think about him.

But Bob forced her to think about him. "Look, I've been in every bar from here to Manila. I'm over twenty-one. How can they tell me I can't go to that one?"

She had to admit the argument made sense, yet he was not the only one concerned. The ban hadn't been made to protect these vets, but the young kids who normally filled the college dorms. "Dottie hasn't." She turned away from him.

Rick joined the argument. "You can do what you want, but not me. I can't afford to get caught. I'd be off the team."

Bob sneered, "Who'll know? You going to wear your BG basketball shirt?"

Rick reached out and touched Sarah's hand. "They all know my face and with Sarah on my arm, who could miss us? We'll pass." He turned a big smile on her. "How about it? The bonfire or the Cla-zel?"

Although Liz couldn't swear she'd moved, Sarah seemed to shrink back into the booth. She spoke in a small voice. "It doesn't matter. Whatever you want. It's fine."

Alan looked from Sarah and Rick to Dottie and Bob, then abruptly asked Liz, "Are you finished? I think I ought to get to the inn."

When they were outside, he opened the door of his dark

blue '39 Packard coupe for her and Liz got in. Of all the cars they made, she liked Packard best. The long hood and sharp nose had the most elegant look of any, short of a Rolls Royce she'd seen once.

And speaking of elegance, she thought, Sarah in particular, and turned to Alan. "Wow. I don't think you like my friends much," then she grinned at him, "except for Sarah."

Alan leaned over and gave her a conciliatory kiss. "I do. I like Sarah a lot and, as you said, Dottie is certainly cute. That young lady is headed for trouble, though, if she doesn't get away from Bob. He's too experienced for her."

"Yeah, well, you haven't heard." She told him of the window escapade. "Ronnie never squealed on Dottie, though. The girl who let them in got in trouble but she's okay. They kicked Ronnie out. Probably if they hadn't been drinking, they'd have just suspended her." Tired of thinking about it, she brightened and rounded on him mischievously. "How come you like Sarah so much?"

He hugged her then started the car. "Not what you think. She is a beauty, but that's not it. Actually, I feel rather sorry for her."

"She's so smart and I think he majors in tiddlywinks."

He laughed at that but said quietly, "Even I can see Rick wants a trophy."

"Mmm. She knows. Did you see her shrink back? You were really sweet. You must be the first guy ever to give her a compliment on her brains. That got a big smile from her!" Liz snuggled close. "I'd love to be as gorgeous as that, but it isn't all fun, is it?"

He pulled up in front of Kohl Hall and took the keys from the dash. "A car's not much good around here, is it? I didn't even have time to shift gears." He had, of course; still, they probably could have walked as fast.

"We are going to the dance tomorrow night, aren't we? I have a new green dress."

He twisted a length of her hair around his fingers and put the strand to his lips. "It smells like lilacs." He kissed her softly then said, "Can't wait to see the dress." He kissed her again and got out and opened her door. "See you at seven." He waited a moment then added softly, "Gorgeous."

They heard a long wolf whistle.

Liz found herself humming "Don't Get Around Much Any More," again. But she wasn't missing this Saturday dance. Alan was in the lobby. Alan waited for her! She walked slowly downstairs, hugging that thought to herself.

He watched with a smile on his face as she came down the final steps. He came to her. "You don't need to worry about Sarah. You are tres chic. Elegant." He took her hand and twirled her around. "Beautiful. That's your color. It sets your hair on fire."

She smiled back but sighed inwardly, tired of having to resist kissing him in public. When he turned on the charm like that, he took her breath away. She brushed her hand down the skirt of her gown. She'd picked the style especially with him in mind. So many of the dresses had the same full sleeves and full skirts with that sweetheart neckline. She'd decided to try to look sophisticated in this slim, princess style, no waistline, tight sleeves with a slit.

He leaned forward and gave her the kiss she'd wanted to give him.

She blushed and stepped back. "They'll see." The housemother and the two hostesses were too busy to notice and she regained her equilibrium. "I guess that's why you decided to be a diplomat, you're full of it."

His eyes went from glimmer to glow. He took her hand and shook his head. "Not always. You really are pretty." Then he handed her a corsage of tiny yellow roses. On the box was a poem by Tennyson:

But the rose was awake all night for your sake,
Knowing your promise to me;
The lilies and roses were all awake,
They sigh'd for the dawn and thee.

For a moment she thought she'd cry. She let him pin the corsage to her waist and take her hand. The touch warmed her as they walked to the dance under the brilliance of glistening November stars.

Orange and brown pennants hung on the gym walls with the bold flourish of a winner. BG had trounced its chief football rival, T.U., so badly at the homecoming game this afternoon, Liz wondered if BG's Toledo population would have the nerve to show up. Would fifteen miles be enough to wipe the smile from a Toledo face?

When they entered, as though on cue, the soulful notes of "Stardust" wailed from the sax and horn, and was picked up by the singer, a kid Liz thought she'd seen in Biology.

Alan drew her, bewitched, onto the softly lit dance floor. "Come on, Lizzie Ellen, that's our song." He put his hand on her waist and moved her to the center. With his cheek against hers, he ignored the band vocalist and sang softly into her ear, "and I am once again with you . . ."

Liz closed her eyes as he crooned the words and wrapped her in their spell. Mmmm. Perfect tune, perfect words, perfect guy. She let the mood carry her until she danced on that cloud of stardust. When it ended she regretfully came back down to earth and took her cheek reluctantly from his. "I don't think I've ever heard you sing before. How come?"

Even in the softly lit room, the light of laughter washed over his eyes. "You notice I don't sing loud."

The music began again. This time it was the horn swinging out with "Polka Dots and Moonbeams." He nuzzled her cheek.

"You're not singing."

"Mmm-hmm. Maybe never again. It was our song that did it." After a moment he asked, "What happened with the snake dance last night? Any trouble?"

"No, the cops were watching."

"Dottie get home okay?"

"Mmmm." Liz hated having the mood interrupted, but she answered to get it over with. "She got in on time at least. I think they did go out to the Center Line. She was chewing gum, but you could still smell the whiskey. Sarah and I both bawled her out, but she just won't be serious. She said, 'No one from the school goes there,' and shrugged us off."

"Mmm. She serious about being an actress?"

"She is good. She's got a part in the next play. Not a big one, but she says she gets to cry, so it must not be too bad. They just had *Arsenic and Old Lace*. The drama department's really good for a school this size."

He chuckled and caressed her cheek with his again. "Ah, well, missed my chance, I guess." They moved slowly and cozily to the strains of "This Love of Mine." He forgot himself and sang, "goes on and . . . ," then stopped and laughed. After a while, he said, "Of course our theater department probably isn't as fantastic as yours, I mean, it's only Georgetown." He brushed his lips across hers and murmured, "I miss you. I think you ought to transfer and marry me even if we do have second-class drama."

Her heart did a quick step and she came to a full stop in the middle of the floor. "I think you just proposed!"

He drew her back to his arms and brushed her cheek with his. "Did I?"

Liz, half-thrilled and half-angry, wanted to hit him. The most romantic moment in a girl's life, and he's teasing her! "No." That would show him!

"No, what?"

"Did you propose or not?"

He didn't move his cheek from hers and his tone still wasn't serious. "Did I?"

"Oh Alan. Stop it." Tears came to her eyes and she walked off the floor.

He followed and took her hand and led her to the fire escape balcony.

How could he! She took a deep breath of cool air, as crisp as the glitter of the stars which looked to be made of ice instead of fire. She shivered.

He kissed her. "I love you, goose." He took off his coat and put it around her shoulders then drew a buried lock of her hair from the collar and held it. "Until the war I spent my summers in Connecticut. Mother would go back in the fall to close the house. The maples were just this color." He put the lock gently on her shoulder then took her in his arms and kissed her, moving his face and lips gently on hers. The fire in his kiss burned away her anger.

"I love you, Liz. Will you marry me?"

She felt her heart stop, then leap. She did want to marry him. She pictured herself walking down the aisle in ivory Skinner satin and Chantilly lace, and then snipping roses from the garden of a mellowed Georgian brick home. Set, of course, on the top of a hill and bathed in autumn. A little brown-haired boy and a golden girl . . .

She did want that dream, but not yet. And she didn't want to go to Georgetown. The door to the gym opened a crack and, for a moment, a streak of light fell between them. The door shut.

She laid her head against his chest. "You'll graduate in June! Then what?"

"Then we'll be together? What else is important?"

Feeling let down and hurt by his lack of understanding, she tried to explain. "I'd be alone at Georgetown and you'd be stuck, a junior junior attaché, in some place like Outer Mongolia or, if you're really lucky, maybe Inner Mongolia. Then what?"

It would never get that far, she told herself. What would her family say? Even Mom, as old-fashioned as she was, would insist Liz finish school first.

"Cold?"

"No. Flabbergasted. Oh, Alan, you know that won't work. I'll have three more years of school and you'll be miles away."

"I think Dad could pull some strings and get me posted in the States."

"That's not what you said you wanted. You wanted foreign experience first. You said Washington would come later."

"Well, I have to admit I'd rather be Ambassador to the Court of St. James, or to Paris. Perhaps as a last resort, Rome." He grinned at her and kissed her. "You could come with me, you know."

"I'll still have to go for my bachelor's, and to do anything interesting at all, I'll have to have a Master's. I ought to get a doctorate."

"There's always liberal arts. A good education. Good background."

"Maybe I should take horticulture and grow your roses!" she snapped. But then the image of the grand dame with a basket of flowers on her arm came back to her. Trouble was, the picture appealed to her. Greer Garson and Irene Dunne passed by with their arms full of roses. In a way, Alan was right. Sooner or later they all did it. Then Katharine Hepburn came along with a diploma in her hand and the dream evaporated.

Alan smiled at her and downplayed her worries. "I love roses." He traced the line of her hair across her forehead with his finger. "We can talk about all that later. Will you marry me?"

She pulled the coat around her. "I'm cold. You must be, too. Let's go in."

As they came in, the last notes of "It's Been a Long, Long Time" faded away. The band leader took the mike and announced, "Ladies and gentlemen, no homecoming coronation dance is complete without a waltz contest, so pick your partners."

Alan raised an eyebrow at Liz and asked, "Do you mind if we don't?"

"To tell the truth, I'll be delighted. I'd much rather watch."

To Liz's surprise, at the other end of the room, Rick led Sarah to the floor. Nearer, but not so surprisingly, Dottie stood with Bob's arm about her waist, her arm poised regally.

The band played "Casey Would Waltz with the Strawberry Blond," as the skirts whirled by in a blizzard of color.

Sarah and Rick were tapped and she smiled, looking glad to be out of it. Liz breathed a sigh of relief. She had been dreading to see Sarah disappointed again.

Bob and Dottie did a spin that made the judges stop

their tapping to watch. By the time Casey had nearly exploded the second time, there were only two other couples on the floor.

"I hate to say it, he is—they are good, aren't they?" Alan said as the first judge took Dottie's hand and led her and Bob to the mike.

"Ladies and gentlemen, the winners . . ." He paused long enough for them to say their names, then handed them each a trophy. "Let's all give them a hand." He put the statues on the piano. "For now, 'Let's Dance.' "

Dottie and Bob took the floor to a big round of applause.

Alan watched the orchestra for a moment, then with a grin quipped, "Your leader's a good man, if he isn't Goodman."

Liz groaned, "Oh. I think I need punch! Come to think of it, I think after that line, it's you who needs the punch." They were at the table by then and she turned with a cup in her hand and almost spilled it on Tom Butler who had just walked up.

Red-faced, she apologized. "Oh, Tom. I'm so sorry. Did I get it on you?"

He looked his jacket and trousers over and gave her a big smile. "No damage. How about you?"

"No. I am sorry." She turned to Alan and said, "Alan, this is Tom Butler. Alan Bannerman." She stumbled over "Tom's in my French class." She could hardly say, "This is the one I told you about, the one at the mixer and the one I bowled with." "Alan's down, ah, up from Georgetown for the weekend."

Tom held out his hand and nodded. The shadow of a smile crossed his face as he said to her, softly, "Too bad." He turned and took the hand of the girl who stood on the other side of him, introduced her, then said, "I think it's safe enough to get our punch now."

As he did, Bob and Dottie walked up to him. Bob said loudly, "Hi, Tom. Heard you give bowling lessons." He smirked at Liz, then got cookies for Dottie and himself.

Liz was sorry it had been Tom she'd missed with the punch. She put down her glass and walked away. Alan followed.

"What was that all about?"

The trombones complained, "Don't Get Around Much Any More." Liz took his arm. That song had been stuck in her head all day. She said, "Let's dance. I love this."

"It's not right for us to be separated like this, you know, Liz. Too much competition around here."

She looked up at him, feeling both guilty and innocent. "You mean Tom, don't you? There was nothing to that." She told him how Rick had arranged things. "Tom's a nice guy and I just couldn't see making a big thing out of it. That's all there was to it."

Alan drew her closer. "I know. But this isn't good, is it? I love you, Liz."

"You are he whom I love, remember?" If he was, though, why hadn't she said yes? Just marry him and forget all this.

Chapter 6

Sarah yelled, "Yeah, Rick," and looked as though she might fly off the bleachers. With the gym packed solidly for the basketball game, she couldn't fall far, but Liz put her hand out to steady her. She could picture a heap of cashmere sweaters and saddle shoes.

She continued to cling to the waving arm, just in case. When the next shot ran the rim and slipped through, she had to let go to cover her ears. The roar of the crowd was nothing to Sarah's bellow.

"I think a hog caller could take lessons from you!" The words were lost in the noise.

The score stood at DePaul 88, Bowling Green 88. Quiet Sarah went right on screaming. "Rick, Rick, Rick!" The cement walls threw back the crowd's thunder as the clock ticked: nineteen, eighteen. The DePaul center dribbled. A BG kid dubbed Toothbrush, tipped it to Rick. Two long bounces and Rick paused, jumped and shot. The gun went off.

The ball looped high and down, sailing into the basket as though on a string. Bowling Green 90, DePaul 88! The house roared; the BG team slapped and pounded each other.

Liz hugged Sarah who didn't stand still for it. "Yeah, Rick! Yeah, Rick!" A sound lost in the near chaos of yelling, stamping and clapping. More than one cried. With DePaul's reputation, this victory showed they were almost certainly bound for the Nationals.

Busy now shaking hands with DePaul's center, Rick didn't turn to look for Sarah as he walked off to the locker rooms. She had told him where she meant to sit, that much Liz knew. Now the girl's look said it didn't bother her at all, but her fingers rolled the pearls on their long strand.

Liz put her arm around her. "Are you going to wait for him?"

"We're going to meet at the Nest. Why don't you come? When he wins like this, I might as well not be there. Everyone comes over." The pearls rolled a little faster.

Liz gave her another quick hug. "I didn't bring enough money. We'd have to stop at the dorm."

They were already among the last students in the gym. It would be useless to hurry. Anyway, Rick would be a while.

As expected, when they finally got to the Nest the booths were taken, but they went through the food line, hoping to luck into a vacancy.

Sarah ordered a malt. Liz loaded up with a hamburger and fries, then, checking her waistband, settled for coffee instead of a cola.

By the time they reached the end of the line, there was a booth with only two couples, empty plates and almost empty glasses. Liz and Sarah hung near trying to pretend they weren't desperately eyeing the level of cola in the glasses.

Engrossed in measuring the rate at which the liquids disappeared, neither at first registered the general noise until it grew too loud to ignore. They turned to see a smiling, bowing and laughing Rick.

Sarah lit up. Liz frowned.

Finally, still grinning from ear to ear, he came over to Sarah. "Great match, wasn't it? Boy, was I surprised to get that ball. Saved that game for sure."

Liz stepped back and glared at him. He hadn't even said, "Hi, Sarah." Her index finger itched but she decided that while the hot coffee on him might pacify her, ultimately, it wouldn't be a good idea.

The four in the booth eased out and reached to shake his hand. "We're done. It's all yours." "Great game." "Great save." "Good shot, Rick."

He bowed, then told Sarah, "I'll be right back. Gotta order."

Liz watched him turn away. Still no kiss, even quick, no hug for Sarah who always kept saying, "He's really nice sometimes."

When? Liz wondered for the hundredth time, pondering the irony of anyone so absolutely beautiful as Sarah being so absolutely insecure.

If Rick were nice, did that make up for the times he was as dense as a London fog? Like now. And didn't he realize he was only one part of a team? Toothbrush had intercepted to give Rick the ball. True, he'd scored about half of those points, but the other four had done the rest.

Sarah put her tray down and between them she and Liz cleared a place.

When he came back, Rick brought Tom Butler and another girl, Ann something. Liz couldn't come up with a last name. They were in the same biology class and Liz had always admired the long straight brown hair. The girl had a habit of tracing it down her face with candy-red fingernails, then cavalierly flipping it over her shoulder. Liz's fingers made a little flip with her own hair.

"Done any bowling lately?" Tom's smile spilled up into his blue-blue eyes. He'd dropped French, said he had too many hours. Liz didn't see him much, which was all for the good.

She gave back a weak laugh. " 'Fraid not." The smell of the browned burger was too much for her and she bit into it. Polite conversation would have to wait.

"Good to see a girl with a healthy appetite!" He put a small salad in front of Ann who had slid into the booth, then unloaded a malt and burger for himself. "Do you all know Ann?"

Sarah and Liz both nodded. Rick reached over to take her hand. "Don't think I do, but I should."

The red fingernail flipped the length of hair. "You were super tonight. Great." Her smile poured on sugar.

Tom ignored the byplay and turned to Sarah. "You need to give Liz bowling lessons, you know."

Liz defended herself. "I did make some spares, you know. It was my first time, after all."

The red fingernail moved to Ann's eyebrow.

Tom went into a long embroidered tale of broken floorboards and gutter balls.

Rick finally joined in as though he'd been part of the fun, not the jerk. He laid his hand on Sarah's shoulder. "We make a pretty good team." He reached into his pocket, leaned over and kissed Sarah on the cheek, and opened a small box. He held out the gold letters of Sigma Chi for her to see. "Where shall I put it?"

Ladies didn't say or even think the thing that occurred to Liz.

Sarah flushed.

Ann oohed and aahed.

Liz bit her lip hard and prayed. Please, Sarah, say no. She knew it was Sarah's business, but Liz hated to see her settle for someone who treated her like an old cashmere jacket, classy but disposable.

Sarah fingered her pearls.

Rick put the pin on her sweater, patted her shoulder and kissed her on the forehead.

Ann stood and clapped her red-tipped hands together. "Hey, everyone. Rick's just pinned Sarah. Let's give them a hand."

Liz reached across the table and clasped Sarah's arm. For a while, the room seemed to have no other table or booth.

Liz and Tom quietly watched it all. Finally, she'd had enough. "I'm tired. Stayed up and crammed last night. I'll see you all later."

Tom and Ann had to stand to let her out. He seemed to hesitate as she turned to go. The expression in his eyes was soft, almost wistful, but still amused, as he said, "How's Georgetown? Still there?"

"He asked me to marry him."

His expression didn't change. "And?"

She gave him a small smile. "I will, but not now." She gave a last glance at Sarah who had a lost look about her, like a beautiful doll in a crowded toy shop.

Liz had not said a word to Rick the entire evening and she was quite sure he never noticed.

The walk from the Nest to the dorm was only a matter of minutes, but the December night wind pushed her along with threats of an early winter. Nothing like a crisp wind to clear the head. Sarah was not a daughter, only a roommate.

For a change, when she got back, Dottie was in bed although not asleep. In spite of the newly remade resolution to doff the mother attitude, Liz couldn't resist asking, "What brings you here so early?" Tempted to add, "Was the Center Line closed?" she bit her lip again. Dottie looked a little green.

"I didn't feel too good. Maybe I'm getting the flu.

Anyway, I think I ought to settle down a bit. Too many chances lately."

"Have you decided whether you're going to Lima with Bob's family or is he going to yours for Christmas?"

Dottie sat up. "He's coming to Rocky River the day after. Our folks'd both have a fit if we missed Christmas." She raised her eyes to the ceiling, "They'd have more than a fit if I went to his." She became eager. "It would be nice to share Christmas with Bob. It's a good thing you and Alan live in the same town. Makes life a lot easier."

"You're getting awfully serious for someone who wants to go running off to be an actress."

Dottie hugged her knees. "I know, but he's hard to resist. It's like a fire inside."

Liz badly wanted to say, "For your sake, I hope it burns itself out," but for the third time that night, bit her lip hard. This time it hurt. She'd either have to get some new roommates or find some other way to keep her mouth shut. Dottie and Bob got along just fine. Perhaps they were meant for each other. She found herself wishing she could say the same for Rick and Sarah.

When Sarah finally came in, she smiled shyly and threw her jacket on the bed. Her gold pin caught the light of the desk lamp and glittered.

Dottie stopped to hang up the dropped coat, then grabbed and hugged her bemused roommate. "Look! Sigma Chi! Oh, Sarah, you're pinned! Rick! Congratulations!"

"Thanks." Sarah kicked off her shoes in the middle of the room, then shoved them under the bed.

Dottie laughed. "Bravo."

Sarah ignored her and got a towel for a shower but stopped when Dottie said, "By the way, I entered my picture in the contest for the yearbook. Gregory Peck's going to be one of the judges, can you imagine?"

"Maybe he'll discover you. Like Lana Turner, you know." The story was that Lana had been discovered in a drugstore.

"Yeah!" Dottie's expression was wistful. "It's a good thing you didn't want to send one in. I'd never have a chance."

Sarah looked embarrassed and Liz put in quickly, "Rick talked her into it. She didn't want to, but it really was a beautiful picture."

Dottie smiled. "Who knows, maybe Gregory Peck himself will fall head over heels in love with you."

Sarah reddened and turned away.

From outside the dorm, male voices floated up to them. The three went to the window and opened it. Liz recognized Tom and some of the other guys from Sigma Chi. Rick, of course. He stood in front.

All up and down that side of the dorm, windows flew open and heads appeared.

Rick tossed a slender box to Sarah who caught it. A red rose. Their clear male voices rose softly in the crisp air: ". . . the girl of my dreams . . ."

Dottie, her arm over Sarah's shoulders, joined them softly. Only Sarah and Liz could hear her beautiful voice sing with the men, "The Sweetheart of Sigma Chi."

When they were gone and Sarah drew in her head, Liz saw tears. She wished she wasn't so sure what Sarah cried about.

Chapter 7

Great downy flakes of snow drifted through the dark like a shower of milkweed seeds. From the deep recess of the Bannerman back porch, Liz snuggled with Alan on the winter-shrouded wicker sofa and looked down the hill at a Currier and Ives Christmas scene. With the Chillicothe winter temperature at a balmy thirty-two degrees, no wind, bundled in down coats, and in love, they weren't the least bit cold.

Liz raised her face to his and nuzzled his neck, then blew softly in his ear.

He drew his shoulder up and gave a small shiver. "Do that again. It's warm."

"If it's so warm, how come you shiver?" She blew again and felt the tremor. She nipped his ear playfully, then licked at the lobe.

"So that's how it is, huh?" Laughing, he turned on her, playfully pinned her back on the sofa and gently pressed his lips to hers firmly enough to feel the soft give. He moved his mouth over hers, gently kneading her lips.

Liz felt like a marshmallow too near a bonfire. She closed her eyes and let her lips melt. In dire danger of becoming toasted, she drew back. Her face flamed.

She gulped and sat up. "Whew. Time out."

"Blow on my ear and I'll follow you anywhere!" Alan brushed back his hair and grinned at her.

"You weren't following."

"If I blow in your ear, will you follow me?"

"To the ends of the earth."

"Paris, London—Bern?"

For a split second, Liz's mind registered the pause in the timing of his answer, but with him nuzzling her neck, the thought flickered and went out. "Sure, but not tonight. It's too pretty right here."

He blew on her ear and Liz looked up at him. "Do you know something I don't?"

He laughed. "Let me count the ways."

"Ugh. We are original tonight, aren't we? How about pride goeth before a fall?"

He gently pulled her up to him and the misgivings that niggled at her flew off with the wind. He took her hand. "Want to go for a walk?"

"Let's make a snowman. It's been years."

The fluffy white crystals packed beautifully and, in between kisses and snow missiles, they managed a respectably fat snowman with stones for eyes and a row of buttons.

Liz stood back. "He needs a high hat. I don't suppose you've got an old one?" She took off her scarf and wound it around their wintry friend.

"As a matter of fact, we do. One of Dad's. Hold on."

Liz piled more snow on until Alan came back with the hat and a pair of worn grey doeskin gloves. He made a snowball for the hands, but the fingers flopped so he pressed them flat against the snow.

"What, no broom?" Liz demanded.

Alan settled the hat. "The only thing ambassadors sweep is into and out of rooms. Didn't you know?" He removed her scarf from its neck, took a broad grey-and-white-striped tie from his pocket. "There now." He fastened it in place.

They stepped back to admire their work. Liz bowed. "Mr. Ambassador, I'm so happy you could come tonight."

Alan shook the scarf, wrapped it gently around her neck then took her face in his mittened hands and kissed her.

"Ooh. You're cold!" She jumped back.

He pulled her close again and his kiss tasted of snow. The icy touch of his lips was like a long cool drink in midsummer. Funny how one could be so warm outside on a winter's night!

After a long moment he drew back and tried to touch her cheek, but his mittens were still in the way. He bent, scooped a handful of snow "Every good snowman needs a good snowwoman behind him. Shall we make her?"

"Behind him, huh?" Liz grabbed a handful of snow and washed his face with it. She ran away laughing. "You look like a panda."

He swiped at the snow. "I think you broke my nose!"

She came back and touched it gently, then twisted it. Just a little.

He scooped snow.

She ran onto the porch but he caught her by the collar and washed her face in it.

She shrieked and his mother opened the door. Smilingly she interrupted. "The neighbors will think you're murdering her. You can't do that on Christmas Eve."

Alan whispered, "I'll get you later." With his arm around her, he led her into the house. "How about some hot chocolate, Mom?"

Katherine Bannerman stood by, brushed the wraps carefully and hung them in the mudroom, then tried to straighten the blond hair that had risen in six directions when he took off the cap. Her son had inherited his blond hair from her. She'd been a Schaefer, one of Chillicothe's old German pioneer families, and at forty-eight if she had any grey hair, it was lost in the northern lights. Kate was proud of her heritage. She was also proud of her petite figure, of her husband, her son, her home and her place in the community. Proud to be a gracious lady.

In spite of all of that or perhaps in a small part because of it, Liz admired Kate even though the snobbery sometimes peeked out of the lace curtains. She was, as she claimed to be, a gracious lady.

And awesome. The Bannerman house had a definite personality, one that said, "This is life as it should be." And whenever she was there, she saw Elizabeth Ellen Chase Bannerman with a basket of cut roses on her arm, standing on the steps of that stately columned mansion high on a hill. Penguinned footmen lit the candles in their gleaming silver candelabra, then served a seven-course dinner. Perhaps she'd be like Elsa Maxwell and have a coffee named after herself, Bannerman House.

And then the voice of the real Liz would come from her toes, barely still on the ground, "Getting a little stuffy, aren't we?" Yet the dream of the perfect home never quite hung out the white flag.

Now, Liz followed Kate through the large kitchen, painted a sunny yellow that managed to warm the room even at night, through a breakfast room, a formal Adams dining room, blue and white this time. As usual, they didn't go into the formal living room but went into the large country colonial den where John Bannerman sat.

If Alan's mother had been responsible for his blond hair, his father, John, had passed along the genes for Alan's good looks. Except for their ages, they could have been twins with long fine-boned faces, straight, rather pointed noses and high foreheads.

His family had better claims on Chillicothe history and society than Kate, but Liz liked it that he didn't really give a damn, that he was patiently amused by his wife's obsession with it all. He looked up from his pipe, slippers and paper as they came into the room. The sound of clear young voices, Liz thought perhaps the Vienna Boys Choir, filled the room with "Adeste Fidelis." He rose when Katherine suggested, "We can use some of that B&B now, John."

While he poured and passed the glasses, Kate skirted the large balsam fir and its antique ornaments to turn down the volume.

Liz wished she could protest. She loved Christmas music and never got tired of it. She drew in the scent of the pine strung along the mantel, the reflections that danced and flashed apple red and holly green on the ribbon there. The room glowed with candlelight, polished wood, the metallic glitter of gold and silver, the earthy, more sensual appeal of bowls of apples and nuts, dark chocolates in crystal dishes.

Her home would look like this. She reached out and took Alan's hand.

He sat on the arm of her wing-back chair, leaned over and kissed her on the top of her head, then turned to his father who had squatted near the tree to pass out the presents.

He asked, "What did you ever do with your Santa suit, Dad? You know the first time I saw it, you actually fooled me. At least until I recognized your aftershave." Pride and wistfulness showed in his eyes as he told Liz, "That was some suit. Not the kind of thing the department Santas wear at all. Came all padded, real fur, only rabbit, I'm afraid."

He laughed a little as he told his father, "I liked the suit so much I didn't care if it was you, Dad."

His father paused for a moment. Liz thought his eyes were dangerously near glistening. He passed the moment off with a smile. "Blame Kate for that. She had it made."

Kate said, "Those department store Santas are so shabby. If they're going to do something, I don't know why they can't do it right. It's not as though they can't afford it."

Liz wondered if Katherine noticed the emotion. Liz seldom saw Alan demonstrative with his father.

Under the influence of B&B, Currier and Ives, and the Christmas tree, Liz asked John, "Do you know where the suit is? Why don't you try it on, just for fun? You certainly can't be much heavier than you were then. I'd love to see it."

He looked up at her, then at Kate and Alan. "I know where it is. Why not?" He put down the presents he'd picked up then paused. "Alan, why don't you put it on?"

Kate rose and took John's hand. "Not until he's a father. Tradition is important. Come along, I'll help you get into it." She patted him on the arm. "Liz is right. I don't think you've gained an ounce."

Alan took Liz's hand and led her from the big chair to the sofa. "Now I have room."

"What's that supposed to mean?"

He laughed and put his arms around her. "Room to do this." He kissed her softly, and laid his cheek on hers. A thump came from the floor above, and the sound of laughter. Alan said, "They're wonderful, aren't they?"

"Mmm. They are." In spite of her fascination, she wondered if she really could live up to such an image. Did she really want that basket of roses? It was what every girl dreamed of, wasn't it?

Liz knew a woman came in twice a week and that Kate had help for dinner parties. Then there was the country club and once a week bridge. The Bannermans somehow made it look so easy.

Sometimes Liz wondered how Kate felt about her. Did she vet Alan's girls for the important role of a wife for the son who must succeed like his father? In such moments Liz knew how Sarah must feel most of the time, on display. Yet Kate had never overtly said a word, never interfered, and Liz knew of no criticism, at least to Alan. If he did know, he kept it to himself.

Liz adored John. Still handsome at sixty-two, he was perfect, too, but not too perfect. There was mischief under all that polish. A dad like John would be a hell of a man to have to live up to.

Kate came back alone, went to the radio, turned it off and put on a record of the Boston Pops rendition of "The Night Before Christmas." Tiny bells jangled. A "Ho, ho, ho" rang out and the most almost-perfect Santa that Liz had ever seen came into the room. While John couldn't come up with fat cheeks, he'd put color on his nose. The thick white eyebrows, a beard like Heidi's uncle and long white wig. Must have been real hair. Works of art.

With a "Merry Christmas to all," John went straight to the tree. He knelt, then handed Liz a slim gold box. On the top, a silver rose pin lay entwined in gold cord.

She touched the pin, reluctant to disturb the effect. "It's beautiful."

Kate smiled at her. "Open it, dear."

She fastened the rose to her green satin blouse. "It's beautiful. Thank you." Inside the box was a gold Parker pen set. Almost every girl she knew had one from graduation. She'd been happy to get savings bonds, but she'd wanted the pen set and now that she had it, she knew she'd never dare use it. What if she lost one? "Wonderful. Thank you so much."

Kate said, "Alan said you didn't have one. Every college girl must, you know."

Alan took the box and with a raised eyebrow complained to his mom, "You muffed it."

Kate didn't turn a hair. "How is that?"

"It was supposed to come with instructions."

Liz stuck out her tongue at him. "When I have my first book published, all written with this pen, you'll be sorry you said that."

Kate said, "Alan said you wrote poetry. But then I think college girls always do, don't they?"

Alan grinned at Liz and gave her a thumbs-up. "She actually had a thing published by *Playmate* when she was a kid."

"Oh." She pushed him, then went to the tree and gave his mom and dad the Cambridge glass bowl she'd found in an antique shop. She gave Alan an oblong foil-covered box, thinking men always got something in a box like that or else a long slender one for a tie or handkerchiefs.

Alan opened it without taking his eyes from her. He had the look of someone who knew a delicious secret.

She drew back and regarded him, half-amused, half-curious. She'd not ask, though. She pointed at the box. "Well, don't look at me. Open it."

He drew out the heavy grey wool sweater and put it on. Perfect fit. "It's great." His look held hers. "Just the thing when they post me to Bern."

Kate rose and motioned for John. "I have some of your favorite cake, dear." Holding hands, the two of them left.

Liz searched Alan's face, thinking of the pause when he'd said, "Paris, London—Bern." She said, "Okay. What's going on?"

He put his hands into his trouser pockets and came out with a small black box in each fist. He held out the right hand. "Say yes and this one is yours. Say maybe, it's the left."

"Oh, Alan. What if I said I don't know?"

He drew her to him. "Then I'll just have to convince you. I love you." He kissed her, pressing hard against her lips, perhaps hoping the warmth would so seep into her, that she would not be able to resist him.

Finally she pushed him gently away. "Your parents . . ."

He reached out and took her hand. "The State Department has offered to post me to Bern as a messenger boy as soon as I graduate."

"Switzerland's pretty good for a start, isn't it?" She studied his face. He looked pleased about going so far away.

He let go of her and gave a pleased smile. "Maybe Dad is a big contributor to the right people. I don't know. Never asked, but I talked to them and they have the opening and that's the offer they made me."

Happy that he had what he wanted, but unsure how it could work for them, Liz played for time and went over to inspect the Father Christmas ornament on the tree. "That's great. I'll miss you."

Alan turned her around. "I want you to go with me. Marry me."

"You know I want to marry you, but what about school?"

"You can go in Europe."

"I don't speak German and my French is not nearly good enough."

"What better place to learn? Besides, look who's there. Jung himself. You won't find that at Bowling Green."

Liz sighed. "Alan, if we married, I'd end up going only part-time. Over there, I'd probably just not do it at all. I want to be a psychologist. Can't you understand that?"

He shook his head. "No, Liz, I don't. I thought you'd want to be my wife." He looked around the room and waved his hand at it. "I thought you liked all this. It wouldn't be quite this grand at first, but we'd be fine. Besides, I'd like your help."

She wanted to cry. She looked down at the floor and took a deep breath. "I do. Want to be your wife, want to help you. You know that. I love you."

"Then what's the problem?"

"What's the hurry? You've been in Georgetown. I've been at BG. We've been apart before." Apart. It wasn't easy. She'd give almost anything to be with him among the Alps, in Europe. All this and heaven, too. Almost.

"Switzerland, Liz."

In spite of her denial, it would be so easy, so nice, just to marry him. Yet, "Three years, Alan. I'm only eighteen. Maybe when I graduate I could do my master's in Europe."

Alan stood there and juggled the boxes but his face was grim. At last he stopped. "You don't need a career, Liz. We'll have children. That's a full-time job. And you'll always have enough money to take care of yourself and any family."

"Alan, I dream of being your wife. Having children. Ours. A boy who looks like you." The corners of her mouth turned up for a moment. "Maybe the girl looks like you, too." She sighed. "But I need to be able to take care of myself. You never know. Besides, psychology is fascinating. Causes. Why people do the things they do."

Alan studied her for a long time. "You can't have everything, Liz." He stooped and put the box in his right hand under the tree. He took out the friendship ring, a wide, intricately carved silver band, and put it on her right hand. "I've already agreed to go. We'll have to marry by August if you change your mind."

As he drove her back to her house they were both quiet. Had she made a terrible mistake in not saying yes? How important was college anyway? She thought of Dottie and the pull between the theater and Bob. Of Sarah, whom the guys steered clear of because she was smarter than they: of the guys who thought she ought to decorate their arm, and didn't want to accept her in the math field. Their field.

Liz heard her mother's voice listing the women who "did something," and at the same time, heard her talking about how things would be when Liz was married. About grandchildren.

A family was something, too, wasn't it?

She gazed down at the ring on her right hand. The white wonder world had lost its magic. Was their—hers, Dottie's and Sarah's—struggle for choice really worth it?

Chapter 8

Liz returned to the dorm on Saturday after New Year's, a day early. Neither Dottie nor Sarah had returned yet. She moped about, glumly going over and over the farewell with Alan. Since Christmas Eve, Alan had been charming but cool. They'd gone to the New Year's dance and done everything they'd planned, but things weren't the same. She wasn't sure if he were truly angry or just hurt.

She was left with the friendship ring which looked as though it might end up being just that, a signal the two were meant to go their separate ways.

Vaughn Monroe's smooth tones rolled out from the radio. "Fools Rush In." Rush. That was the problem, wasn't it? Alan was in such a rush. Now or never. She turned the mellow complaint off. She and Alan had seen Vaughn at Loew's in Columbus. They'd sat through the movie three times to hear him twice.

She curled up on the bed, flipped through the pages of *Life*, then tossed it aside to dwell on her misery. She could always go for just an AB (Awaiting the Boy—spending time in college just to get a husband) in arts and sciences. It might even be fun to go to Universität Bern or, one day, the Sorbonne. When she listened to Alan, the degree really didn't seem worth the trouble. As he kept saying, his mom didn't have one and look at her.

Liz did look at her. Everything was so right, the marriage, her place in the community, her son. She'd probably placed an order with the Fates to have a successful son, one just like his father.

How could anyone win an argument against all that?

But then there was her own mom who raved about Jeannette Rankin in Congress, the only one to vote against going to war after Pearl Harbor. Not that her mom agreed. But the woman had done things. Eleanor Roosevelt and Amelia Earhart, too. Trouble was, her mother's messages were mixed. Her life showed what she really thought—it is a man's world.

There never seemed a final answer. Her mom, and probably Alan's, too, spent their time playing bridge and volunteering. Somehow, Liz knew she wanted more. And she didn't want to settle for some job a man didn't want.

She rose and poked about the room then, finding nothing to satisfy her, fled to the common room where she found a couple of other strays to play cards with.

Sarah finally returned on Sunday, all smiles. "We had a wonderful time. Rick came down the day after Christmas, then Sunday we drove up to Rochester to meet his parents."

"How'd he get along with your mom and dad?" Liz figured that was a rhetorical question since they'd allowed Sarah to go to Rochester. Sarah's dad was extremely protective. They drove up from Columbus to pick Sarah up for the breaks instead of letting her take the train, or ride with anyone. She wasn't even supposed to ride in a car while she was at BG. Mostly Sarah went along with that. Luckily, there was little in Bowling Green one couldn't walk to or from. But then the housemother didn't spend all her time looking out windows.

Sarah stuffed two new cashmeres into her drawer, then whirled on Liz and hugged her. "They loved him. He was so sweet. Treated me like a princess. He gave me this for Christmas." She opened the gold locket that replaced the usual strand of pearls around her neck.

Liz thought that even in the photo, Rick's grin had a cocky look. Sarah's picture, just off-focus, had an ethereal look to it. Liz bit her lip to keep from saying aloud how beautiful Sarah was.

If only I could like him, Liz thought. As much as she wanted to see Sarah happy, she couldn't bring herself to praise Rick. She hated being at odds over the guy. The best she could do was smile and try. "Your dad must really have liked Rick if they let you go home with him. What happened in Rochester?"

Sarah stepped out of her shoes, leaving them where they were, then draped her skirt on the bed. Evidently the visit home had revived the Mom'll do it habit.

"His folks were really nice. His dad drove us to see the falls. Kinda cold. I thought I'd turn into one of those icicles. How about you? Bet you and Alan had a great time. Must be nice living in the same town. Not having to run all over the country."

"Yeah. Great."

Pushing the skirt aside, Sarah plopped down on the bed and crossed her legs. Eyeing Liz, she said, "That didn't sound thrilled. You're pretty quiet. Didn't you have a good time? What'd you do New Year's?"

Liz rose and scrabbled through her desk to avoid Sarah's scrutiny. "Went to the country club."

Sarah drew her knees up and clasped them. She rocked dreamily. "We did, too. I never danced so much in my life. All his friends asked me. I thought he'd get mad, but he didn't. He actually seemed pleased." Sarah looked dreamily into space. "We had the last dances, though. He was so sweet."

Liz curled again in the corner of her bed, then reached

out and hugged Sarah. "I'm glad." Perhaps he could make Sarah happy. Considering the state of her own affair with Alan, Liz Chase was obviously no authority on men.

A heavy clunk outside the door relieved Liz of the need to say more. Dottie's face and form appeared, followed by two big suitcases, one of which landed on Sarah's shoe.

Sarah said, "Oops," and grabbed her shoes and skirt. "See? Putting them away!" She scurried to do it. "My New Year's resolution. Hang up my clothes so Dottie doesn't choke me!"

Dottie gave her a weak grin, shoved one of the bags into the closet and put the other on the bed. "I'm too tired—tomorrow maybe. Had to take the milk train. You guys have a nice Christmas?"

Sarah bubbled her story over again.

Liz carefully edited hers, then asked, "Did Bob come up to Rocky River?"

Dottie took an armful of skirts to the closet and began to hang them, but she had none of the ususal Dottie-bounce. She leaned against the door frame and fiddled with the hanger. "Yeah. We got three feet of snow Christmas Eve. Live on the wrong side of the lake. Thought maybe he wouldn't make it."

"I take it he did."

"Yeah." The tone seemed so down Liz dropped the subject.

Sarah, probably still wound up from her own triumph, didn't seem to notice. "How'd Bob get along with your folks?"

Finally, finished in the closet, Dottie started on the drawers. "You know Bob. He was a real cool cat." She smiled as she said that. "I didn't know his folks were Baptists, too. He'd never even said anything. So, naturally, he

97

and Daddy really hit it off. Then he kept telling Mom funny stories about the Marine Corps. She keeps saying he's braver than MacArthur. The general's her big hero!"

Dottie gave up on the clothes and pushed the suitcase in with the other. "I'll do it later. Promise. I'm tired."

Liz wondered, tired or dejected? The gloom in the room was cloying. She said quickly, "You guys going out tonight? I've got cabin fever."

"Rick's supposed to meet me at the Nest at seven. Why don't we go there?"

Dottie turned her back. "I'm going to sleep."

Liz studied her. "Don't you feel well? You look tired."

Without turning, Dottie mumbled, "Ever ride a milk train? I swear this one stopped at every barn in between every town."

Liz gave up. She and Sarah bundled into their jackets and braved the cold to find a sparsely populated Nest.

As they settled into their booth, with burgers and malts, one of the Sigma Chi's walked past. "Hi, Sarah. Rick was wondering if you were back yet. I'm just leaving. I'll tell him."

Sarah, almost totally wound, smiled and nodded, then unlike her usual quiet self, chattered happily about Rick and Christmas, New York state in the winter, cars sliding, and about anything and everything.

Liz let her ramble. At least they were out of the room. They'd almost finished eating when Rick slid in beside Sarah.

Tom was with him. "May I?" His blue eyes either reflected the lights in the Nest, or some inner pleasure. Liz tried not to think about the possibilities as she moved over.

Rick pecked Sarah on the cheek, then got out again. "We're going to get something to eat."

Tom rose but left his jacket next to Liz.

When they returned with their food, he gave her a sly grin. "How's the bowling?"

She laughed and shook her head. "Got a one-track, excuse me, a one-lane mind?"

Rick hooted and gave Tom a kick under the table. "Gotcha there, pal."

Tom tilted his head at Liz, then asked them all, "Well, as long as I'm in a rut, how about it? Want to go bowling tonight?"

To Liz's surprise, Sarah spoke up, "How about something not so physical. I've been riding all day. I don't think my joints can stand any more."

Rick snickered. "How about chess?"

Liz said, "Anyone play bridge?"

Sarah put in quickly, "Contract?"

Liz shook her head. "I started to learn it, but mostly I fly by the seat of my pants. How about auction?"

Tom pulled a deck of cards from his pocket and riffled them. "Told you I was always prepared!"

Liz shook her head. "I didn't think that was part of the Boy Scout routine."

"To tell the truth, some of the guys at the house were talking about a game and so I swiped these for the fun of it."

Liz complained halfheartedly, "That's a dirty trick!"

He only grinned. "They'll just have to shuffle more often. Besides, it came in handy, didn't it? Let's go over to one of the tables so Rick can't look at my cards."

Since Tom had the cards, he spread them and came up with the deal. Liz looked at her hand and hoped the rest of the night wasn't going to be like this. The highest card she had was a ten.

She wasn't far wrong. The battle turned out to be between Tom and Sarah who fought for the bid at almost every hand. Liz was no help at all and Rick proved to be a disaster. He raised the bids with hardly any support for Sarah.

At first Liz figured he just didn't know how to play, but she decided his problem was his attitude. He raised Sarah's hearts over Tom's spades. When Tom bid again, she went to game at four hearts. Rick laid down three small hearts, and a queen, ten in a string of diamonds. At least he had no spades. The count wasn't worth a single raise.

Sarah didn't even flinch. Tom raised an eyebrow at Liz and shook his head.

A passing kibitzer looked at the dummy spread and walked around to check Sarah's hand. "Hope you didn't raise her, Rick!"

Rick scowled but Sarah dived into the game. She quickly took Tom's ace of spades but she couldn't use Rick's only queen with Tom in the catbird seat. Still, she made three of the four she'd bet.

Rick complained, "You should have left it at three, Sarah."

Stunned at his denseness, Liz blurted out, "You raised her." She bit her lip and looked quickly at Sarah who did not react.

Rick glowered. "Not to four."

Liz took a deep breath and clamped her mouth shut. She wanted desperately to say he never should have bid at all, let alone three. That asked for four.

Tom said quickly, "All things considered, Sarah's sharp. Don't think I could have done as well."

Sarah smiled gratefully, then tried to pacify Rick. "Win some, lose some. I like to gamble."

Actually, Liz figured Sarah didn't like to gamble. She knew exactly what she was doing. Too bad Rick didn't.

The whole evening seemed to be a repeat of that hand. Whenever Sarah went down or Tom won his hand, Rick reverted to his old self and grumbled. When she made her bid, he baited Tom.

By the end of the evening, Tom and Liz had beat Sarah and Rick, but not by much. When they left the Nest, Tom hugged Sarah. "Great game." He grinned at Rick. "You're a good player, Sarah. Get a decent partner and we'll do it again."

Rick bristled. "What do you expect when I don't get good cards?"

"Learn how to bet?"

Rick glowered at him and pulled Sarah away.

Liz and Tom looked at each other and had a laughing fit. "Just like old times." She knew he meant the bowling fiasco. In spite of Sarah's Christmas view of Rick, it didn't seem to Liz he'd changed much. For a moment she wanted to cry for Sarah.

Tom took Liz's hand. "Do you mind?"

The night air on Liz's skin had the crisp snap of cold air from an open refrigerator. Just being with Tom warmed and comforted her. Something she'd missed since the argument at Christmas. Still, she could not allow herself, nor did she want to let go of her relationship with Alan. The thing could be worked out if they tried hard enough. Perhaps Alan was right.

Tom interrupted her reverie. "Considering the lousy cards you got, you didn't do badly. At least you knew what to lead."

"I really like bridge but I don't play much."

"Auction's old hat. No one plays it seriously anymore.

Why don't you learn contract? I can show you. Much better."

She shrugged. "Alan."

He squeezed her hand then let go. "I don't mind if he doesn't."

Considering Alan's coolness, perhaps it didn't matter. At least she'd have something to do. "You talked me into it."

When he gave her a quick hug, she asked, "How's dear Annie? Still see her?"

His look said he knew something she didn't. "Once in a while. She's a busy girl." Then he laughed. "She isn't, nor was she ever mine, you know."

"Oh." They stopped and sat down on the bottom steps of Kohl Hall. It was too cold to stay but Liz wanted to. Tom was comfortable, comfort.

She could feel his gaze on her. Perhaps she ought to go on in. She moved to rise. He leaned over and kissed her. The kiss was gentle. He didn't push. Like him, it was warm and, well, not passionate, but pleasant. Too pleasant in her present mood.

She drew back. Tears came to her eyes. She said, "I'm sorry, Tom," and rising, rushed up the stairs.

As she reached the door, he shouted, "Be my partner again?"

She stopped in the doorway and looked down at the friendship ring. Nuts! Why not? She wasn't engaged and Alan was definitely cool. She turned and nodded.

Chapter 9

Dottie lay on her bunk, face to the wall, apparently asleep as Liz clumped into the room and threw her books on the bed. She was tempted to toss them in the wastebasket but couldn't afford to. She'd just left the bookshop and what she really wanted to throw was a stream of nasty words at Ann, then maybe call Rick a few names to his face.

The store had been crowded. Liz had turned the corner of a book stack to find Ann's red fingernails curling Rick's hair. He lounged against the wall looking like Tantalus as the grape neared his starving lips.

They didn't see her. She'd slipped back around and stood shivering with rage. When she got the nerve to move, the two of them were leaving the building.

Dottie, obviously asleep, didn't move when Liz had clumped into the room. She frowned now at the immobile figure. The kid had looked so tired lately. Big circles under her eyes.

Liz settled at the desk to work, but she'd hardly started when Dottie rose and went across the hall to the shower room. When she came back, her face was pink and wet. "Didn't know it was so late."

Liz put her hand against her friend's cheek. "Do you have a fever? Don't have mono, do you? You ought to see a doctor."

Dottie sat back down on the bed, drew her knees to her chin and buried her face. After a moment she looked up. Tears dropped onto her knees. She brushed at them and sniffed. "I'm okay, only . . ." Her words tailed off and she buried her head again.

Liz sat, put her arm around her and drew her close. "Is it Bob? Did you break up?"

Dottie shook her head. "It's not him. It's just . . ." She swallowed. "It's just that I need to borrow some money." Tears started again.

Liz bit her lip. Oops. She did have a little of her allowance left, but lending and borrowing were bad business. Boys and money, the chief makers of enemies. Still, she hadn't the heart to turn her down when she looked so bad. "I can lend you twenty. Would that help?"

Her roommate waved the offer away and shook her head. "I mean real money. At least a hundred and fifty. I've got about forty."

Liz sighed, partly in relief, partly in sympathy, and certainly from surprise at the amount. What on earth could be that serious? "If you can wait till the first of the month, I could make it forty."

"Oh." Dottie lay back down on the bed with her face to the wall again. Her shoulders shook.

Liz pressed her hand on Dot's shoulder. "It can't be that bad."

Dottie jerked away and said, "Never mind. I'm just tired."

Liz let go just as Sarah came in, paused for a moment, taking in the scene, then sat and hugged Dottie. "What's the matter?"

"Nothing. I'm tired." Dottie turned her face to the wall and closed her eyes.

Raising a brow at Sarah, Liz shrugged slightly and picked up her purse. What with Rick and Ann, and now Dottie, she was in no mood to do any paper. She needed something sweet to take away the taste of all this. She reached for her jacket. "I'm going to the Nest. Anyone want to go?" She frowned at Dottie's back.

Sarah looked from one to the other. When Liz shrugged again, she said, "Yeah. I will. Rick's supposed to meet me there." She looked at the curled form on the bed. "Come on, Dottie, you need to get out of the room."

The only answer was a sniffle.

When they reached the end of the hall, Sarah said, "What's the matter with her?"

"She wanted to borrow some money."

Sarah raised an eyebrow. "Is that all? I've got maybe thirty if she needs it."

Liz shook her head. "I was really surprised. It isn't like her, but she looked so awful I offered her twenty. That's about all I can spare." She bit her lip. "It has to be serious. She said she wanted a hundred and fifty. She has forty."

"Wow! What for?"

"She wouldn't say. Just got mad."

"Um. You think maybe she hasn't got tuition money for next semester? Maybe her dad's in trouble."

"If that's what it is, even a hundred fifty might not be enough." Liz scrunched down inside her coat. A bitterly cold wind made for a deserted campus. "I'm glad January's almost over, but then February always seems worse. I sure hope old what's-his-name Phil will see his shadow this year."

Absentmindedly Sarah answered. "Punxsutawney."

"What?"

"Punxsutawney Phil. The groundhog who sees his shadow."

February. Valentine's day. Liz sighed. What would Alan do or say this year? He had written a chatty letter. Ordinarily she'd think nice, chatty letter but under the circumstances, chatty wasn't much of a recommendation. Friday when he'd called, he'd not given her an argument, just said, "I love you." He'd sounded hurt.

The Nest was as deserted as Liz had ever seen it. Evidently everyone was hiding from the cold. The smell of browning burgers and bubbling oil was no temptation. She needed chocolate. Hot chocolate.

Unburdened by any knowledge of faithless men, Sarah ordered the cheeseburger. She looked so content, Liz forgot any debate about telling or not. She'd not volunteer that bit about Rick and Ann, for now. Perhaps Sarah would ask some question, allow her to be honest. Sometimes things were not what they seemed, but how could anyone misconstrue the look on Rick's face?

Sarah dug in. "It's a good thing I don't gain weight easily. I can't seem to get enough food." Between mouthfuls, she turned the conversation back to Dottie. "You know I could probably get fifty from my dad without a big thing. I mean without having to make excuses. He's a sweetie pie if I don't push him too far."

"I told her the first of the month I could come up with forty. That would probably do it. I'd hate to see Dottie have to drop out."

"I'll tell Mom I need a few things, which is never a lie. Just won't name them. Unless I'm talking a hundred she probably won't ask. I do need some stuff and if Dottie pays it back, it won't be a fib." She shoved away a plate that hadn't so much as a crumb on it and checked her watch again, something she'd been doing regularly since they'd been there. "He said three. It's three-thirty now."

Liz flinched. Maybe she ought to say something. Ann probably still had her fingers locked in his hair. She checked her own watch. Maybe . . . She looked up into the face of Bob.

He slid into the empty space next to her. He had no food. "Hi. Where's Dottie?"

"Sleeping, I guess. At least she was trying to when we left."

He frowned. "She was supposed to meet me here."

Sarah snorted. "That seems to be a communicable disease."

"What? Isn't she okay? She isn't sick, is she? She was fine this morning."

Liz looked at him with a kind of awe. Was he blind or something? She couldn't help herself. She snapped, "She's just dandy. That is, if you don't count the dark circles and the crying all the time."

He paled. "What do you mean? She has been tired; I thought maybe she might have the flu."

A red-faced Rick came up to the booth and interrupted. "I'm sorry I'm late. I had to see the coach."

Liz scowled at him, but he looked at Sarah.

Sarah tipped the last of her chocolate.

Perhaps flustered by the silence, Rick mumbled hastily, "I'm going to get a burger. Be right back."

Bob followed him.

When they got back from the counter, Sarah rose and walked out.

"Bravo, Sarah!" Liz crowed silently. The look on Rick's face, as her mom would say, warmed the cockles of her heart. Sarah had snatched a sure shot from his hands, leaving him red-faced with surprise. Now thunder.

While Liz watched that transformation, Bob unloaded his tray. "Do you think Dottie can see me, if I come over?"

She glowered at him. "You two need to do something

besides neck all the time. Like talk! She's worried about money." She pushed away her cup and moved to stand. Bob flushed and let her out.

She left, feeling like a jerk. I'm really turning into a bitch, she thought, but she continued to grumble as she walked toward the library. She didn't want to face Sarah or Dottie.

Liz wandered around the American history stacks, hoping that by some magic there might be a new volume that turned Alexander Hamilton into Cary Grant or Clark Gable, someone romantic. That didn't happen and it didn't make any difference anyway; she had no paper, no pen and no space at any of the tables.

As she came out of the stacks she saw Tom sitting with his back to her at a table in the far corner. He wore grey just like the rest of the world. She fled the room. Not that she didn't want to see him, but he reminded her that she had not heard from Alan since Friday.

She stood outside and let the cold wind brush away the tears that gathered on her lashes. Everything seemed to have gone wrong with everybody. The girls coming up the steps all looked cold and sad and the boys sly and self-satisfied.

She ought to write a play like *Lysistrata*, only about male fickleness and not war. No girl would have anything to do with any boy until he wore a big medal around his neck saying to whom he belonged. If he took it off without his girl's permission, he could be tarred and feathered, maybe hanged.

She'd have to figure out a label for the ones like Tom who weren't attached. Maybe a scarlet A for Available. She started to giggle at the thought but stopped to swipe at the tear that quickly froze on her eyelash. She decided she'd call the play *The Scarlet Letter*. So much for Hawthorne.

She shivered. Alan's voice would warm her. Maybe she

could call him. She never did. She didn't want him teased about it. The drugstore on Main had a booth that would be private. She checked her wallet. She had enough if they didn't talk too long. She set off down Wooster toward town. It was almost 4:30. Would he be in? She turned up her coat collar and walked faster.

As it happened, Alan was in. She listened impatiently as the boy who answered whistled his way to pass the message. Finally she heard Alan's pleased baritone say, "Hello? Liz?" He didn't wait for her acknowledgment. "I was just thinking of calling you."

She apologized. "I didn't get a chance to write. There's this term paper . . ." She trailed off. She was having a lot of practice making excuses lately. Fibs, too. But that excuse was partly true. If she hadn't been in the dumps, she'd have it done by now.

Alan said, "I thought maybe I'd drive up this weekend."

Her heart leaped and for a moment Liz forgot she was in a dilapidated telephone booth. She wanted to reach out, feel his cheek and curl his hair with her fingernails. Maybe she'd even paint them bright red.

Then he said, "I guess it's a bad time, though. Forgot you had semesters. With our quarters, makes it awkward."

Her excuses were about to trip her. Liz hurriedly tried to repair the damage. "I'll hurry and get it done. I really want to see you. I'm so lonely and everything seems to be going wrong."

For a moment the smile came back in his voice. "Poor baby!" He sounded hesitant, though, when he said, "Well. If you think it's okay I can make it Friday about six. When's your paper due?"

It was due Monday. Today was Tuesday. "Not until

next week. Maybe I can finish it by Friday. How are you doing?"

"I'm okay. All caught up. I've been thinking about you so I really dug in. It's been a lot of pressure, though. I still have to come out at the top for the State Department boys. You girls have it easy."

She frowned and flared at him, "What's that supposed to mean?"

He laughed, a little embarrassed. "Nothing. Only a girl's whole life doesn't depend on her standing, does it?"

Liz saw red. "You mean since she's only going to get married anyway, this is all fun and games. Right?" If words were fists, the "right" would have left a few teeth missing.

"Uh. No. Look, Liz, I'm sorry. I thought maybe we could talk things over, but it doesn't seem like anything is going to change."

Part of her wanted to cry, but the rest of her was too angry. They needed to get things straight, once and for all. "I really think we do need to talk. We can't over the phone." She took a deep breath and tried to control the desolation she felt. She didn't want things to go this way. "I do love you, Alan."

"I love you, Liz. Desperately. Look, I'll see you Friday at six. Wear something green for me."

"Okay. Friday then. Bye. I . . . I . . ." She hung up. He was gone. She let the tears fall.

Chapter 10

In the backseat of Bob's Plymouth, Dottie huddled in the blanket to hide from the icy January air. It didn't help much that the top was up.

Bob crawled in and scooted under the blanket with her. "It's Alaska in here. Why don't we go inside somewhere?"

"No." How could she tell him? Would he feel trapped? Probably! Be angry? She didn't have any idea what his reaction might be. She'd made up her mind not to cry, but she was past that. A sickness that had nothing to do with the baby swamped her. Just about every unpleasant emotion she could think of raised its fist and threatened a riot in her stomach. If she'd had the money . . . but Liz and Sarah hadn't been able to help. Their thirty or forty dollars wasn't enough and she couldn't wait too long or it would be dangerous. Was there some fib she could tell her mom and dad?

Bob brushed the back of his hand against her cheek. "Liz said you were sick. I don't want you to get pneumonia!"

"That would be one way out!"

He put his arms around her and drew her close. "That better?"

His arms did make things better, but didn't cure anything. "I wish things were that simple."

"What do you mean? Nothing can be that bad. If you need money or something, I have a little."

When she spoke, her breath made a patch of fog in the icy confines of the car. She wished the cloud were bigger and she could lose herself in it, let it cover her face so that he could not see her shame. "Bob, I do need money."

He reached in his pocket, counted out fifty dollars and handed it to her. "You short of tuition? Something happen to your dad? He didn't lose his job, did he?"

She looked at him as though he were a kindergartner who asked "Now?" when he'd been told three times to wash his hands. "He owns a print shop, for Pete's sake. You know that!"

"Then why do you need money?" His hand twitched as though he'd like to take the fifty back.

She threw it at him, turned her back and sobbed. It didn't matter if he didn't have any idea what the trouble was.

He put his hands on her shoulders and tried to turn her.

She threw back the blanket and beat on his chest with her fists. She choked the words out between sobs. "I'm pregnant." The weight of the words, said aloud for the first time, sent a violent shudder and a storm of sobs through her.

He took her fists and held them tightly. When she calmed a little, he took her in his arms. "Don't, Dottie. It's okay."

She struggled against him, trapped in her guilt and misery. "Don't," he'd said. Did he mean, don't hit me or don't have a baby? Either way, it wasn't the right answer. "No. Damn it, you jerk. It's not okay. I'm pregnant. My life is ruined. You can let me out of this car and drive away, but I can't run."

He pulled her tighter so she couldn't struggle. "I'm not going anywhere. Are you sure? Have you been to a doctor?"

She could hardly move but she tilted her head back and snapped at him. "I've missed two periods and I've been sick for weeks. I don't need a doctor to tell me."

When he spoke he only sounded unhappy, not mad. "Look, Dottie. You don't need to . . . well . . . have it, you know. But I'll marry you. It's okay. You know I love you."

Her anger dissolved into a flood of tears.

He held her and let her cry until she quieted. "Look. They have trailers for married couples. We could go down to Kentucky, get married this weekend and sign up for one."

She sat up and drew away from him. "I don't want some man to marry me and be trapped, maybe even think I did it on purpose."

"Dottie, I love you. I do."

"But this will ruin everything for you."

His soft laughter came as a surprise. He said, "No. It won't. We can work something out."

"I couldn't stay here at BG and have everyone count on their fingers. Besides you only have your GI bill. We can't afford to get married. Dad would never go on paying. When he finds out, he might disown me."

He kissed the tip of her nose. "I don't think he'd go that far."

The kiss and his tone should have been reassuring, but nothing would change the reaction she knew would come from her father. "Hah. You've never listened to him go on about fallen women. Mary Magdalene and those other ones, the one they wanted to stone in the Bible, they'd have done it for sure if Dad had been Jesus!" She wiped her eyes. "Anyway, even if Dad did let me in the door by some miracle, I couldn't face all the gossip. His friends, our neighbors, all whispering or shaking their heads when I left the room!" Shame kept her from saying that this would end any hope of her ever being an actress.

"That's a load of shit. We're human, that's all. Besides,

I'll bet probably half of them held their breath when they counted the days."

She studied his face, trying to figure him out. "Aren't you upset? Aren't you even mad? I thought an abortion would be the first thing you said." She put her hands over her face and waited. "If you said anything at all."

He took her hands down. "You didn't think I'd just leave you, did you?"

Dottie gulped. "I didn't know. You just got back from the war. You wanted a good time, not to be stuck with a baby."

"A couple of months ago, I might have. Only I love you."

She pressed her cheek against his and turned slightly so that her lips brushed his skin. The beard scratched and she rubbed her face against it. "I couldn't marry a guy who never shaved! My face would be red all the time."

He wrapped her in his arms and held her. "When's it due?"

The word "due" sent a shudder through her. She wasn't ready for this. She had four years of school yet. Four years in one of the best drama classes around. This would certainly put paid to all that. Willing or not, this was no way to do things.

She'd be nineteen next week. She'd hardly tasted life. Bob was twenty-four and had been around a lot, and he certainly had not spent all of the last five years fighting, even though there'd been enough of that to toughen him.

When she'd thought he wouldn't want to marry her, the thought of an abortion had almost been a relief. Now, the choice was worse. She closed her eyes and tried not to think, but guilt and fear hammered at her. She'd be damned for all eternity, but how could she have it and ruin everyone's life, including an innocent baby's?

Bob had said he didn't feel trapped, but in a couple of years, well . . .

Marriage would ruin a lot of things, for her and Bob. She didn't even want to think what her life would be like if she had the baby but didn't marry. She could put it up for adoption, but meanwhile, she'd have no place to go. She couldn't imagine her father putting up with it in the house. Her mom? She'd probably quit her bridge club and hide in the basement.

Dottie pictured herself, scrawny and starving, scrubbing dirty diapers in a tin pail with one of those tin washboards, a sink full of dishes waiting to be washed, the baby screaming because he was hungry and she had no milk.

The baby was bound to be a boy.

The thought of a little Bob softened her. She had a nephew she bathed sometimes. She loved to nuzzle him fresh from the bath. He smelled so wonderful on the back of his neck. Maybe it wouldn't be the end of the world.

But it would be the end of Cara D'Talia, actress. For a second the thought came that the name was a bit much, even for a stage name, but now, she might never have a chance. If . . . Not that she didn't like kids, or want any. In a way she even might like to marry Bob, too. He was fun and down deep she knew he was a good guy. In spite of his baloney she had a hunch he'd make a good father.

Maybe he bragged and acted goofy because he was mad that he'd lost almost five years of his life, the good years when a guy was supposed to be young and wild. With the baby, he'd never have that chance. Yet, he would marry her. Some guys would have said right off, "Get rid of the baby." She'd been so sure he would, too. He'd surprised her.

Was she ready to be a mother? She really wanted to stay in the drama class with people like Eva Marie Saint. She permitted herself a moment of dreams. Hollywood would probably snap Eva right up. They'd be crazy not to. If they took notice of one Bowling Green star, why not two? They all said, "Dottie, you are good." She wanted to go to New York and try the stage so badly she ached. If she had this baby, how would she feel toward it when her dreams were dead?

She closed her eyes, shut out her feelings of guilt and said it. "Bob, I can't get married now. I can't have this baby. Will you help me?"

His voice was bleak. "Whatever you want, Dottie. I love you. Let me talk to some of the guys. Find out who."

"I've got fifty dollars. How much do you think it will cost?"

He shrugged but he drew her closer. "I can take care of the money but I don't like the idea. It's dangerous."

Dottie buried her face in his coat. "My life is ruined anyway. I might as well die."

"Don't say that, Dottie. I'll find out."

"You sure you have the money?"

His hand made gentle circles on her back. "Enough."

She raised her eyes to him then put her cheek against his. For a moment she thought his face was wet, but decided it was her own tears. After a while she said, "I'd better get back. It's getting late."

They got into the front and he put the car in gear.

When she got back to the dorm, she pulled her collar up and kept her face down. It had to be red and blotchy and she didn't want any questions.

Liz and Sarah were both studying and barely looked up as she entered the room. She tried to keep her back to them as she hung up her coat, took off her skirt and put it on a hanger. To avoid having to go to the dresser, she threw her sweater on the bed.

She thought she heard Sarah gasp but ignored it. Another time that might have made her laugh, but now Dottie draped the towel over her head and went across to the shower. By the time she got back, she figured she'd look fairly normal.

When she did, Liz stood and put her books away. She said, "Dottie, if you still need the money, Sarah and I can get some more at the first of the month."

Dottie swallowed and blushed. "Thanks, but it's okay."

Sarah came over and felt her cheeks. "You're kind of flushed and warm. You sure you're okay?"

Dottie smiled a little at that. "You two. You're like a couple of mother hens. I'm all right. Really."

Liz, evidently still either curious or concerned, said, "We were worried maybe something happened to your dad. Is he okay? Do you have enough for your tuition?"

Dottie took a deep breath and jumped into the fire. "No. I mean, yes. I think. Dad's okay. I wanted to buy something for Bob and I didn't want to ask my folks."

Her roommates both gave her annoyed looks. Liz opened her mouth, then clamped it and turned away.

Dottie blushed but couldn't help being relieved by their reactions. They must have talked it over, but neither had guessed what she wanted it for. Maybe they'd be mad, though, because she'd made a big deal about it. That excuse was a bit lame.

She turned away and climbed onto her bed. She tried to sound normal. "But thanks a lot. I'm sorry if I worried you. It was just that he's been broke lately and worried. But it's okay now."

She figured that little lie was the best she could do to smooth things over. Miserably, she wondered what they'd say if they knew the truth.

Wednesday after class Dottie and Bob met at the far corner table in Harvey's. She ordered vegetable soup. The rich broth made her stomach churn. She pushed it away.

Bob shoved it back toward her and said, "You've got to eat."

She sighed and took a sip of the liquid then asked for extra soda crackers. They were the one thing that could keep the nausea down.

Bob had ordered a cheeseburger but, like her, he wasn't in the mood. He shoved it around on his plate and picked out the onion and nibbled on that. Finally, he said, "Well, I got two names. One guy is just outside of town and charges a hundred and fifty. They say he runs a practice on it. He's really old.

"Then one of the fellows told me about this woman doctor in Toledo. But she charges three hundred. She has an office in her house and you can stay there overnight. He said she's a really good doctor and doesn't do it all the time. The guy says he heard her sister died from an abortion by some drunk. He didn't know if it was true, but it makes sense. Anyway, she's fussy about who she'll do and won't take chances. You have to know someone she knows but the kid thinks he can fix it up."

He put out his hand and took hers. He didn't look at her. "Are you sure about this? I guess she'll have to see how far along you are."

"I've been sick for about three weeks straight. I figure about nine weeks, maybe ten."

He heaved a big sigh. "She won't do it after twelve."

Dottie took her hand from his and rubbed the back of her neck. "Let's go see about this guy outside of town. Three hundred's a lot of money."

"Are you sure, Dottie? It's not the money. I don't want anything to happen to you."

"I know. But we can talk to him. See what he's like. Do you have the address?"

He pulled it from his pocket. "It's down 25. We'll drive past and see what it looks like."

They left the food almost uneaten. When they got to the door, Bob stopped. "I forgot." He went back to the table and laid the tip down. He came back and held her hand as he helped her into the car. The top was up and he turned the heater on full blast.

It took only a couple of minutes to reach the south edge of town once they passed the last traffic light. They both watched for the number. Finally they passed what once must have been a nice, big white house. Now dirty paint peeled and left patches of long-ago grey. In other places, bare wood. The porch steps dipped. The roof was pockmarked with missing shingles.

The number wasn't visible from the street. It had to be close, but Dottie hoped this was not the one.

The next building was a deserted cement block gas station. That number was too low.

Bob backed up and the two of them stared at the gloomy relic they'd just passed. There was no doctor's sign, but on one side of the door a square spot showed where one might have hung. The rusty mailbox said Dr. Green.

Dottie swallowed and looked at Bob. Tears rolled down her face.

He said, "Shit," put the car in gear and made a fast

U-turn. His tires squealed. "I have a telephone call to make." He stopped at the drugstore.

She went in with him and waited while he called from the booth. He talked for a couple of minutes then hung up, opened the door long enough to say, "They'll call back." He shut it again and sat there, cracking his knuckles.

She chewed her lip, thinking this is how people on death row must feel. Finally she turned away and went to leaf through the magazines. Anything . . . The phone rang and she went back to him.

The muscles in his cheek worked but he wasn't talking, just listening and writing. Finally she saw him say, "Okay. Thanks."

When he came out, he said, "That was the guy I told you about. He called her. She wants to talk to you first. She'll see you Friday morning but won't promise anything. Can you cut classes?"

Dottie sat in the inner office and chewed her nails, then realizing what she was doing, tucked her hands under her. She hadn't bitten her nails since she was in the second grade. They'd been down to the nub then. She pressed her hands hard against the chair and squirmed.

A dark-haired, middle-aged woman opened the door to the inner office. "Miss Cook? Come in."

The office itself did not fit the practical waiting room. It was simple but soft with a sea-green carpet and sofa, the walls a lighter shade. Long drapes were closed over high Victorian windows and ought to have made the room darker, but the satiny finish danced with reflected lights.

In spite of the room, there was nothing short or soft about the doctor's looks. She reminded Dorothy somehow of a wooden spoon.

"I'm Doctor Short. Are you sure you're pregnant? Have you had a test?" The authority in the voice had the male Bible Belt ring to it.

"No, ma'am."

"We'd better do that first. If you're more than three months, I can't help you."

"No, ma'am."

When they finished the exam, they went back into the office. "We'll make an appointment for Monday." She leafed through the appointment book. "About five, I think. Chances are you're right, that you are pregnant." The doctor paused, let out her breath. "You know, abortion for no medical reason isn't legal. I'm not sure it's moral, but I don't know either how moral it is to ruin three lives." The next words came angrily: "Or lose one."

She looked away. "Too many girls die at some butcher's hands."

For a while she said nothing more. Dottie waited.

"There are options. For one, adoption. Two, keep it. Three, abort it. None are pleasant. Does your family know?"

Dottie gulped. "My mother would die and my father would send me out to be stoned, if he didn't do it himself."

"I doubt if either of those things would happen. I'm sure they love you."

The censorious face of her father condemning a friend of Dottie's who suddenly quit high school, turned up married, then had a four-month baby, made the question moot, as far as Dottie was concerned. She wasn't sure whether the tight lips of her mother came from disapproval or the attitude of her father. She and her mother had talked about marriage and good girls and bad girls. Had her mother had any sympathy for the plight of the friend? Dottie wasn't sure but even if there would be sympathy now, it wouldn't be enough to stem the tide of rejection let loose by her father. Her mother would be silent, a silence steeled by shame. "I can't tell them."

Dr. Short reached for a pack of cigarettes and abruptly stopped. "Why the hell do you kids get yourselves into this? Didn't your mother tell you anything?"

Dottie wasn't sure whether the words held anger or sorrow, probably both. She stared at her hands and blushed. "She gave me a book."

Short snapped, "Did he have a book, too?"

"He had a rubber. And, well. It might have been . . ." She gulped and said lamely, "Sometimes they leak, don't they?" And sometimes people get too much to drink and don't put them on, she admitted silently.

The doctor said it. "And sometimes you kids don't use them."

Dottie looked down at her hands and realized she was wringing them. She sat on them again.

Short looked up at the ceiling. "God."

Somehow Dottie didn't think the woman was swearing.

"Are you, as the saying goes, 'in love'? Will he marry you?"

Tears filled Dottie's eyes and she nodded without raising her head. He said he loved her, but how could she be sure?

"Does he have any money?"

She jerked her head, but why should the question surprise her?

The sigh Short made sounded like a steam kettle. "Not for me. You. The two of you!"

"I don't know how much he's got. He always seems to have some. He's going under the GI bill."

"Look, Dorothy. I'll do what needs to be done. Not because I like it. And it isn't only you, either. Most of the times it's the kid who suffers. I sometimes think kids should be made to do community work as part of their education. Get out there and see the hungry, unwanted, neglected kids out there."

Dottie would never want a kid to suffer. Could she ever be sure she wouldn't hold it against the child? She'd hope not, but she was afraid, too. And Bob? Somehow she didn't think he would. "He's nice. I think he'd make a good father. He didn't ask me to do this."

"But you want it?"

"Yes. No. Well, I'd have to quit school." Her face flamed. She was so ashamed to admit that she wanted with every fiber of her being to be a movie star. "I'm a good actress, I wanted . . ."

The doctor was quiet for a while then in a resigned tone said, "Well. Along with everything else, resentment over broken dreams is never good baggage for a child. First the test results, then we'll see."

Her tone effectively ended the interview.

As Dorothy rose, the doctor added, "There is one thing we haven't spoken about. I don't want to make you feel guilty, I only want you to be sure. Someday you're going to look at a child and wonder 'what if.' 'How old would it be now?' Do you understand?"

Dottie nodded.

"There is always adoption."

"If I ever saw it, I'd never be able to give it away."

"Like babies then, do you? I think every time I look at one that God knew what He was doing when He made those faces."

Dr. Short stood, came around and put her arm about Dottie and raised her up. "Just be sure. Getting married to the right guy, having babies isn't the end of the world. You could always go to night school, you know."

Dottie wanted to lay her head on the woman's shoulder. The spoon had acquired some padding. "You seem healthy enough. Five o'clock, Monday afternoon. We'll decide then. If your mother and father could be told, we could arrange a medical reason for the abortion and have it done in the hospital."

Dottie jerked her head. "They'd never."

Grimly, the doctor shrugged. "It's the poor and deserted who have to rely on the quacks. There are always ways when you have connections. You'd be surprised how many are done in hospitals."

"My parents are strong Baptist."

"I gather that. Well, if you decide to go through with it, we can at least make sure it's safe and clean. If you're truly pregnant, we might as well do it as quickly as possible." She handed Dottie a list. "Bring these things. You'll be here overnight."

As the door shut, she said, "Pray about it."

Chapter 11

Friday, at exactly six-thirty, the telephone rang on the third floor of Kohl Hall. Liz dashed to answer it. "May I speak to Elizabeth Chase, please?" She smiled at the sound of Alan's voice, so smooth. The baritone sort of hummed around her ear for a moment then settled in to make her heart purr.

She told herself to come back down to earth. "Would just plain Liz do?"

"I'll take three if you've got them, please." He laughed back at her.

She wanted to break into song, but to sing you had to be able to breathe. It had been a whole month since she'd seen him. "Where are you?"

"Down at the inn. Have you eaten?"

"Yeah. I did. I wasn't sure when you'd get here."

"I'm starved. I only stopped long enough to get a hot dog at a drive-in. Why don't I go on over and get something at Harvey's? I'll pick you up in an hour. Okay?"

"Seven thirty-three. I'll be ready." It would be thirty-three, not thirty-two or thirty-four.

"Are you wearing green?"

"You'll see."

Since she'd already broken her "no borrow, no lend rule" for Dottie, or at least had agreed to, she had gathered her courage and borrowed a green cashmere from Sarah that happened to match her nicest Forstmann wool skirt. She sniffed in her best "I can do anything you can" manner and laughingly told Sarah, "I have pearls of my own." She'd even splashed on her precious LeLong's Indiscret perfume.

Sarah tossed her coat to her and said approvingly, "Wow, Liz, you look swell."

Evidently Alan thought so, too, as he swung open the door of the blue Packard for her. He bent forward and nuzzled her. "Perfume only goes so far."

She turned her face and kissed him on the mouth but cut it off quickly. These kisses were nice but getting warm. To distract both herself and him, she opened her coat to show the green outfit.

He stood back and shook his head. "You're too much for this heap. For you I need a Rolls."

"No. This has class." She liked the long pointed nose and winged hood ornament. "I have wondered why you didn't buy another. It's not as though you can't afford it."

"It runs. Waste not, want not." He put on his Oxford accent: "It isn't the thing to be too splendidly obvious. Just not done, my dear."

"Yes, well, I can't see the U.S. Ambassador to the Court of St. James drive up in a '39 Packard, lovely as it is."

He laughed and climbed into the driver's side. They leaned together and this time she didn't pull back. His lips made her wonder how there could ever be a problem between them. Surely such heaven was meant to be.

Alan pulled back from the moment and took a strand of her hair in his fingers. "A rare fire."

And what did she say to that? She knew what he meant but wanted to hear him say it. "Where's the fire?"

He counted on his fingers: "You, your hair, that outfit, and me. Only, not in that order. It's me first, even if that isn't good manners."

She snuggled against him. "I've missed you."

"I know. Me, too."

In moments like these she could easily chuck college and marry him. But, Bowling Green State University, Bowling Green, Ohio, Bachelor of Arts, Psychology, MA, Ph.D., those were real dreams, too. Somehow she had to work something out. Surely she could talk to him.

The continual emotional battering made her dizzy. His face, so earnest even when he smiled, so . . . what? So maddeningly lovable. She wanted to run her hands over that cheek he must have just shaved, touch those eyes that had such a nice warm glow in them. Shake those shoulders, so manfully stubborn. She sighed without realizing it.

"Why the sigh?" A bit of fire from the kiss still lingered in his eyes, turning the hazel to a warm sienna.

"Because I love you and things seem so complicated when they shouldn't be, I guess."

From the radio, Kitty Kallen sang, "Kiss me once and kiss me twice . . ."

He turned it off. "Yeah, a long time." He lowered his head and pressed his lips on hers, softly at first, then with the fervor of a man too long in a desert. "Too long."

Liz, too, burned with the heat and the longing of it. All the anguish and tumult of the last months melted into hunger for love. She trembled both from the impact of his kiss and the cold.

He drew away and scooted back to the driver's side. "It's cold out here. Isn't there someplace we can talk?"

Liz swallowed. He'd never kissed her quite like that before. He was always warm and sweet, and . . . careful. He'd never demanded. That kiss came as close to demanding as Liz cared to experience just now. But it had been wonderful. She had to force herself to come back from that Eden and answer him.

She couldn't think of anyplace really private other than

the car and even his kiss couldn't warm that up. The downstairs lounge of Kohl would probably be empty right now, but some kid or the housemother would be wandering through, maybe have her door open. They could easily be overheard. The only private place she could think of would be in the midst of a crowd too busy to notice them. And other than the theater where they couldn't talk, the bowling alley was the busiest place she knew.

The alley with its polished barn look, the smell of banana oil, the thud and roll of the balls and sharp clack of falling pins, all the hard sounds ricocheting off the slick surfaces, was about as unromantic a place as she could imagine. Still, no one would pay attention to them in the confusion.

When he found them a table in the corner, she managed to grin at him. "You can't kiss me here like you did in the car."

"I could. But I'll enjoy it more, later." He squeezed her hand then went and brought back a couple of Cokes. When he sat, he looked at her with eyes that had lost the sienna and were now dark brown.

She shivered a little and told herself it was still a chill from the January cold, not an omen even though his eyes had turned dark. Perhaps it was only a trick of the lights, or the lack of them. He loved her. She loved him.

He took the ring box he'd had at Christmas and laid it between them. How could so small a thing take up so much space? The table suddenly became crowded.

She had not even held the box that other time. She picked it up, opened it and gasped. Even in this dim place, arrows of fire made a halo of color over the brilliantly white solitaire. It must have been at least a carat. "Alan, it's beautiful."

"Put it on."

She swallowed hard and clenched the box, then dropped it like a bad joke in church, a temptation and a dare. It meant giving up. Should she?

"Liz, they'll give me the summer off before I have to go. Please say you'll come. I love you. I want to marry you. Now."

She gave him a tiny smile. "This minute?" All the weeks away from him had not resolved the issue, nor made thinking about it less painful. After she'd come back, the lure of his so-perfect life and a white columned house had weakened while the happy confusion of BG and the dorm pulled harder. Now, his love tugged full force at her heart. His voice . . . his face . . . the kisses. It would be so easy to say yes and forget everything.

What would Mom and Dad say if she quit? Dad would probably say it was just as well; after all, catching a husband was what girls went to college for anyway, wasn't it? Mom? There were always the women who "did" things. When her mom said things like that, her eyes, normally filled with warmth, maybe not too much humor, held a trace of envy and even perhaps a little anger.

She looked at Alan and saw his mom. The word that came to mind for Kate Bannerman was placid. Her mental thesaurus finished the thought. Placid. Undisturbed. Becalmed. The last made Liz shiver.

The clack of balls and pins from the alleys filled the space around and between them as Alan waited for her to answer. The lights from his diamond did their own dance, flashing out to lure her, darkening and withdrawing to deny her.

Back in her own tug-of-war, Liz reminded herself there were women doctors. They managed.

She squared her shoulders. "It's not that simple. Look,

what do the husbands of women doctors do? They marry. Does the man come home every night and complain?"

"I don't know." He picked up the box and turned it, then laid it down. "Let's not argue, please, Liz. I love you. I want you to marry me."

He doesn't want to think about the options. Professional women could have cooks and someone to clean once or twice a week. Send their laundry out. Why not her?

Still, except for Tom, she didn't know any man who might like that, a wife not waiting when he got home. It was the nature of things, they said. But why should it be?

She could accept a time-out while the kids were small. What, ten years? There ought to be some way to do it.

She picked up the box and fingered the stone, challenging the fire that shot at her. Her fingers burned. She put it down.

"It sounds so easy when you say it, Alan. 'Marry me.' Your mom and mine had no choice. But now women can do things beyond changing diapers."

"You make it sound as though you don't want a family. You said you liked kids."

"Kids grow up, you know. Fast. Babies are adorable, but pretty soon they go away to college and get married. Then what?" Red Cross bandages?

Alan sniffed. "Mother keeps busy."

Liz wanted to say, "But doing what?" Instead she tried to put the argument practically. "The war showed that sometimes a woman has to support herself. I wouldn't want to have to wait tables for a living." She held up her hand to deflect the answer she knew was coming. "You say if I was widowed I'd have enough money. What would I do with the rest of my life? Sit around and twiddle my thumbs?"

He kissed her quickly on the mouth. "Marry again."

"Oh. Of course. How silly of me not to figure that one out! A woman's only existence is through a man! Is that right?"

"Liz!"

Exasperation steamed from her. "Suppose after we're married, you hated me? Suppose we'd get a divorce?"

Hurt smoldered in Alan's eyes. "We'd never. I'd never leave you, Liz."

He looked so sweet when he said it, she almost believed him. She gave him a half-smile. "You can't say that for sure until you've eaten my cooking. I even burned the bacon in my cooking class. I hate cleaning house. I do love kids, though."

He picked up her hand and kissed it. "I can get a maid and cook."

Irrationally she demolished her own argument that professional people could indeed have help. "The only cook I'd allow would be some old woman who couldn't make eyes at you when my back was turned. None of that Lili Marlene stuff."

When he laughed, she said, "I'd never want to leave you, either. I'd never want a divorce."

She could see that he thought he'd won.

Perhaps he had. She was running out of steam and willpower.

Her dad hadn't liked it when her mom wanted to work during the war. So she hadn't.

The others, the ones whose husbands had been overseas, well, they were all coming home now, hoping for babies. What happened if there were no babies? She said it aloud, "You know it could be we couldn't have children. What then?"

"Liz, it's you I love, no matter what."

She looked away and saw Tom with Miss Red Finger-nails. Tom's glance met hers. He smiled and gave her a tiny wink. He knew why Alan was there. Tom's eyes seemed to say, "Be careful." When his eyes held hers for an extra-long moment, his message read, "I'll take you if he doesn't."

Embarrassed that it was Tom who understood, she looked quickly back at Alan. He's only waiting for me to agree with him!

"Look. If you could wait only two years. That's not so long. I could do the last year in Switzerland." If he was still there. How long would the government leave him at one post? Desperately she tried a different tack. "As the buck private in the line, they'll keep you busy. And there'll be a lot to see and do besides work. Just remember, though, blonds aren't an acceptable part of the scenery."

He said, "How about brunettes?" but she could see he wasn't pleased with her answer.

"I'll come over and visit and you can show me Europe. You will get a vacation, won't you?" She rejected the thought that her mother would never let her go alone. She supposed maybe they could afford it. Prices in Europe were cheap enough, considering the dollar's value.

Alan closed his eyes and shook his head. "You don't understand, Liz. I'd be too lonely over there. I keep saying it, 'I love you.' 'I want to be with you.'"

He leaned back and the corners of his mouth turned up again. "Besides, I think marriage would make the State Department think I'm more stable, more reliable. You know how odd they can be."

She sighed. Adults kept saying eighteen was too young to marry, yet they pushed just by giving their approval to Alan's views. "Just two more years, Alan. I'd be a senior. I'll take German along with my French." She went through the whole roster of "I could's." When she was finished, his eyes were darker than ever. She looked away.

She met Tom's eyes again and turned abruptly back. Tom had encouraged her when he'd said, "I don't think it's fair for a man to walk all over a woman's feelings. My mom wanted to be a nurse." He'd qualified that, said his mother was happy, that with seven children it was problematic anyway. He swore his mom would make lawyers or doctors out of his sisters whether they wanted to or not. All six of them. Then he'd laughed but he wasn't kidding.

Liz wanted to cry. Why is it the wrong guys were always right? The problem was, she loved Alan. If there was a Prince Charming, well, he was. Maybe everyone else was right and she was wrong. Certainly tradition was on their side.

The ring winked at her. She put it on. The first time. She held her hand out to look at it. Beautiful. And a perfect fit. The resolve in her threatened to melt. But she couldn't. She took it off and set it back in its slot.

Alan's eyes clouded. "Wear it, Liz."

She shook her head at him. "Can't you give a little? You know how important school is to me."

This time, he shook his head as though puzzled by her. "You can get a BA in any place in the world."

She said bitterly, "Like Cambridge?" Sarah had told her how awful Cambridge was to women. Liz wondered if Alan, the future diplomat, knew? Perhaps he approved. "Do you know they won't award a degree for women even when they complete the same work as the men? They give them a certificate. And it's only because if they did, the women could vote in the college. You can count Cambridge out." Sarah had said the tide was changing, but still.

He smiled a little as though such things were irrelevant.

"Cambridge isn't the only place. London won't be my address for a long time yet. There are plenty of other colleges."

"Sure. And at any one of them I can get a BA to make me conversant with literature, give me an inside view of pickled frogs, 'educate me to amuse men.' "

She took a swimmer's breath and plunged on. "I could always play the clavichord and paint."

"Liz . . ."

She shook her head. "Parents want girls to go to college, but what they really expect is for them to be a teacher—a proper job for a lady who has to work. Failing that, there is always the BA, the great time filler and social polisher. Colleges are filled with girls looking for the right guy."

When she finished, she looked up at him with tears in her eyes. Why couldn't he understand? "I don't want that kind of a degree. I want a Ph.D. in psychology. I don't mind entertaining white-haired old men and blue-haired women, but is that all there is?"

"I think you really mean you don't want to get married."

The tears threatened a downpour. She looked up at the ceiling. How could she make him understand when she didn't understand herself? Of course she wanted to marry. Marry him. But she also wanted to be out there and dig into the brain of the universe. Do something so that men and women could understand each other, talk to each other so that they understood what was said, not just hear their own prejudice. And write so that other people could see, too. Was that so wrong? Was it only a man who counted? Couldn't women do things other than raise babies? Why shouldn't she have her cake and eat it, too? Men certainly did.

She shook her head. "Of course, I want to marry. And I

want children. Only I don't know what to do about it." Her look implored him. "Alan, can't you ease up? Wait for a year or two? Please?" She wanted desperately to say, "If you loved me, you'd wait," but bit her tongue to keep the words and the hurt back.

It was Alan who said it. "I thought you really loved me. It just isn't natural for a woman not to want to get married and have a family. Maybe you should have been a man."

Liz's hand tightened on the glass of melted ice in front of her. How could he have said that? That she wasn't natural? That she wasn't a true woman? Just because she wanted something more than a kitchen for the rest of her life? For a wild moment she hated him. How could he?

She bit her lip to keep from crying. If she cried, she'd only get angrier. "I didn't know a kitchen defined a woman."

He shook his head in frustration. "Well, Mother is at Dad's side every step of the way. I don't think he could have done it without her. It just seems to me that's a woman's strength." He stopped and looked her in the eye. "And her full-time job."

"Alan, your dad would succeed at anything he did."

"But she helped." His lower lip jutted as he said it.

"All I want is time."

"I don't have it. In September I'll be in Switzerland. It's been bad enough being at Georgetown with you here."

Liz thought of all the old movies where a loyal man loved a woman from afar for his whole lifetime. But even she knew that was too much to ask. But two years? She'd only be twenty.

"Lots of men wait two years. Look at all the guys in the war. Some of them waited four. It's not like I wouldn't be true to you."

"But that's not the entire problem, is it? I wait two years. We get married. You get your bachelor's. That's fine. But then you'll want a master's and a doctorate. And you want a career. I won't be in the same place long enough for that." He took her hands in his and drew them to his lips but he didn't kiss them. "Share my career, Liz."

She weakened again.

"If I thought there was a really good reason for it, I could wait, but it all seems so unnecessary. I'll take care of you. I promise."

She withdrew her hands and said bitterly, "Snow White and Cinderella. What a real woman wants."

"Well. No. I'm sorry I said that." He reached across and took a strand of her hair in his fingers and said, with a look in his eye and a warmth that most times would melt her, "You're very much a woman." He picked up her hand and held and kissed it. "You smell like one."

Liz drew her hand back and wished she hadn't put the perfume on. "Would you have said that to Sarah? You've been so nice about knowing the way she feels like a flower in a buttonhole. You seem to understand that she wants to be a mathematician. She's brilliant and she's going to do it in spite of being a woman in a man's field. Or do you think she'll get over it when she grows up? That she ought to stay home and wash dishes, too, even though she is twice as smart as most guys in her classes?"

"I'm not marrying her. Anyway, she's a genius, isn't she?"

She looked hard at him for a long time. "You mean there are different laws for them? Well, I might not be a genius but I am on the dean's list."

He put his hand on her arm. "You do get defensive, don't you? You know I meant nothing of the kind. We need to get out of here and be alone. Even Kilroy wouldn't want to stick his nose in here."

She smiled a little in spite of her misery. She hadn't seen a picture of those peeping eyes and nose for a while. Once they'd been peeping over fences and walls everywhere. "Kilroy was here" meant the GIs were, too.

When she smiled, he did, too. "You know I love you."

There it was again. The argument to end all arguments. But it didn't. "I'm not sure you do. I think you care about you." As she said the words, her heart settled into her toes. She knew it was over. They didn't even hear the same words in the same sentence.

She handed the box back to him and shook her head. "It isn't going to work, is it? I love you, Alan, but it's hopeless."

He put the box in his pocket and stood. "I guess you're right."

On the ride home, Hoagy Carmichael's "Stardust" filled the car. Tears tried to fill Liz's eyes but she squeezed them shut. She wasn't going to cry in front of him.

It wasn't until she got to her empty room that she let the tears stream.

Chapter 12

Even if the sun had shone brightly, and it did not, Monday could only be a dreadful day for Dottie. She climbed hesitantly aboard the Greyhound for the dreary ride into Toledo and the doctor's appointment, desperately wishing she had Bob to hold on to. She'd give anything to bury her fist into his big hand, lean against his burly chest, but panic told her she could not face him. She must make this trip alone.

Until Route 25 reached the Maumee River and Fort Meigs Park, the road ran like a dark ribbon through flat, grey, snow-covered farmland. Dottie could not help but contrast this trip with that glorious arch of gold and bronze, the bonfire of reds mirrored in the river. Now the white frame houses along the road looked dirty winter-white and shabby. The few Victorian leftovers of redbrick stood dull and numb in the cold gloom.

Numb. The perfect word. Perhaps she would remain that way for the rest of her life. If she did this thing, how could she ever allow herself to feel again?

But she had never been good at closing herself off, locking up pieces of her mind and heart into little cubbyholes where she could visit and then leave. In spite of herself, all the parts of Dottie went headlong into happiness or disaster at once.

Until she stepped onto the bus, she'd made up her mind to have the . . . She couldn't even say the word. She took a deep breath and steeled herself to think it, abortion. But, in spite of that resolution, her heart would not be still. What then? She had no idea. She could neither do, nor not do. Her mind felt like the snow looked, a grey dreadful mush. She didn't want to think of Bob. She dare not think about herself. She closed her eyes and gave herself up to the formless pain that stopped thought.

From the Greyhound station she managed to find the right city bus, the right street and the right office, on time. At five o'clock, she had to be the last patient for the afternoon. No one else was in the office at all. Not even a receptionist.

Dottie rifled the magazines. *Good Housekeeping, Ladies Home Journal.* Both names, with their hint of happy homes, sent a wave of nausea through her. She finally found a *Life* magazine and stared blankly at the pictures.

She pulled out a pack of cigarettes, put them away, then got them out again and lit one. Maybe she ought to leave, return later when she could accept what her mind told her she must do. Would she ever accept it?

She checked her watch. Five-fifteen. Maybe Dr. Short had been called away. Dottie twitched in her chair. If she left now—she stubbed out the cigarette she'd taken only two puffs from and rose. Later. Maybe she'd come back another day.

She reached for her coat then froze as Dr. Short walked into the receptionist's space. "Let's go into the office."

Dottie followed orders but did not sit.

The doctor adjusted the neat dark bun of hair at the back of her neck. "It won't be easier standing."

Dottie sat.

"You are pregnant. The test is positive." She opened the folder.

Dorothy's heart thudded. Pregnant, she knew. But the

file . . . it was history. A short interval of her life. A story. The story of a kid, a baby. Unborn, but a real baby. If it lived, it would have a name and a story. If she aborted it, it was nothing with no name, a blank space in the file.

Her heart told her she could never relegate this baby inside her, for it was a baby, a part of her, a part of Bob, to the status of a blob, a blank. A calm swept over her. She said quietly, "I know I'm pregnant. But I'm not going to have the abortion. I thought I would. I thought I had to, that my life would be ruined. But I can't."

In a way, this strange calm was as bad as the storm. It left all those unanswered questions. Yet there was a freedom in it. The big one was answered.

Dr. Short came around the desk and put her arm around her. "I'm glad. I really am. Now, what can I do?" Gently she maneuvered her so that they sat on the sofa.

Dottie shook her head. "I don't know. I haven't told Bob."

"Will you go home?"

"Not if I can help it." Dottie gave a short laugh. "I don't know if I can stand having the door shut in my face."

The doctor's expression looked less sure than the words that came from her. "Surely your parents won't do that? They must love you."

Dottie shrugged and stood. "Well, I may or may not find out." She heard Bob's voice again: "We can go down to Kentucky and get married."

Her own voice whispered that marriage would solve a lot of problems. Shame for one. In her mother's eyes, being a Mrs. would take part of the sting from it. If they never went back to Rocky River for a while, no one need know.

She pictured her father waving his Bible, threatening to stone her. Would time allow him to accept it, too? Maybe the sight of a grandson would do what she could not. It would be a boy, she knew it.

Dr. Short shut the folder and tapped it. "If you stay up here, we can work out an arrangement. Let me know what you decide to do. I can pass this along. Where are you from?"

"Rocky River. Cleveland, that is. Bob's from Lima. He has an apartment in Perrysburg."

The doctor nodded.

Dottie rose. "I'll be in touch." She turned back from the door and held out her hand. "Thank you. You've been really nice." Tears filled her eyes. "How much do I owe you?"

When the bill was paid, Dr. Short hugged her and, with an arm still around her, walked her through the waiting room.

Dottie decided to stop at Harvey's rather than go back to the dorm, or face Bob. She needed time to think. He would not think to look for her there. She had no idea what she would order. Her nausea was the nonstop kind. If food settled it for the moment, it only came back worse afterwards.

The heat in the room slapped her in the face as she opened the door and the odor of browning meat made her want to bolt. She held her breath, headed for the booth in the corner and ordered a Coke. "With soda crackers, please."

The slow anger at Bob that rose in the pit of her stomach surprised her. She'd already been through all that rage, at him, at the Fates. Why this inexplicable anger now? She sipped at the soothing fizz and examined her feelings. Perhaps not so inexplicable. She was angry at him because she hadn't the faintest idea what to do now.

A different kind of panic held her. Maybe not panic.

Terror. Bob had said he'd marry her. In spite of her protests, she knew she'd been depending upon that promise. Depending upon it even though she knew that, if she took him at his word, she would always wonder if he married because he had to.

The rush of blood to her head and the cramp in her stomach told her there was no easy answer. Perhaps none at all. She drew up sharply and tried to calm down, breathe deeply. No. Not that way.

Desperately she went over the options or lack of them again. Even if her father didn't disown her, she couldn't face that burden of disapproval. The gossip. There was no chance she could bring it up as a single mother. Adoption? The soda gushed back to burn her nose and throat. How could she ever just give her baby away and walk off?

Big tears rolled down her cheeks and she ducked, hoping no one could see. She reached into her purse but the tissues were gone, so she reached blindly for the tiny napkins crammed into the steel box. They came out in shreds.

In exasperation she picked up the stainless steel box. The brand letters shouted at her, "Made in Temple, Alabama." Temple down in the Bible Belt. Word from God? She began to laugh and cry together. Between the hiccups that followed she mumbled, "Even the damn paper napkins condemn me."

She was still hiccuping when a flushed Bob sat down in the booth opposite her. "Where the hell have you been? I've looked everywhere." His shoulders slumped, and he softened his tone. He came around to sit beside her and put his arm around her shoulders. "Did you go to Toledo? I've been so scared. I'm sorry I barked at you." He picked up one of the larger shreds of napkin and wiped away her tears. He hesitated then looked around quickly, said, "Oh, to hell with them," and kissed her soundly. "It'll be okay. Really."

She hiccuped again and tried to quiet her sobs.

"Hey. I love you. It's okay." He drew her close. "Did you see the doctor?"

She looked up at him through her tears. "Oh, Bob. I'm so sorry."

"You've nothing to be sorry about. It's my fault."

"I do. I was going to—well, you know—but I couldn't. I mean, I saw the doctor but I couldn't go through with it."

"I'm glad you didn't." He hugged her hard then moved opposite her in the booth. He reached for her hand and smiled slightly. "It's hard talking to your profile."

Her face crumpled again.

"It's okay."

"Don't keep saying that. It isn't."

"I've said it before. I'll say it again. I love you, Dottie." He rubbed her cheek with his thumb. "Look. The semester ends Friday and the new one won't start until Thursday. We'll go down to Kentucky this weekend. You won't even have to tell anyone here if you don't want to. Are Liz and Sarah going home for the break? Maybe you can check out while they're gone."

She raised her head and studied him. Was he telling the truth? He didn't look mad or anxious, only soft and warm. Could he really love her? Immense relief and gratitude flooded her. And yes, now that she didn't have to fight it, she could admit that she did love him, too.

Still, she had to say it. "I don't want you to marry me because you have to. That would be an awful life. I couldn't stand looking at you across the table all the time if I thought you were trapped."

"Come on. Let's get out of here. I want to show you something in the car." He picked up her ticket, rose, went to her side of the booth and pulled her up.

She waited while he paid. His car was in front of the building and he let her in and slid in beside her. He reached into his coat pocket and came out with a small black box. "I got this just in case." He opened it. A plain wide gold band lay tucked in white satin. "One more time. I love you, Dottie."

She didn't take it right away. She cried.

He handed her his handkerchief.

She blew her nose and laughed. "I'm sorry. I feel as though I've been chopped and stewed for dinner."

"I know. I'm sorry. It will be all right." He put his arms around her and held her.

She drew her head back and looked into his brown eyes. She'd never noticed before how warm they were. She laid her face against his cheek and slipped on the ring. It fit perfectly. "Don't be sorry. I'm not. Not now. I hope he looks like you."

Chapter 13

"Ugh!" Liz pushed on the pile of sweaters, trying to make room for one more in the drawer. "Boy, this is swell!" she muttered under her breath. "When I get a house, I'm going to have a whole closet with shelves just for these."

"What's all the mumbling about? Didn't you have a good weekend, either?" Sarah struggled into the room and plopped her suitcase in the middle. "I should have stayed here. Boring!"

Liz frowned at the light knit in her hand and the full drawer. Finally she tossed it down on top of Dottie's bare dresser. "Oh, I had a great time. That is, if 'great' is trying to avoid lectures on what a real woman wants; on a miserable, lonely old age; and how to be feminine." She didn't mention Alan. Not yet.

She gave the offending sweater an annoyed tap and said, "I'll get that later." She shoved her suitcase under her bed, then stumbled over Sarah's, still parked in the middle of the room.

"Ouch! Sarah!" She nursed her toe for a moment then began to laugh.

"I'm sorry. Really, I am." Sarah obligingly moved the offending case.

"It's a good thing Dottie's not here. Do you think you'll ever get the hang of putting things away?" As she said it, she looked back at her own sweater and blushed. "Oh nuts, let's go to the Nest."

Sarah grinned and shoved the case back to the center.

"Let's leave it and see what she says!"

"Why stop there?" Liz took a pair of shoes from the closet and set them in front of Dottie's dresser, then two of her fattest sweaters and piled them on the dresser top with the stray she'd left before. "There."

Sarah draped a pair of stockings over the desk chair. "This is fun. We ought to do it more often! It's just like home, except Mom isn't here to clean it up!"

For a moment they were lost in a fit of laughter. Between gasps, Liz said, "Let's put some of her stuff out!" She opened the drawer and froze. "It's empty!" In a near frenzy, she pulled out the others. "They're all empty!"

Sarah dashed to the closet Liz shared with Dottie. "Her clothes are gone! Didn't you notice?"

Tears came to Liz's eyes. "No. It did look different, but there's so much junk in there, I didn't pay attention. Do you think she's gone? Maybe she just took it all home to wash. Maybe she was going to bring her spring stuff?" But even as Liz said it, she knew she didn't believe it. She stared at the spaces as though she could make the missing things materialize.

"In February? Oh, Liz!" Sarah opened and shut the empty drawers of the chest as though she had to prove it to herself. "She's gone. And she didn't even tell us."

Liz plumped down on Dottie's empty bed. She didn't know whether to cry or be scared. "She said she had enough money, that nothing was wrong at home." A dismal tear filled the corner of her eye.

Sarah sighed and joined Liz on the bed. Absently she plucked at the cover then suddenly pulled it back. A bare mattress. "I didn't even notice the pillow was gone."

Hurt and anger at Dottie deserting them overwhelmed Liz. She pulled her feet under her and leaned her chin on her fist. "Do you suppose she's seriously ill? She wasn't well at all for the last couple of months." Month. Two. The thought hit her so violently she bumped her head on the overhead spring. "Oh, Sarah. Do you suppose she's . . ." She couldn't say it.

The same thought jolted Sarah. "Pregnant? Do you think she's pregnant? Oh, no! No! The money! She said she wanted it for Bob, but, she wouldn't. She can't . . ."

Liz paled, unwilling to accept abortion. "The poor kid. She didn't even say anything."

"That Bob. Wait till I get my hands on him!"

Liz flushed. "Maybe we're jumping to conclusions." A little voice told her they were not. Fear, anger and hurt jostled to see which could hurt most. Fear won. What if Dottie had gone to some sleaze? If she meant to and was short of money . . . All the horror stories she'd ever heard ran riot in Liz's head. But if Dottie had done that, where would she go? That Bob! Where was he? Had she even told him?

Liz gulped. "Where do you suppose she is? I can't imagine her going home after the way she talked about her father's Bible thumping. She could be with Bob, but, oh, Sarah, do you think she's just run away somewhere?"

Sarah rose and pulled and pushed at Dottie's dresser drawers as though things might suddenly change. "There's nowhere to run to. I don't even want to think about it. With her clothes all gone, she must have gone home. Besides, maybe we're wrong. Maybe she's not even pregnant. Maybe she got discouraged and quit. Do you think we should call her house?"

Liz shook her head. "If she's not there, what would we say to her mother and father?"

"If she just quit . . ."

"Not Tallulah. Not a chance." She jumped up and

grabbed her purse. "I'm going to see if that Bob's back." She plowed through it and triumphantly came up with a small red book. "She asked me to call him one time. I've got his number."

Both of them dashed to the hall and stood biting their lips, hopping from one foot to the other while the girl on the phone gave them a dirty look and kept on talking.

Sarah nodded toward their room and they went back to wait. In a rare burst of venom she muttered, "That stupid Marge! She'll only take longer if we stare at her."

Surprised at Sarah's spite, for a millisecond Liz wanted to laugh, but the two of them were too busy vying for the best spot to peer through the almost closed door.

Finally Marge hung up. She dashed across the hall and gave a quick knock on her own door, but Liz and Sarah tumbled from their room and grabbed the phone. "We've been waiting."

Marge and her friend sniffed, said, "Hmph! So've we!" They went back into their room and slammed the door. The floor monitor looked out, frowned, then withdrew.

Liz sighed and dialed.

A woman's voice answered. It wasn't Dottie. Too old. "Is Bob Arnold there, please?"

There was a snort, then an abrupt, "He moved out. You kids have no consideration at all. He didn't even have the courtesy to give me notice and it's too late now to get another student. I don't know where you get your morals." The woman punctuated her annoyance by slamming the phone down.

Liz jerked the receiver from her ear, stuck out her tongue, and hung up not too softly herself, wishing the witch was there to hear it. The words, though, rang in her ear: "He didn't give me notice." Surely he hadn't run out on Dottie if she was in trouble. But, "They're both gone. That must be a good sign."

They linked arms and went back into the room. Both of them dived for the box of tissues. "Now what?" Sarah managed. "Do you suppose they got married?"

Liz sniffed but before she could answer, a tall bony girl, all sharp planes and long angles, came into the room and plopped two suitcases down. Even her brown hair was long and straight. Without a word, she turned, went out and brought back two more boxes.

Liz gaped and Sarah gasped, they looked at each other and stifled their giggles.

The girl pushed the hair from her face and gave an appraising look around the small room. "Oops. I hope there's storage somewhere!" Her grin was as full as she was thin. "I'm Jenny. Sort of short notice. Registration called and said they had a vacancy so I grabbed it. Looks like you're stuck with me for a while at least."

So Dottie had quit! Officially! Liz and Sarah gave each other a worried glance. Was this good or bad news? Liz wasn't sure.

Jenny turned and brought in one more box. At least that one was small!

In spite of her worry, Liz had to swallow hard to keep from laughing at the array. She introduced herself and Sarah.

From the middle of her stacks, Jenny asked, "Where do I put my stuff? Kinda crowded, isn't it?"

"Oh." Sarah reddened, shoved her own suitcase to the foot of the bed and grabbed the clothes strewn about. "We weren't finished putting things away."

Liz snatched her sweaters but dropped them on her bed. Jenny was like a small hurricane. Liz felt a bit winded already. "We're not really this sloppy. It was a joke. We'll get this stuff later. We were just going over to the Nest."

She threw a pleading look at Sarah for support. They couldn't talk in front of this new girl.

Sarah didn't catch the look. "Yeah. We were just going. You're welcome to come if you want to."

Liz held her breath, hoping for a "no." Not that she didn't like Jenny. She and Sarah had to talk.

The girl gave them her big grin again and the planes in her face softened. She motioned at the suitcases. "I think I've got work to do. But what do they keep in the Nest, baby birds?"

Laughter bubbled up in Liz, bringing with it the relief humor always does. "It's the Falcon's Nest. The unofficial student union. Name of the place. Falcons are the BG mascot. We eat there a lot. The dorm's okay but there's a long time in between."

They explained about the arrangements in the room and the storage.

"Do the Greeks have more room than this? Which sorority's the best?"

Sarah and Liz looked at each other. Both tried to keep a straight face. Sarah mumbled, "Dunno," and the two of them beat a hasty retreat.

They were still laughing when they unloaded their trays of burgers and fries in the booth. Liz said it first. "Okay, so she's not Greta Garbo, but I think I'll like her."

"She just walked in the door and already has plans for the best sorority." Sarah chuckled. "But you know, she's got a lot of personality. She might just know what she's doing."

"With all that luggage?" Liz's laugh was interrupted by a guy she could only describe as a smoothie, a wolf.

He gave them a sly smile. "You're Dottie's roommates, aren't you?"

Liz drew back in the seat and felt Sarah do the same. No good news could come from this guy. "Yeah," she said. "I'm Liz."

He turned to Sarah who stared blank-faced at him. "Have you seen Bob? He owes me some money." Unaffected by their rebuff, he asked, "Where's Dottie?"

Liz bristled. The tone and smirk implied he knew something they didn't. She sat up straight. She could tell him about the call to Bob, but she most certainly would not.

He puffed up his chest and proclaimed, "Dottie's not coming back."

He slid in beside Sarah who was already as far back in the corner as she could get. "I called Bob's apartment. I know he's not there. Wondered what you knew about the affair."

Affair? Liz glared at him. How dare he?

It was Sarah who answered. "What's that to you?"

"Didn't you know?" He reached out to touch her hand. She jerked it back.

Liz glared but bit her lip. She tried to scrunch farther away from him as well. She knew she didn't want to hear anything he might have to say.

He said smugly, "My guess is she had an abortion."

"I don't believe you!" Liz shouted, then looked down, embarrassed by the noise and the attention she knew she'd drawn.

He raised a brow and gave a lopsided leer. "I suppose they could have just gone off and got married, only he asked me for the name of a doctor." He rose. The look on his face Liz could only describe as a simper. He said, "I just wondered. He's a friend of mine."

"Save me from friends like you!" Sarah muttered.

"Babe, you can be my friend anytime you want." He patted her hand, smirked again and walked off.

Sarah made a grab for the salt shaker then sniffed. "Jerk."

Liz made a hex sign at his back. A clapping behind her made her turn. Tom rose from a booth away. How long had he been there?

"Make a sign for me, too. Mind if I join you?"

When he sat down with them, Liz asked, "Who is that creep?"

"No one you want to know. A jerk who thinks he's a big man. Someone once told him he was a human being. I heard what he said." Tom took her hand and held it.

"Dottie's gone." They said it at the same time.

He nodded gravely. "I know." He took out an envelope with Liz's name on it. "Bob asked me to give you this. Said he couldn't do it himself and didn't know who else to ask."

Liz stared at it for a moment and started to cry.

Tom handed her a napkin and gave her a small smile. "Here. If you're going to cry all the time, you really ought to carry tissues."

She sniffed then wiped the tears away and opened the note. She read it softly, trying to keep the sound of her voice within the booth.

Dear Liz and Sarah,

I'm sorry to do this to you, but Dottie didn't want you to know. She is too embarrassed. I just can't let you think anything bad of her. We are going down to Kentucky and get married this weekend. We won't be back. She is expecting a baby in July, maybe early August. When everything was settled, we decided we were happy about it. I love Dottie . . .

Her voice broke and Tom took it and finished:

. . . and I'll take good care of her. I'll see she has time for acting. We'll live in Cleveland but not near her parents. I'll go to Northwestern and she can join some little theater. I'm sure Cleveland will have some.

Anyway. I know she'd want you to know she's all right even if she can't face you now. I don't know where we will live, but here is my mom's address. She'll forward anything and I'll let you know. Only don't write until I tell Dottie you know.

Thanks, Bob

This time it was Sarah who pulled napkins from the box and wiped her tears.

Liz had her own stack of crumpled paper in the seat. She said, "I always thought he was a jerk. A big wolf. But I was wrong. I hope they'll be happy."

Tom folded the paper and slipped it under Liz's plate. "There's nothing quite like getting in the family way to make you grow up."

Sarah giggled in spite of her damp eyes. "In the family way? Oh, Tom. What's the matter with expecting a baby?"

He laughed. "I collect euphemisms. Like 'a bun in the oven.' Like that one better?"

Liz put her hand on his. "Thanks, Tom. I feel a lot better."

"Then how about going to the Valentine's dance Saturday with me?"

She had to take her hand away to wipe away the last tear. She smiled at him. "What? And hurt Ann's feelings? Those red fingernails would probably claw my eyes out. I wouldn't dare!"

Mischief glinted in his eyes as he turned to Sarah. "Well, she didn't say no, did she?"

Sarah nodded as though the matter were of grave concern. "I heard her say yes under her breath."

"Traitor!" Liz threw her an amused glance then looked back at Tom. "Well, what about Ann?"

"History. Like Boleyn. I chopped her head off. What about Alan?"

Liz looked down at her plate and the cold hamburger. She shoved it away. "I thought I was hungry but what with one thing and another, I can't eat that." She barely paused as she said, "Seems Alan's history, too. Evidently I'm not woman enough for him."

Sarah looked at her as though she were Thor and had loosed a bolt. "Maid enough, I think."

Tom reached for Liz's hand but didn't touch her, just lay his own near hers. "Some people don't know when they're well-off and his loss is my gain. Will you, Liz?"

She looked up at him and steeled herself against the thought of Alan and the past. "Yes." College and history sort of went together. She might as well make some of her own here at BG.

Chapter 14

Liz watched the delivery boy unload the flower truck. One, two—thirteen boxes and bouquets. Valentine's Day. She leaned forward as though by getting closer to the window she'd be able to read the names, see if one was for her. From Alan. Silly. Why would he? She'd not heard a word since that Friday and, the way things were, she couldn't call him.

She sighed and sat down at the desk and tried to work on her psych paper. The big romance was over. Over. She might as well get used to it. Alan would never change, and why should she?

From the corner of her eye, she saw the truck move off. Maybe . . . No. Maybe she'd mosey down and see if by some miracle there was something for her. She could pretend she had something to do outside. She grabbed her jacket and hurried from the room.

As she reached the bottom step, Mrs. Greenway, the housemother, looked up from the card in her hand. She put it down. Liz's heart sank.

Mrs. Greenway half-turned and pointed. "Liz, there's one for you. That little one over there."

Alan! He had! He'd sent her flowers! Wow . . . maybe . . .

She trembled as she reached for the small square box. Hastily she tore open her card and read, "A rose is only a rose, but these are Venus's own flower, Tom."

Her heart skidded to a stop. Tom. It was only from Tom.

At that thought her conscience chided her. He had sent flowers, at least. She opened the box. Violets! The scent rose as delicately as the curl of the tiny purple petals against the green. "Venus's own flower," so romantic. But all she had thought of was Alan! If only all guys were like Tom. She was touched in spite of her disappointment. He was so sweet.

Trouble was, no matter how sweet, Tom wasn't Alan. Her heart told her she still loved Alan, despite the racket in her head vociferously insisting she mustn't, it would never work. They wanted different things.

But that wasn't exactly true. She wanted all the things he represented, love, a family, even travel if he stayed in the foreign service. But she also wanted at least the possibility of a career. That little piece of paper that said she was qualified and could be a psychologist if she chose, or if need be. It could be that, after going to all that trouble, she might not practice, but who knew what life would bring? And besides, psychology was interesting. People were fascinating. If nothing else, she could use her understanding in writing.

It was a moot question by now. There were probably a lot of Georgetown girls who wouldn't mind spending a life cutting roses from the garden of a Georgian house on a hill. If Alan wouldn't even send her a bouquet on Valentine's Day, well, it really was over. She swallowed and scolded herself. She would not cry over flowers unsent.

Burying her nose in the violets, she willed herself to enjoy them. How could it be so hard to like a guy who was so sweet and thoughtful? As she ascended the stairs to her room, she told herself, from now on, it won't be. "Deep Purple." Maybe that should be their song. Tom's and hers. Forget "Stardust."

Tom brought her more violets on Saturday for the dance. A corsage of them.

"They're beautiful." She told him what she'd thought about their song.

"I like it." He pinned the flowers to the shoulder of the winter-white velvet dress she'd bought in a fit of shopping after her quarrel with Alan at Christmastime. He'd never even seen it.

Tom gave the corsage a last flick, shook his head, held his hands up in front of him and backed up two steps. His grin belied his words. "They're horrible. You're horrible."

That grin saved him. "Thanks a lot!" She cuffed him gently. She knew the long sleek lines and slightly flaring skirt flattered her figure.

"I'm just being careful not to tempt the gods. Remember what happened to Psyche when she made Venus jealous."

Liz blushed but stood on her toes and kissed him quickly.

His eyes sparkled as he held her coat for her. "I don't suppose you'd want to walk? It's not cold."

He held her hand all the way to the gym. And for a change it did look as though spring planned to come early this year. Valentine weekends in Ohio were synonymous with snowstorms and blizzards. But tonight the walks were dry. The crisp cold points of winter starlight did their own dance.

Inside the gym, they shouldered their way through the stags standing in the doorway. As they did, the lead horn played the opening notes of "Stardust." Those long notes hung in the air and Liz seemed to hang there with them, frozen. There seemed no way to get away from that song. From him.

She mentally shook herself. No. She would not moon over Alan anymore. She lifted her chin and when the ache lingered, forced herself to turn up the watts on her smile at Tom.

At least he understands and cares how I feel about things, she told herself. Her hand strayed to the violets.

He led her to the floor and took her in his arms and held her close as though to claim her, as though he didn't know what the song meant to her. When the orchestra slipped into "Someone to Watch Over Me," he relaxed his hold.

Sarah and Rick danced by and Rick stopped long enough to tap Liz on the shoulder. "Next dance."

She didn't want to trade partners, but they did. She had forgotten how good a dancer Rick was. She wished him away and slipped into a vision of Alan, of dancing in his arms to their song. For a miserable moment she wished she hadn't come. What good did it do to go out with Tom, when she loved Alan?

"Hi, Liz!" The voice came from Jenny. Liz couldn't help but grin. Her new roommate stopped beside her. Perhaps only an inch taller than her partner, with her straight-line princess-style dress, she looked even taller. Nothing, not a seam or belt or a line ran crosswise anywhere on the girl, except perhaps for her brows and lips. Everything was vertical, even the straight dark hair added to the going-on-forever look. Until she smiled. Then again, the lines softened.

Jenny's partner hugged her, nodded to Rick and held out his hand to Liz. "I'm Ray."

Surprised, Liz took his hand. She knew who he was, only one of the most popular guys in Sigma Chi! Blond and muscled enough that he could get away with his brand of mischief, he had a round impish face that matched his reputation, that of the unofficial campus clown. How in the world did Jenny, a brand-new freshman, end up with him? And he definitely looked in tow.

His reputation prepared anyone who knew of him to laugh when they met him. Liz was no exception. "Nice to meet you at last. I keep hearing these rumors . . ."

He held up his hands. "I'm innocent. Ask Tom." He motioned at Tom who stood in back of them, now with Sarah.

Jenny said, "Ray and I are both from Cinci." The tone of her voice claimed him. "He was the one who talked me into coming here."

Ah, that explained it, Liz thought. There was a look in their eyes . . .

The band broke the meeting up with "Cow Cow Boogie" and Ray and Jenny swung into a jitterbug. A Catherine wheel couldn't have spun better.

For the next dances, the six of them kept trading partners and Liz almost forgot Alan. She hated to stop even for the intermission.

"I haven't had so much fun in a long time." She grabbed Sarah's hand. "I need lipstick. Come on. Coming, Jenny?"

Jenny linked arms with Ray and tugged at him. "We're going to eat. See ya." The two of them made for the tables.

With wistful eyes, Sarah watched them. "I did wonder how she was so sure of herself. Knew from the start what she wanted. Boy. Wish I could be like that!"

"You know what you want. Don't worry. You'll get it." Liz took her hand and they went into the rest room.

Sarah's eyes clouded, then she shrugged and unpinned her hair from the ballerina roll at the nape of her neck and combed it. "There. I think I'll leave it. Does it look okay?"

Liz eyed her friend quizzically. "You could wear a mop and still look great. Don't you know that?"

Sarah sighed. "I guess. But that's not exactly my ambition in life. Have you heard of Howard Aiken, Harvard?"

"Thinking of going there?"

"No. Of course not. He's a math whiz."

"Oh, well. You're kidding, aren't you? The only people in your field I ever heard of are Euclid and Pythagoras. They're dead and I think I'm relieved. Except for you, that's all I want to know about math, thank you."

"Well, Aiken has done something they call the Mark I, Advanced Sequence Controlled Calculator."

"Huh?"

Sarah laughed. "Technology and math. That's what I want to get into."

"What does Rick say about all that?"

Sarah shrugged. "We never talk about it."

Liz looked closely at her friend. She didn't seem upset but neither did she look happy. "Doesn't he care?"

"I don't know if I care if he cares."

"Sounds serious."

"Not really. Sometimes I just get tired of it all." She gave her hair a last flip. "Technology and math. It's the coming thing. If I were a man, I'd have no problem!"

"Well, it looks like I may have to go through life wearing green and smiling a lot."

"You don't mean that."

Liz sighed. "No. I don't. Let's get something to eat."

When they got back to the floor, they couldn't find the guys. Liz said, "Well, I know how to fill a plate," and headed for the tables.

The line had thinned to nothing by the time they made it, as had most of the food. Liz took a couple of cookies and a glass of punch and turned to see what Sarah had found.

She stood, ashen-faced, at the end of the table, near the screen that shielded the serving area. An empty plate dangled from her hand.

As Liz went up to her, she heard Rick's voice from behind the screen. "I'll meet you on the fire escape in a minute."

There was a short silence then a moan.

A girl giggled, then in a low wheedling tone said, "But you're with Sarah!"

"But it's you I want to be with. She's such a bore. A real prude. I never even get to feel . . . like this . . ."

In something that amounted to a stage whisper, she said, "Keep your hands to yourself." Then another low laugh. "Until later. I don't want to get messed up."

"When?"

"What about Sarah?"

"Oh, her."

"You go with her. You're pinned. Of course, if you like me so much . . ."

"Mm. Well. You know how it is. She's bound to be the freshman beauty in the yearbook. We could be the couple of the year. Good publicity."

"What good is that?"

"Makes you look good. All these guys in school, you've got to stand out if you want a place in a good law school." He laughed. "They call it leadership, I think."

At last Sarah moved. Her face flamed as she picked up two cups of punch and walked around the screen, Liz close behind.

Sarah said, "Ann!"

Rick turned just as Sarah dashed the contents of her cup in Ann's face. She threw the second cup at his open mouth. "You're not a leader, Rick. You're a leaner!"

Ann gasped as cold liquid splashed over her. Pink froth ran down the front of her blue dress. She sputtered and flew at Sarah. Liz threw more punch at Ann who came to a dead halt, then evidently feeling outnumbered, fled.

Rick stepped toward Sarah just as Tom came up and put himself between them. Rick grabbed a napkin, wiped his face and furiously strode off.

Gasps and titters filled the gym.

Tom, Sarah and Liz slid quickly around the edges of the crowd and out the door. They fled to Tom's car still parked near Kohl.

"Jerk!" Sarah threw Rick's Sigma Chi pin across the lot and climbed into the backseat. Liz got in with her.

Sarah buried her face in her hands. Her shoulders shook.

Liz put her arm over Sarah's shoulder and hugged her. "It's okay. He wasn't worth it. I think you've always known it."

Sarah looked up. She wasn't crying. She was shaking with laughter. "I . . . know. I can't help it. That punch on his face!"

They all collapsed into a fit of near hysterics.

"Did you see her face? I thought she was going to hit you."

"She might have if you . . ." Sarah giggled again then sighed. "They deserve each other."

"And Rick! I think I'm glad you came up, Tom," Liz said.

Sarah leaned back and closed her eyes. "I'm just glad period."

Chapter 15

The trig paper said Sarah Johnson. Nelson Ames fingered it and laid it down to watch her walk back to her seat. New, but a full professor expecting tenure quickly, such elementary stuff as this class wasn't his bailiwick. He owed Wilson a favor and had agreed to sub for him this Friday to make a long weekend. At the moment, he was glad he had.

Wilson had blathered on more than once about how gorgeous Johnson was. That certainly was true. A blond Greta Garbo, and from her demeanor in class, just as cold. Cold? Or shy? Did it make a difference? When she'd brought her paper to his desk, the first in the class, he'd figured she was a washout. But the answers were all neatly filled in. He wondered if prim was more accurate than cold, and was that good or bad for his chances? For the chance he intended to take.

If she were repressed, he might get lucky; if prim, well, perhaps he could smile a lot. That sometimes worked with that kind. Most of them weren't used to much attention.

With nothing else to do but keep on eye out for cribbers, he ran down her answers. Amazing! All correct!

He looked up and raised an eyebrow at her but she was putting her book into her pack. Well, Wilson certainly had not mentioned that she had brains. Interesting. There were strings a guy could pull for that.

In a way it was a shame. A girl who looked like this Sarah didn't need brains and shouldn't have them. That only upset the balance of things. Sooner or later, she'd find she hadn't a chance in the real math world. Of course, she could always teach. Wouldn't have minded having a teach like that when he was a kid!

"Miss Johnson, can you stay for a moment?"

Sarah, her books piled ready to leave, looked up at him when he spoke, wondering why a sub would want to talk to her. This one in particular. His reputation preceded him. It couldn't be her test. A snap, the score would be perfect. She hesitated, then put her books down but kept her hand on them. "I have to—I was, well. Never mind." She sat and waited until Ames cleared his throat and said, "Time's up. Papers, please."

The students dribbled past his desk and dropped off their work. Most gave a sigh or grunt.

Ames paused to give her an encouraging smile then turned to glare at the slow-moving students, some of whom he was sure lingered to hear something interesting. He waited until they'd gone then rose and came to her desk.

Pulling a nearby chair close, he sat next to her and handed her the test paper. "I'm impressed. I guess I shouldn't show you yet, but you must know you aced it."

Sarah nodded and turned pink. Wilson never made a fuss about her work, never said more than, "Good work, Miss Johnson." This Nelson Ames was a new professor, a vet, and rumor had it he had good credentials, maybe too good for BG. He also had already earned a reputation as a wolf. At the very least a flirt. She didn't know anything for sure about him, but the way he bent toward her and held on to the paper . . .

"May I call you Sarah?"

She nodded, edged back. He kept the paper in his hands. "Is all of your work in other fields this good?"

She shrugged, said, "I guess," and looked at her watch.

"What are your plans?"

She thought about rising to leave but she hesitated. In spite of those stories, she hesitated to be too rude. Yet. She said, "Lunch."

His blue eyes held a shadow that made him look sly. "I meant career plans. I'm done for the day. Maybe we could combine lunch plans with a talk of goals."

She flushed, but it was anger, not embarrassment. It looked as though the gossip was true. She could see why he flirted. He counted on his good looks, a rugged face with a strong jaw and good nose, hair almost as light as hers. She'd expect such a face on a magazine, not a math prof.

"Oh. I can't," she mumbled.

He grinned at her. "Your career? What are your goals?"

In spite of herself she found herself telling him about Aiken, Harvard and the Mark I. She couldn't keep her delight from dancing in her eyes when she talked about it. "I think that's the future. Really exciting. That's what I want."

He sat back and gave a quiet whistle. "You do know women and the higher math fields don't mix, don't you?"

She bristled. "Why not?" She wanted to say, "I'll show you all." By the time she was through, these closed-minded math jerks would have to eat their words.

He shrugged. Condescension sat in his smile. "Women, most women, just don't have that kind of a mind. You'll have a tough time getting into a good grad school even as smart as you are. Women, most of them, waste space and make it harder for men who must make a career. Most of you quit to raise families."

Glaring at him, she picked up her book pack. "If there is nothing I need to know about the test, I'll go."

A feisty one, hmm? Ames shrugged. "Be honest. You do go off and have babies. When you take up space in the grad programs, you do keep good men out." He tilted his head at her. "You definitely have the brains, but it just isn't a woman's field."

"I'll pit my mind against yours any day." She supposed she shouldn't talk that way to a professor, but she was tired of this crap. As for the good men, well, she equaled any in the class and she was entitled. She'd never admit to any of these creeps that the family bit might be a problem, even though perhaps the war had changed things a little. A lot of mothers had worked. She'd work something out because she loved math and its challenges. Maybe she'd stay single anyway. With jerks like this, she wouldn't miss much. Tom's face smiled at her. But he was taken, wasn't he?

She snapped, "I suppose it's too much to ask that a college support talent." She tried to rise but the chair with its big flat arms was awkward to slide out of, especially with him so close. Her chair fell and she dropped her books trying to catch it. Damn him anyway! Angry tears hovered. She grew even angrier.

He stooped and put his hand on her shoulder and said softly, "I'm sorry. Let me."

Go ahead! Let him get down on the floor where he belonged!

"I am really sorry. I didn't mean to upset you." He straightened the books and papers and handed them to her. "I suspect you could hold your own anywhere and I am interested in your future. I'd like to talk about it."

He did look sorry and concerned. She wanted to believe him but with her record, and what she knew of him, the odds were against it. She shook her head. "I have to go."

"Which way are you going?"

"Why?"

"I wondered if you were going by the mailboxes." He

gathered the test papers and stuffed them into an interoffice envelope. "Wilson can grade his own tests. That wasn't part of the deal."

"Oh. Okay." She took it and left without looking back.

Used to the kids eyeing and smiling at him, her coolness aroused his hunter's instinct. He waited only a moment. If she went to the boxes, he could get downstairs first and see where she went.

Thanks to Ames's delaying tactics, the big rush was on at Harvey's. Luckily a couple left as Sarah entered. She slid into the booth. This bit of luck didn't put her in a better frame of mind. Nor had the walk down Wooster, or the brisk March wind been able to clear the smell of rat from her nostrils. The more she thought, the madder she got. A professor had no business discouraging a good student in any field.

The waitress cleared her table and flopped the menu down. She held her pad and pencil as though Sarah should have known an hour ago what she wanted to eat. Actually she wanted the cheeseburger, but the attitude angered her and, with no big plans for the afternoon, she studied the menu in detail. The waitress tapped her pencil then snipped, "I'll be back."

Sarah's conscience pricked her after the girl left, but that niceness was hard to sustain when the girl still hadn't come back after ten minutes.

By that time, Professor Ames stood at her booth. "The place is full. Mind if I join you?"

"Oh. Well. Yes." She had meant yes, you may join me, but she never meant she didn't mind. She wondered if he ever worried that people might talk about him sitting with a student. Now, though, he could always say the place was crowded.

The moment he sat, the waitress appeared with a big smile, and this time placed the menu gently in front of him. "Do you need a moment or do you know what you want?"

He smiled at Sarah. "What are you having?"

In the mood to chew nails rather than a cheeseburger, she ordered the sandwich and a milkshake.

"I'll take the same but with coffee." His teeth flashed.

It took the girl a whole thirty seconds to show up with coffee.

Sarah wanted to throw up. To distract herself, she rifled through her purse. The only thing interesting was the rubber band. She took it out and tied her hair back with it. She didn't like people who messed with hair at the table, but this time she definitely hoped one of hers would land on his space or on him.

Oblivious to her feelings, or seeming so, he asked, "Do you eat here often?"

Oh, Lord, don't let him hang out here. They've got the best burgers in town! She shook her head and snapped, "No. I study all the time."

He said blithely, "When I don't eat in the faculty cafeteria, I usually run into Perrysburg."

"Isn't that a bit far for lunch?" The farther the better!

He shrugged and gave her a big smile. "Fifteen minutes. But then I like to drive. There's something about a yellow convertible with a top down, I can't resist."

While the waitress delivered their burgers Sarah fumed. That figured. A Cadillac with a winged hood ornament, a bird in flight, if she remembered correctly. She took a bite and chewed slowly. Extra slow. She wouldn't have to talk with her mouth full.

Ames picked up his sandwich and leaned back. "As a matter of fact, I thought I'd go into Toledo tonight. The

Commodore's got a very nice restaurant." He put the burger down uneaten and fiddled with his empty cup. He looked for the waitress who promptly showed with coffee in hand.

He gave her a big smile. When she'd gone, he said, "Do you ever go into Toledo?"

"No." She stared at him. "Never heard of it."

He gave her a magazine cover smile. "It's one of the better hotel dining rooms. It's funny how many people show up at a place like that. I was hoping we just might run into each other there. I'm the last of the big spenders, you know."

Sarah reached for her purse. Oh, sure. She'd hurry right over. A hotel yet! She took a deep breath and counted to ten, then turned and signaled the waitress who hurried over, smiling at Ames all the while. Sarah pushed her plate and glass forward. "Would you please put these in a bag to go? You can leave them here. I'll be in the rest room."

Without looking at him, she went to comb her hair until she thought the food would be ready. It was. She picked it up and walked out.

She tried to eat the burger as she walked to the dorm, but it was cold and the malt runny. She threw them into the first trash barrel she passed.

When she got back to her room, Jenny was rummaging in the closet and Liz nowhere in sight. She groaned inwardly. Not that she didn't like Jenny. She did. She just wasn't in the mood for enthusiasm.

Sarah tossed her books on the nearest chair, kicked off her shoes and left them in the middle of the floor. Boys. Men. She'd just about had it with them. Tom was about the only guy she could stand. And Alan. He'd been nice, too, actually complimenting her on her brains, not her face. But he'd been going with Liz then. But he was one of those who didn't want a working wife. A guy could afford to be understanding about some other girl. She lay facedown on the bed. She wasn't sleepy, but she didn't want to talk.

Jenny had no such problem. "I don't know what to wear. Sigma Chi's got a bash tonight. Ray says there'll be lots of Alpha Gam's there. I think that's the sorority I want. What do you think? Which shall I wear?"

With no options, Sarah turned to look.

Jenny held a peacock-blue wool dress in one hand and a Kelly-green skirt and sweater set in the other. "What do you think?"

For Sarah's taste, they both were blindingly bright but at least the pleated skirt and sweater would be two-piece. Any line going across would help to cut off some height, a definite plus.

The other, the dress, did have a belt, but the soft, clingy material and straight lines wouldn't flatter Jenny's rangy bones. Sarah wondered what the girl's mother must be like, why Jenny obviously got no good advice.

Sarah pointed at the green. "That, I guess. Do you have anything else?"

"Lots of stuff but I just don't know." Jenny went to her dresser and rummaged through the drawers, pulling out a red cashmere and a matching sweater set, more of the peacock. "How about these?"

Sarah thought she knew defeat when she saw it. Those things were so flashy and Jenny was too tall for anything of hers, except maybe a sweater. They finally settled for a black skirt with Sarah's fluffy white angora sweater with the big padded Joan Crawford shoulders. Sarah gave Jenny a mini-lecture on lines.

Looking in the mirror Jenny agreed. "This looks swell. Sure you don't mind?"

Sarah shook her head, then laughed at the sight of Jenny kicking the stray shoe from the middle of the floor on her way back to the closet. Remembering Dottie's attempts to train her, Sarah smiled and put them away. She missed Dottie.

Jenny evidently saw the smile. "Feeling better, are you? What are you doing tonight?"

"I've got some trig to do." She hadn't, but no one had to know that. She hadn't had a date since she'd broken up with Rick. Most of the guys in her classes treated her as though she were made of ice and might melt if they touched her. Except the ones in math. They kept their distance, probably out of fear, fear she'd get a better grade than they would. She did.

The punch business with Rick and Ann had been worth it, though. She was actually glad to be rid of the two-timing schmo. Without realizing it, Sarah snorted.

Jenny gave her a strange look but asked, "Do you want me to ask Ray to get you a date for the frat's bash? There are some real Hubba! Hubba! guys. I'm sure one's available. Any of them would be thrilled to be with you."

"If they're so thrilled, why am I studying tonight? Besides, Rick'll probably be there." Liz and Tom, too, maybe. If only she could find someone like him.

Jenny turned away. "I'm glad you got rid of that Rick. I asked if he'd be there. Ray says he doesn't hang around the house. Seems he and Ann like to be alone."

"Good. I hope he catches something."

Jenny put her hand over her mouth, then giggled. "I've never heard you say anything like that before. You're always so nice. Ladylike as Mom would say."

Sarah laughed and, unable to restrain herself at the mention of Mom, asked, "Do you have a picture of your family?"

Jenny gave it to her. Sure enough, Mom must have been all of four feet eight. The dad was a little taller than Jenny, not as tall as her brother. Evidently Mom liked tall. No wonder the girl dressed as she did!

She handed the photo back wondering what it would be like to be someone else. Like Jenny, maybe. "You said you came here to BG because of Ray. What do you want to do when you graduate?"

Jenny grinned. "Marry. What else?"

"Then why bother?"

"Mom wanted me to. And then Ray is a real cool cat and I don't trust all these little kitty types around here." She grinned and grabbed a towel. "Besides, I plan to have a good time." She glanced quickly in the mirror, swiped at her hair and headed for the door. "Sure you don't want me to call Ray?"

Sarah shook her head and curled up in a corner of the bed. "Thanks, but I really do have to study. Put out the 'don't disturb,' will you?"

When Jenny left, Sarah let the tears come. Damn it. Stupid men. Why couldn't she be awkward and plain like Jenny? Plain girls knew they had friends who liked them for what they were.

Well, she'd show the jerks, Rick, Ames and all the rest. She'd go it alone. Be a math wizard. She knew she could. She'd set her sights on a Nobel Prize. Beat the jerks at their own game. Was there some organization of women mathematicians? It would help if she didn't feel so alone out there.

She rose, crossed the hall to the lavatory and splashed her face, then stuck her tongue out at her image. Returning to her room, she took her sweater and headed for the Nest. Friday night was the pits.

Chapter 16

Sarah scanned the Nest but only three of the booths were occupied. Four kids filled one, one of them a girl from Kohl. The girl hailed her but Sarah smiled and shook her head. Boy, girl, boy, girl. No comfort there. In the second, a kid from her math class slouched over a messy table. She had dubbed him Mooch because he always begged the answers for his trig problems from anyone who would stop long enough to talk to him. In the other, a gentle-looking kid she'd never seen before divided his attention between his book and his burger.

She got a malt and two hot dogs, loaded them with onions—after all, who was there to care—and went to a corner, studiously avoiding Mooch's eye. She dumped her sweater on the bench facing her. Make it look occupied.

The juke box played Vaughn Monroe, "There, I've Said It Again." Usually she melted when he sang, but now she wished he'd stop. She'd seen him once in person, at the Loew's in Columbus. He'd sung "Racing With the Moon" and she'd fallen in love. Now, please, Vaughn, shut up.

It took about four seconds for Mooch to pick up his glass and plate of food scraps and arrive at her booth to override the sound of Vaughn's voice. "Hi, Sarah. How come a gorgeous thing like you is alone on a Friday night? Can I sit down?" He moved her sweater.

Sarah sighed mentally, drew in a breath and said, "Uh, I am expecting someone."

"When she comes, I'll go."

"What makes you think it's a she?"

Her haughtiness went over his head. He smirked. "Saw Rick and Ann."

A glare was just as wasted. Why couldn't it at least have been the other kid who wanted to sit here? But that one looked like he hadn't enough nerve to pick a goldfish from a bowl. She looked desperately at the door, praying for someone, anyone to show up.

"What did old glamour boy Ames have to say today?"

"Ames?" Then she remembered. Mooch had been one of the dawdlers. "He just told me it was a good paper."

"Uh-huh." He leered. "You know he's supposed to be a big wolf."

The onions on her hot dog glistened at her. She took a bite and sighed hard, hoping her breath would chase him away.

"I heard he was making out with one of the Delta girls, Dolores Brown. Then he dropped her. Of course, with Dolores, it could have been the other way around. Anyway, she complained to the department head but she's got such a reputation for being fast, no one believed her. She bats her eyes at anyone who looks her way. They all know that."

Sarah sipped her malt and kept her glance on the table. What was she supposed to say to all of this? What was he suggesting anyway? That she batted her lashes, too? She tried to turn the conversation from Professor Ames to Dolores. "I don't know her very well. She is pretty. Seems like a lot of fun."

He snorted.

Pipsqueak. He had a lot of room to talk about anyone! Funny, no matter what a jerk a guy is, he feels totally free to rate and berate the girls.

"Hi, Sarah, sorry I'm late."

174

Sarah looked up and almost choked. "Tom!" She tucked the last bite of hot dog into the corner of her mouth and grinned, mouth full and all. If he'd brought her roses, she could not have been happier to see him. "Mooch was just passing time." She pushed his glass toward him. "Weren't you?" Good manners only went so far and these had plenty of miles on them already.

He rose and gave her a buddy smile. "See you in class." He moved as though to leave his dishes and Tom handed him the plate. "Don't forget these."

When Mooch reluctantly cleared his mess, Tom sat. Sarah fought down the urge to kiss him in gratitude. Well, perhaps not only gratitude. "You have a knack for rescuing people." She glared at Mooch's back. "He's such a schmo."

Tom laughed. "You didn't look too happy."

"I am now." She meant it. She liked Tom. A lot. But . . . He was Liz's. Liz. Whom Sarah thought really wanted Alan. What a mess. Still, this particular moment had its pleasure.

He pointed to her full plate. "Do you always eat when you are miserable?"

She thought she'd better not pursue that. She rubbed the back of her neck. "My lunch was ruined. Where's Liz? I thought you . . ."

"She had a headache." For a moment Sarah thought his eyes darkened. Just a shade. Then he laughed. "I don't suppose you've had the chance to notice, but women have more headaches than an alley cat has fleas, I think."

"Sometimes they really do." Headaches or heartaches. There were only three letters that made them different words. Three letters—because of three other little words—I love you.

He nodded. "Yeah, I know. Anyway. I'm free and you looked like you needed me."

"My hero!" Yeah. She did need him. But then that was her problem. "That Mooch. He's such a schmo it's hard to feel sorry for him!"

"Want to go to a movie? I don't think Liz would care. She did dump me for the night."

"I don't think we . . . She might care more than you think."

He gave in with a small shrug. "Well, at least I can get something to eat. Can you stay for a while?"

Should she? Shouldn't she? Their meeting was accidental.

Tom rose. "Don't go away. I don't want to sit alone and have all the gals in here hitting on me. I need your protection now!"

"Turnabout is fair play. Okay. Get your supper! I'll wait."

While they ate, she found herself telling about Mooch and his remarks, then went into the story of Ames and the restaurant. As he listened, a silent film of emotions ran in his face, ranging from sympathy to annoyance and anger, then laughter when he ended up by saying, "On behalf of the men of the world, I apologize for ones like Mooch and Ames."

Sarah gulped. Would she ever have a fellow like Tom? Someone who really cared what a girl felt and thought? But that strayed into dangerous territory.

He said, "So, anyway. Tell me about this Aiken and his wonderful machine. I really am interested."

"Well, you put codes on punched paper. It all comes out on cards or a typewriter. Just think how that can speed things up."

"Mmm. Yes, just think, it would make it easier for the government to keep tabs on things. Like taxes. That'll make a lot of people happy!"

"No." Her hand waved the absurdity away. "It's not that kind of punched cards. It's a faster way of computing. I want to get involved. I think it's so exciting. Who knows what we can do with something like that? We can maybe prove all the things Einstein figured out but we don't really understand. Be able to solve problems it would take the human mind too long to calculate." She held her breath.

"Look at you! You're glowing!"

His smile made her blush. "Sorry. Can't help it. It's just the idea . . ."

"Don't apologize. I think it's great. I sometimes feel that way when I see a particularly beautiful building."

"Beautiful? I guess I'm surprised. I expected you to be all excited about the new stuff. All sleek and modern. Functional."

"I like anything if it's done with integrity and an eye to design. As for functional, well, that covers a lot of territory. Useful? Or just without any trim? Take a look at the stuff the Russians build to be useful. They're terrible!"

"Maybe they think cheap is useful!"

Mooch passed her table on what she hoped was his way out. She nodded toward him. "I'd say he's neither functional nor beautiful! Probably cheap, too!" She laughed but couldn't stop the pink that crept into her cheeks. "That really wasn't nice. I couldn't resist." She rubbed the back of her neck again. "Aiken's mind must be like a machine."

"I have a hunch you have a pretty good machine in your head, too. You mustn't get sidetracked. Don't waste it."

For a moment Sarah wanted to cry. Don't get sidetracked. Easier said than done. "Life is so complicated for us women. We have all these extra things to tie us down: the home, marriage and children."

"Well, men get married and have a home and children."

"Sure. But his only responsibility most times is the paycheck. Old Aiken can spend twenty-four hours a day in his lab and all he'll get is a complaining wife. A woman now, she'd have the whole world down on her head. Unnatural. Mannish. Maybe even a dyke." She blushed after she said it.

Tom only looked amused.

"I do want to marry and everything. Even fanatical little me knows a math book may be fascinating but not very warm."

"You should be able to do both." He put his hand on hers. "I hope you make it. If anyone can, you will."

The praise silenced her and she played with her crumpled napkin while he finished his hamburger. Another thing she liked about this guy, she didn't have to jabber all the time. Of course, this evening he might not have noticed any lack of jabbering.

He finally sat back and fiddled with his few leftover fries. "Going home for Easter?"

"Not much else to do, is there?"

"Where do you live?"

"Columbus."

"Ah. We're practically neighbors. I'm from Springfield."

She never quite knew what to do with such little gems of knowledge, especially when the informer smiled like that. "Come up and see me some time," came to mind, but she hadn't the nerve.

She steered him back to safer tracks by asking about his family. She knew he had six sisters, all younger than himself. Sometimes it was nice being an only child, but there were times she wished . . . Well, maybe that was why he was so nice and considerate.

He answered the unspoken thought. "The trouble with being part of a big bunch is you only got to color three

Easter eggs. I used to keep dipping mine in all the colors just to make it last longer." He laughed. "You should have seen some of the eggs I ended up with."

"You can come to our house. We always do a dozen each. Mom and I, that is. Dad did one, once. He complains he gets tired of boiled eggs." She stopped and reddened. She'd just invited him to her house! But, of course, that was a joke. He hadn't meant it.

That he wasn't entirely kidding, though, came through with his next words. "I'm driving down and could drop you off if we're going on the same day. Columbus is on my way."

It wasn't really, she thought. Normally he'd probably go down to Dayton, but he could go to Columbus almost as easily. Her heart did a little dance then settled down to pout. She couldn't, shouldn't. "Dad or Mom always drive up. I can't leave until late Friday." She took a deep breath and gave him an extra-warm smile. "But thanks."

"If you change your mind—"

Time to go before she did.

Sarah's guilt over her appreciation of Tom didn't go away when they'd finished eating. He offered to walk her home but she thought better of that. "Thanks, but I don't think I'll get lost." Actually a walk alone on a warmish March night might be just the ticket to cure the "if only's."

Tom had helped but he had also opened up a whole new landscape of blues. Why was it everyone seemed to end with almost what they wanted? Liz wanted to want Tom, not Alan. Dottie had wanted the theater and ended with her Bob and a baby. Neither outcome was bad, they just strayed from the dream. As for herself, she had her math, half of her dream. Would there be another half?

The thin night air was not as warm as she expected. It

still held stubborn traces of the dying winter and the stars snapped in the clear darkness. Sarah pulled her sweater tightly about her and hurried to her room.

Liz sat cross-legged on her bed, reading *Lady Chatterley's Lover*. She gave a sheepish grin and flourished the book as Sarah came in. "Might as well read about romance."

Sarah gave her a weak smile. "Tom said you didn't feel well. Are you okay?"

"I just had a heavy case of the down in the dumps." Liz put down the book, flopped over onto her back, and reached up to fiddle with the springs of the top bunk.

"Et tu, Brute." Sarah dropped her sweater on her bed and her shoes on the floor. "Must be the weather. In the spring a young girl's fancy . . ." She laughed. "That must be where all the old clichés hang out, in the blues room. Ever notice how they come pouring out when you're depressed?"

"Umph. You said that Tom said I had a headache. Where'd you see him?"

Sarah picked up her shoes and put them in the closet so she wouldn't have to look at Liz in case she was mad. "I was at the Nest and . . ." Then she laughed, remembering Mooch. "He rescued me from a jerk."

"Yeah. He's a born Galahad." She paused then added, "That's the trouble." She plucked at the springs again.

"What do you mean?" Sarah came and sat at the foot of Liz's bed. A glimmer of hope flickered in the back of her mind. What if Liz really didn't want him?

What then? Oh! What then?

Liz sat up, crossed her arms over her knees and rested her chin on them. She stared at the blanket, not Sarah. "He's too nice. That's why I told him I had a headache. I do like him a lot. He thinks the way I do about life and everything."

She chewed her lower lip, then added, "I used to think

Alan and I thought alike, too. Maybe we still do except that he is so old-fashioned about a wife. Sometimes I wonder if he believes women should vote. You'd think there'd never been a war. That women had never worked." She sighed deeply then was silent for a while.

Sarah didn't hurry her.

"I know Alan wants someone like his mother. I'm not her. And anyway, what's the use of all this talk. It's over." She brushed a tear from her eye. "But Tom really thinks women should be able to do what they're good at, what they like."

Sarah had been down this street so often she'd parked a bench there.

Liz swiped at her eyes. "I feel so guilty. Tom knows I don't love him. He never pushes me. I just couldn't face him tonight."

"It'll take time to get over Alan. Anyway, how can anyone not fall in love with Tom." As soon as she said it, Sarah thought she'd put it rather badly but the implications weren't something she could explain away. Nor were they something she'd want to.

If Liz noticed, she gave no sign of it. She flopped down on her back and picked up her book and raked the springs, then slapped them sharply with it. "I'd better get over Alan. Quick! Trouble is, I don't want to. Oh, blast!"

"Maybe you'll run into him when . . . Well, Easter vacation." Sarah rose and got her towel. Maybe she could shower the blues away. Somehow, though, they didn't seem as dark. That tiny flicker of hope had shed a bit of light. What if Liz and Alan made up during the break?

Chapter 17

Liz carried the dark green wool dress into the kitchen. With all her stuff at BG, her closet at home seemed empty. The things she'd left here had been things she didn't like much. "Mom, I can't wear this to the Easter sunrise service."

Her mother, Peg Chase, looked up from her cookbook, gave an amused sigh and said wryly, "I guess then, we'll have to do some shopping. We all know that closet of yours needs filling." She smoothed the cotton print she wore, then put the book away. "I'll have to change."

When she came down in her three-inch heels and a light wool dress, she'd lost the cookie-baker look. One more confusing thing about her mom. A lot of the moms she knew seemed to stay cookie baker. Except the ones like Alan's mom who probably had a lifetime contract with a bakery.

But Mom wasn't always what she expected. Sometimes she seemed like two women, the one who did bake and the other who could still turn a few male heads. If she'd done anything about her suppressed desires, Liz figured she would have succeeded at anything.

Her mother interrupted her reverie. "Do I look all right?"

"You look great. I hope I look as good when I'm a mom." Although her mom complained about being short, Liz thought of her as petite and pretty. The once-blond hair was brown now, but it lay softly about the small face, as well-trained and well-mannered as she was.

"Can we go to Schachne's?" Chillicothe's best in Liz's mind.

"We could go to Columbus, but it is late."

Liz hugged her. "Schachne's. We can make a day of it. Like old times." A stab of pain told Liz "old times" wasn't quite true. They'd gone shopping at Schachne's sometimes, but they'd never really made a day of it. Mom always hurried home to get supper on the table on time.

"I can't be too long. George will want his supper."

The little lady waiting for her man. Liz bit her lip. It had been nice, though: Mom always there, oatmeal and peanut butter cookies, laundry always done. "Responsibility" was the operative word around the house, a virtue that included buttering her husband's dinner rolls. Not a virtue Liz intended for herself. If she ever got married.

For a moment she wished she'd never come up with the "day out" thing. Everything just reminded her of Alan and Tom and her problem.

She turned away from her mother, then anger overcame the self-pity. Not only should she get over it, Mom, too, ought to get over this "yes, dear" routine. It was time she stood up for herself.

First step: "Mom, leave a note. Or call Dad at the drugstore. He can eat there at the lunch counter."

"A man needs a good meal after a hard day."

"He can get the tuna plate. Good brain food. Or for Pete's sake, make a peanut butter and jelly sandwich here!" Grinning at her mother, she went to the refrigerator and set out the jars. "See. It's easy!"

Her mother put them away.

"Mom, if worse comes to worst, Dad can learn to cook. He doesn't like to, but then, do you?"

"Well, yes. I do." Her mother actually smiled. "I do get

tired of it. Only I feel I ought . . ."

"Today you ought to take off and shop with me. Call him. We can eat down on Paint Street, maybe take in a movie, too."

Did her mother's face actually pale? Liz laughed, got out a piece of paper. "If you aren't that brave, here." She scribbled a note and put it on the counter next to the refrigerator.

Peg Chase straightened her shoulders. "You're right. I deserve a day off." She found her purse and checked it for money. "We'll have to go to the movie another night. Maybe we all ought to go together."

Liz hugged her. "Sure, Mom." One step at a time.

The satisfaction of winning even a part of this particular battle stayed with Liz through the shopping. At first she'd thought she wouldn't get anything green. She needed a new color for her new life. She held a navy sharkskin suit to her waist. One more battle to win. One of these days I might even forget him. Melancholy and pride pitched a war in her stomach.

In the end, she bought a green suit—it was livelier—and headed for the hat department. One straw sailor matched the outfit, but with a perverse impulse she reached for a purple felt. Purple, violets, Tom. It was even on sale! From now on, I'm going for violets and Tom. I will.

She put it on and peered into the triple mirror. The hat with its round crown and two-inch soft brim framed her face perfectly, but the purple with lavender flowers against her red hair forced an "Ugh" from her. She tried to keep a straight face as she turned and preened for her mother.

Her mom said it for her. "Honey, that's awful. You don't really like it, do you?" Then she gasped.

Liz laughed, thinking the gasp was for the hat. "It is

awful, isn't it?" She put it down and picked up the green. She turned to bump into Alan. A high heat began at her toes and worked upward to turn her face the color of her hair. "Oh!"

His look of chagrin might have told her he still cared about her, had she looked into his eyes instead of just over his left shoulder. He said, "I was supposed to meet Mother here. How are you, Liz?"

Forced to look into those hazel eyes, she melted for a moment, then told herself, It's over. She put down the hat and took a deep breath to steady her voice. "Fine. How are Kate and John?" If Kate was coming up here, she wanted to get out of the store. She snatched the hat without trying it on. She could always bring it back. "It's late and Mom has to . . ." She turned toward the hovering salesgirl. "I'll take this."

Alan took a step toward her. "You . . ."

His eyes were honey-colored. Sometimes they were dark, but it was the gold tones that made her melt. Anyway, eyes or no, if he didn't care about her, she didn't care about him. Besides, there was Tom, wasn't there? She paid for the hat, then, without meeting his glance, said, "Good-bye, Alan."

He said, "Liz . . ."

She fled.

When they reached the street, Liz, pulling her mother by the hand, took off down Main.

Peg Chase halted. "Whoa, honey. It's okay."

Liz stood for a moment trying to pull herself together. Just when she was doing so good, he had to show up. Oh, damn him! She took a deep breath to try to still the tears that pooled behind her eyes. She closed them tightly for a moment, then started down Main again.

"Liz, stop."

She stopped.

185

Her mother came up to her. "I'm sorry, dear, but it was bound to happen sooner or later in a small town like this. Where else would Kate shop? Schachne's is the best."

"I know, but I . . ." She wondered if Kate would be steely if they met. Why did he have to meet her, anyway? Without forethought, she said aloud, "He had to get her home to fix his supper for him, didn't he?"

Her mom looked hurt and a little angry. "You don't mind when I cook your supper, do you?"

Liz flushed. She had been mean. "I'm sorry, Mom. It's only . . . Well, it was a stupid thing to say, wasn't it? I'm just so mixed up. I love Alan." She bit her lip, "Loved Alan."

Her mom put her hand on Liz's arm. "There are other fish in the sea. At least that's what they say."

Liz looked down at her packages. Green. Both of them. She had meant to get over him. She raised her chin. She had gotten over him, was getting over him. She handed her mom the suit and untied the ribbon from the hatbox. "Oh. hell! I'll show him."

The "hell" brought a disapproving frown from her mother. "Please! That's hardly ladylike."

Liz laughed. "Oh, Mom! As if I never . . . As I recall, I've had my mouth washed out with soap for saying it before. Fels Naptha, too. Laundry soap!" She took the hat from the box and put it on. The green straw didn't exactly match the white sweater and black skirt, but then who cared.

"It really isn't nice, is it?" Her mother didn't give in. "A reputation is important. You know that."

"Do you like it?" Liz turned in a circle.

"Like that word?"

"The hat!"

Peg Chase sighed. "You're hopeless."

"Let's go eat." She kissed her mother on the cheek, resisting the temptation to say, "To hell with it all," aloud.

The small restaurant they entered was relatively new and plain, but it had tablecloths and smelled like roast beef and apple pie. Cinnamon, too. When they were seated, with that mouthwatering smell, they had little trouble making up their minds what to order.

While they waited, Liz took off the hat, tucked it in the box, then said, "Mom, why did you really send me to college?"

"That's obvious, isn't it?"

She didn't want to hurt her mother's feelings but she had to know. "No. It isn't. I get mixed messages from you. You keep telling me about women who do things, but you refuse to do them yourself."

Her mother turned pink, played with the silver, but she didn't frown. "To be honest, I'm not sure why I didn't do more. The easy way out, I suppose. In my generation, being a wife, being home for their husbands and children, that's what women did." She looked sad when she said, "To be honest, maybe I just didn't have the courage to do more. If I can get mad at your father for keeping me in the kitchen, then I have an excuse, don't I? Maybe I wouldn't like to work. I'd probably just have a guilty conscience for running out on George like that."

"Mom, that's not running out. You'd probably be home every night for supper. It isn't as though you'd be a traveling sales agent. And even if you did, for Pete's sake, lots of men have to cook. They can when they have to, not to mention chefs and stuff."

The uncertain light in the room gave her mother's eyes a misty look. She turned to look out the window. The hand on the table suddenly seemed vulnerable. Her mother wasn't old. Forty-five, but the hand was a worker's hand in spite of how petite and pretty she still was. Liz reached out and put hers on her mother's. "I love you. I'm sorry. Don't let me bother you. I'm just so mixed up." A woman, maybe her mother's age, interrupted the thought by serving their dinner. When she'd gone, Peg Chase nodded toward the woman's back. "That's why you had to go to school."

"Alan keeps telling me I'd never have to worry about money."

"Never is a big word sometimes."

"I don't suppose there'll be another big depression again. Besides, if he works for the State Department, that's pretty steady unless he goofs, and he's not the type. He ought to be able to take care of his family."

"It's not about money always. These days you need to know you can do something."

"Why bother with a degree if you can't ever use it? Alan obviously doesn't think it's important."

"The Bannermans have old money. If they worry about a degree, it's for social reasons."

"Even if I could convince him to wait, he'd never be in one place long enough for me to use it."

"It's still good insurance. What if something happened and you didn't marry? What if, God forbid, you got a divorce? You don't want to end up like our waitress, do you?"

"I love school. I like BG, Sarah and Dottie. Even Tom."

Her mom raised an eyebrow. "Even Tom?"

"He's so nice. I won't have this trouble with him." She let the whole problem spill out. "I'm sick of fighting with myself and feeling stupid and selfish for holding out. Tired of being accused, even implicitly, of not being normal. What's normal anyway? I wonder how many people marry because they think they should? Did you ever not want to get married?"

Her mother laughed at that. "And be an old maid? That would never have done!" She pushed her peas into the pile of mashed potatoes. "I know I shouldn't do that, but I like them together."

In her turn, Liz chuckled. "Did you ever notice how Dad eats? A bite of meat, then potatoes, then peas, more meat, more potatoes . . . Very orderly." Both of them giggled.

"Honey, we can laugh, but it's been a good marriage. George is a good man. Steady. Loving. And he's done well. We aren't rich, but even in the Depression we had enough." She stopped eating. "He's been a good father, hasn't he?"

Liz nodded. "He has. I love him. And you. But have you ever been sorry?"

Her mother smiled but was it wistful? "The grass is always greener, isn't it? But no, I'm not sorry. I've got you and George. It's been a good life."

"But then why did you always want to work?"

"I thought when I finished high school I'd like to be a book editor in a big publishing company. It sounded so exciting. But then, I met George."

"But during the war?"

"War work sounded so brave and helpful. I even applied at the paper mill. But George . . . He thought rolling bandages did just as much. And I think he always felt someone would criticize him. As though he couldn't make enough with the drugstore."

Yes, Dad did want everything neat and in its place. And like Alan and Mrs. Bannerman, a wife's place was at home. In her dad's case, in a neat white frame house. The only thing that was missing was the rose trellis over the door. Lilacs were in the backyard.

"But what about you? Didn't you care?"

"I loved having you. We wanted more, but it never happened." She paused, then said, "One child doesn't fill up the time. Not like your grandmother with her six. We all had to pitch in at home then. If any of us girls hadn't gotten married, though, Mother would have blamed her. She would have felt a failure."

They talked about Grandma White for a moment, then Peg said, "You don't have to get married these days, but I think it would be an awfully lonely old age. If it weren't for her family, I don't know what Mother would do."

"She's lucky with six kids still living. Excuse me, daughters and sons." With her mother's three sisters and two brothers, and a dozen cousins, Liz had always felt part of a big family even if she was an only child. "Grandma does keep busy."

Still, she didn't want to be just like Grandma, depending on someone else to make her happy. "It looks as though I might be an old maid anyway. Unless I do marry Tom. I'll write books in my old age." That would show them all, wouldn't it?

Her mother's face turned red. Liz thought she'd shocked her.

"Don't turn around."

"Why not?" Liz turned.

Kate Bannerman stood point for Alan and John. "Hello, Liz, Mrs. Chase. This is a surprise. I don't think I've seen you here before. The food is delicious and, since we first discovered it, we come often."

Liz wished she could disappear. She really didn't feel like being polite. She was relieved when her mother spoke up. "We are celebrating."

Alan smiled at Liz but she couldn't read his expression.

190

Either his emotions had battled to a standstill or he was perfectly happy with his life. Probably the last, she thought. The Bannerman ethos was success: family, business and social. Liz's stomach twisted like clothes in the washer-wringer. If he was fine without her, she was fine without him.

He turned back to her mother and asked politely, "What are you celebrating? I know it's not Liz's birthday. Must be yours, Mrs. Chase."

Alan had always called her mom Peg before. Now he was being formal and distant. Smug maybe. Liz flared up, putting her hands under the table as she did. "We're celebrating my engagement." She could have bitten her tongue as soon as the words came out.

If ever Alan had looked smug, he lost it. He flinched, paled and turned away. She thought he mumbled something.

His mother filled the void. "My best wishes. I hope you'll be very happy." John, Liz thought, looked dismayed. The three hovered for a moment in the corner of the restaurant then went out.

Their dinner spoiled, too, Liz and her mom left without the cinnamon apple pie.

On the way home, Peg said, "Honey, I'm sorry the dinner was ruined." She hesitated.

Liz answered the unspoken question. "No. I'm not engaged. I just got angry."

"That was foolish."

"Yeah. Well, he just looked so satisfied. I figured he didn't care anymore."

"From the look on his face, I'd say he does."

"Well, East is East and West is BG, or something like that. I hate this vacation."

Chapter 18

Kate Bannerman, in the midst of putting the final touches on the Easter dinner, gave Alan a gentle shove away from the refrigerator door. "Go brush your teeth or shine your shoes or something. Please. I need to get in here."

He moved but not far enough.

"Alan! Stop moping and please step aside. Haven't you anything to do? I don't mind you in the kitchen, but . . ." When he moved she retrieved a bottle of Grave which she held out to him. "Here. You can open this and fill the glasses, then call your father. Everything is ready."

He looked at the label. Chevalier. Good stuff. He made no move to open it.

"Alan!"

"Liz doesn't like dry wines." He didn't know why he'd said that. Not like she was coming to dinner. How could she be engaged already? They just broke up at Christmas.

Tom! It had to be him. Why him? Why get engaged when you don't want to marry? The jealousy that already ate at him, took a bigger bite. How could she? And Tom was such an ordinary guy, too. How could she?

Kate turned the oven off and opened the door a crack, then on the top of the stove lifted the lid to check the candied sweet potatoes. Finally she turned to face him. "Perhaps you ought to talk to her."

Talk to her! The thought of speaking to her, hearing her voice, set his heart drumming, but a man had his pride, didn't he? "I have! We're all talked out. She's marrying that Tom."

"She loves you."

He looked at his mother in surprise. Ever since they'd left the restaurant, he'd thought she'd seemed relieved to know he and Liz were finally through. Not once since the breakup after Christmas had his mom stood up for her. Not that he cared. It was his life, wasn't it?

As for her loving him, "Obviously she doesn't!" How could she not? His lips tingled where she'd kissed him when they built the snowman. He brushed the feeling away.

His mother turned back to the oven to bring out the ham. "It was written all over her face when she turned and saw you there in the restaurant."

He shook his head. "She looked embarrassed to me."

"Open the wine, Alan." His mother never argued. She'd just get that "You're being silly" look on her face, an arched eyebrow and pursed lips that barely held in the sigh hovering behind them. He knew she had it now, even though her back was turned.

He absently watched her give the ham its final glaze of brown sugar, orange and pineapple juice. On another day he might have reached for one of the pineapple rings or cared that the scent of golden brown juices filled the kitchen. He reached for the corkscrew.

In spite of his professed disregard for his mother's opinion, the stubborn boy in him insisted on hearing her say it. "You don't like Liz, do you?"

"You know better than that."

He and his mother talked about some things, but his love life wasn't one of them. Now he said what he'd thought a few minutes ago, "Well, ever since Christmas you've acted almost relieved."

Her whole posture told him she didn't like this conversation. "I just wonder if she is right for you. Look. It's all very well when the song says a man found his million-dollar baby in a five-and-ten-cent store, but in life, well, for a man in the position you'll be in, it doesn't usually work, does it?"

He pictured Liz behind a dime store counter in a print cotton dress. Strangely enough she looked at home, but then she'd look good anywhere. He never thought of her like that. His version ran to a vision of her greeting their guests, stunning in green silk with an emerald necklace. How much did emeralds cost? He'd have to check that out. If she'd only marry him, maybe he could exchange the ring he had for an emerald.

How angry she'd been that time at the dance, the first time he'd proposed. He'd said it lightheartedly but he'd meant it. He knew better, knew girls were sensitive about things like that, wanted shining armor on their knights and a man on his knees when he proposed. She'd been so angry her hair had practically burst into flame! Damn it. He loved her. Why couldn't she see that?

Perhaps it was time for some honesty. "Mom, you talk of a dime store, but you know Liz isn't that type. It sounds as though you're being a snob."

His mom stopped what she was doing and sighed. "Alan, is it the time for this? Dinner's ready. We can talk later." She reached up and got the bowls from the cupboard.

He put his hand on her arm. "It can wait for a minute. Mom, I'm going crazy. I want to marry Liz. She can't marry that guy."

His mother stopped and hugged him. Something she seldom did, then she smiled a little. "You know, we parents are warned about traps like this. We only get into trouble no matter what we say. I love you, Alan. You're a big boy. She's your girl."

He said it again, as though by digging his toes in, the sand would turn into a castle. "I can't let her marry that guy."

"Call her."

He turned toward the hall where the phone was, but shook his head. "We're back where we started, aren't we? It's too late and, anyway, it won't do any good." He still fished. He wanted his mother to be on Liz's side. Confirmation might end all this. "If you were Liz, would you want a career?" He couldn't imagine that.

"Perhaps she's insecure. Her father is a self-made man. If they're comfortable, it's new."

She'd said it in such a small voice, reinforcing his belief she thought Liz wasn't good enough for him. His mother was a born grand dame even if she'd had only a silver-plated spoon. He used to yawn when she got going about her family history until one day he realized that the confident mother hadn't always been so sure. Her old pioneer Chillicothe name was good, but wasn't sterling and didn't match his dad's.

His dad had never bothered to justify anything. His was old money. Not Rockefeller tons, but a lot more than most in their small town.

"She probably needs the security of knowing she can control her life. People do get divorced or die."

"I'd never divorce Liz and, if anything happened to me, she'd never need to worry about money." How many times had he said that to Liz?

Kate turned from dishing the dinner to grin at that. "Unless you disgrace us and your father disinherits you and he might if you don't open that wine."

"Do you or don't you want me to marry Liz?" That might be a moot question, the way things were, but he had to convince Liz. One way or another. In the long run, he figured it didn't really matter what his mother thought, but needed her to agree with him. He got the corkscrew and went to work on the cork.

"She's a very nice girl."

"But . . . ?"

Waving away the implications, his mom said, "I only want to see you happy. It seems to me, the two of you want different things. I do think you're right when you say she could go to school in Europe. You need to talk to her."

He pulled the cork too soon. "Oh, blast!" He threw the broken piece, then when his mother turned and frowned at him, went over to pick it up.

She took the wine from him. "Alan, if you want to be an ambassador, you'd better learn to open wine!"

"Well, is she?"

"Is she what?"

"Right for me." A "no" might put finish to this thing.

Kate sighed and reinserted the corkscrew, opening the wine while she talked. "I do think a man needs support from his wife, especially a man who is planning a career in the State Department. Men need so much!" She handed the bottle to him. "Pour."

There it was, the truth! She never had liked Liz! The confirmation both pleased and depressed him. She had agreed that Liz was being stubborn and foolish. As for the dime store bit, that was silly. Liz had a lot going for her. Charming, personable, caring. She would make a good ambassador's wife. If only she would put off that career idea. She could get a bachelor's for status. She'd have years and years for that.

"Alan, dinner is ready. Are you going to pour that wine or not? I really have my hands full here. Call your father."

She carried the sweet potatoes and carrots to the table and he followed with the wine. White linen and crystal caught the sun that streamed through the open window. The pale Grave poured into the glass like a liquid moonbeam. All this: family, the things that gave stability and order to life, beauty. He treasured it.

He sometimes went into the men's department of Schachne's just to look at the formal wear. He'd done it that day before he met Liz in the hats. But the store never carried the morning greys. He hoped such things wouldn't go out of style by the time he was important enough to wear them.

"As elegant as ever, Kate." His father wandered in from the living room, leaned over and kissed her on the cheek. He winked at Alan as he gingerly touched the blade of the knife.

The wink was meant to be conspiratorial. His dad was far less worried about traditions than his mother. He'd confessed to Alan earlier, "You know, some Easter we ought to have a crown roast or lamb instead of this. Ham isn't really one of my favorites."

Alan had almost choked. His mother would never conceive of such a departure. Thanksgiving and Christmas meant turkey, Easter, ham. There ought to be some kind of moral here, but he wasn't sure. Would his dad be so casual if his mom was not who she was? What if she had not wanted to be the grand dame for him? Well, maybe for herself? What if she'd wanted to be . . . Alan thought for a moment. He couldn't imagine. Of all the women he knew, in the country club and out, only the town librarian managed to wear that mantle of grand but gracious authority. No one, child or adult that he knew, questioned or disobeyed the librarian. In that genealogical warren, were the two related?

He busily put sweet potatoes on his plate to distract himself from laughing aloud. He could never explain that thought to his folks.

Yes, his dad could afford to be relaxed. He lived with a thick red carpet to cover all the pesky little pebbles of life. Isn't this what every man wanted? Well, serious and ambitious men, that is. That Tom probably was neither, probably the kind who would settle for an Easter dinner of ham sandwiches, potato salad and beans. The very thought made his temples throb. Probably served on paper plates, too.

Would Liz be happy with someone like that? Alan thought the life he could give her would be so much better, filled with the finer things and security. That Tom was probably going under the GI bill. If he had money, he'd be at one of the Ivy Leagues. He could never give her the life, he, Alan, could. How could she love someone else after only three months?

He cut his ham and swished it about, stopped and drank his wine, then pushed his food around again. The thought that she might be in love with someone else took away what little appetite his confusion had left him.

He needed to call her.

His mother, who had stopped talking, frowned at his still-full plate. "Alan, go make that call. You'll feel better and then you can come back and eat your dinner."

Not now. He wasn't ready. Nor did he want to talk about it. "Dad, what would you have done if Mom hadn't always been here?" He steeled himself not to crack a smile. "What if she'd wanted to be a librarian?"

His dad looked at Kate and laughed. "I would have been very surprised!"

Some of Alan's tension melted for a while and he did eat, even though a little voice inside kept tickling his brain. Call her. Call her.

He spent the rest of the dinner deciding then undeciding, until his mother passed him the tail end of the coconut-iced lamb cake. She always gave him that piece, ever since he was four and had licked it clean when her back was turned.

His watch said two o'clock. He pushed the cake from him. "I'll eat it later, Mom. I promised Bob Martin I'd call. I'd better do it before he gets away." He didn't like her gaze following him. It wasn't a fib. He had said it, and he would dial the number. It would be the literal truth.

He headed for the phone hoping they'd be eating cake for a while yet. He never gave Bob Martin a thought as he dialed her number. At the first ring, he panicked and hung up. What if she wouldn't talk to him? If she did, she'd only say the same things again. Besides, she was going to get married. How could she? She mustn't.

He picked the receiver up again, then placed his finger on the cradle, stared at it, let go. This wouldn't work! He rose, then sat. He knew what he could do. He dialed the operator. "Operator, get me long distance, please." Then, "Information, please. Columbus." He caught his breath and hung up even before the operator could ask for the name. The phone wouldn't be in Sarah's name. How many Johnsons were there in Columbus? He thought he'd heard there were almost as many Johnsons around as Smiths.

Maybe . . . He dialed the number for Kohl Hall at Bowling Green. The ring sounded hollow as though it echoed into an empty place. Please, Sarah, be there! He had to talk to her, convince her to talk Liz out of marrying that guy. Liz would not listen to him.

"Be there," he told the phantoms who must lurk in the empty halls. At least the housemother. Someone. At the sound of a soft click he sighed. Yes!

"Kohl Hall. Third floor." The voice wasn't young enough to be Sarah's.

"When does your Easter vacation end?"

"Classes start Wednesday. No one is here right now."

"You are there and I love you! Thank you."

Laughter came from the other end of the line and the amused voice said, "Tell me who you are, maybe I could love you, too!"

Alan sounded a big smack and hung up.

Wednesday! He was supposed to be back Wednesday, too, but he could miss a day. With his grades, he wouldn't even have to explain.

Chapter 19

Four past two o'clock. Sarah had agreed to meet him here, at the Nest, at two. According to her, Liz had a class that should keep her busy for now. Alan looked anxiously at the line rapidly getting longer at the counter. He was down to his last two drops of coffee. If he left the table, he might miss Sarah. He took the final sip and slid the cup about. Maybe he shouldn't have even come to BG.

What if Liz cut a class and showed up? His heart lifted at the thought but settled back with a thump at the realization of futility. Sarah had assured him, she would not.

If he were going to get through this afternoon, he needed coffee. He left his coat on the table and took a chance. Luckily there was a pot at the end and the cashier waved him away. His coat still lay where he left it and he slid gratefully back into the booth, telling himself to relax. If it hadn't been for the seconds, he would have sworn his watch had stopped.

The Nest itself hadn't changed. The strains of "Stardust" rolled toward him from the jukebox. He wished he could throw something and break the damn thing. If he lived to be a hundred they would probably still be playing it. This one with Dorsey's mellow tones and Sinatra's voice would haunt him for the rest of his life. He clenched his teeth against the recollection of that weekend. Liz with her autumn-leaf hair and green dress at the dance, the feel of her in his arms as that song filled the gym, the softness of her cheek, her smile.

He must have smiled at the thought. A couple of girls passing his booth smiled back at him with curiosity rocketing from their eyes. He gave them a weak grin. Please, Sarah, come on!

The thought materialized quickly as the tall blond came toward him. Sarah. She was even more beautiful than he remembered.

She smiled, too. Everyone smiled. But he didn't feel like smiling. He felt like running. He was embarrassed to be here pleading.

"Alan? It's been a while."

He half-rose and she shook her head and slid into the booth opposite him. "I was flabbergasted when you called." She got up again. "I think I'll get coffee."

"Let me." But she was gone.

Flabbergasted, she'd said. He wished the word had been "delighted." Was all of this a waste of time? He pushed his coffee from him. It already tasted like rusty lead.

When she came back, Sarah looked at him expectantly, or perhaps more accurately, curiously.

How should he start? He was afraid he was about to look like a colossal fool. "How are you?" He took a deep breath. That hadn't been too hard. "I wanted to talk about Liz . . ."

She smiled at him.

Even her teeth were perfect.

"I didn't suppose you wanted to ask me out. Not that I wouldn't like that, but . . ."

His face flamed. She was certainly the prettiest girl he'd ever known, but if Liz and her wanting to work was trouble, this one was a barrel of it. He liked her and sympathized. It had to be hard being so beautiful, but some things he'd never understand. She was going to be a mathematician for heaven's sake. He wondered for a moment if she were normal, but looking into those soft blue eyes that held a certain gentleness, he thought yes. Normal. Maybe odd. But then even the men mathematicians he knew, he thought odd. Something about all that order in the mind. He preferred the domestic kind where the world ran smoothly on cogs and wheels already in place.

Sarah said, "Well?"

"Oh. I'm sorry. I was thinking. Look, Sarah, I need you to talk to Liz. She can't . . . He wanted to say "marry that Tom," but Sarah interrupted.

"Why don't you ask her yourself?"

He shook his head. "She won't listen. We've been through it too many times before."

"Have you changed your mind?"

The absurdity of the thought showed in his face. "About what? Marrying her? No. I'd give anything to get her to say yes." He added under his breath, "To me. Not him."

Sarah evidently didn't hear the last of that line. She gave a small laugh, not necessarily of humor. "I'm sorry, but if you want her to say yes, maybe you should ask her something simple, like, 'Would you like a cheeseburger?' "

"Sarah! I'm serious."

"And so am I. You say you love her. If you did, you'd give some thought to what she wants."

"What does she want? Who knows what any woman wants?"

She shook her head. "She wants time. Time to finish school. I don't think that's so much to ask."

"You don't understand."

"Oh, I do." She looked at him for a long time while he sat there feeling sorry for himself. This was not the way the conversation was supposed to go. If this was the best he could do, he'd make a sorry diplomat. Why were women so difficult? They were supposed to be soft and caring, warm and yielding, giving at least.

He opened his mouth to speak.

Sarah cut him off. "What are you afraid of? You can tie your own shoes, can't you? If you can't boil an egg you can always walk or drive to the nearest White Castle. If you don't know the way, call a cab! You know how to read. If she's out working some evening, pick up a damn book."

Alan knew he blushed furiously, from anger, embarrassment and surprise. Her answer had muddled his tongue. "But . . ."

She put out her hand and touched his. "Sorry. I didn't mean to yell at you. And I don't usually cuss. Lost my temper."

"Sarah, I'm going overseas. Who knows when I'll be home?"

"You'll be busy then, won't you?" She shook her head at him. "You men really ought to grow up. What if we were still at war and you were in the army? Would you say, 'I'm invading Japan but I can't be apart from you so you'll have to come here'?"

He slammed his fist on the tabletop. "Damn it, Sarah! A man wants a wife, not a part-time servant."

"Oh. I wasn't sure you knew the difference."

"I don't know why I came." He knew he sounded sulky but it was true. He should have known that a girl wouldn't help him.

"Why did you? You haven't changed."

"Because she can't marry him. Mom said she was sure Liz still loved me from the look on her face. She can't love him."

"I'm not sure I follow all that. By 'him,' do you mean Tom? What do you know about him? They've been dating, that's true. But how do you know? You must have had time to talk to her."

Alan wanted to curl up in a ball and roll the hell out of here. He had a feeling he'd already rolled into a gutter. He rose.

"Sarah, please. Talk to her."

"You're talking to the wrong person. I'm on her side."

"I'm sorry, Sarah, we seem to be at cross-purposes here." He wanted to shake her or something. Make her get Liz and talk to her, but the intractable look on Sarah's face told him it was hopeless.

He took a deep breath and steeled himself to say the words he didn't want to say. "Look, tell Liz I will always love her and I hope she'll be happy with that man. I came because I thought maybe you could talk her out of marrying him." He turned and walked out. He meant it. He did want Liz to be happy. But he was sure her happiness did not lie with Tom.

He was a fool for believing he could change things, and angry that Sarah—no, women—were so impossible. He had tried, hadn't he? If Liz made a bad marriage, it was her own fault, wasn't it? A wave of self-pity settled over him. Women at least could cry when they were upset. All he could do was rage. It wasn't possible that Liz no longer loved him. Or was it? His own gut burned with longing for her. But no matter, there was little hope that he could change things.

Unless he did call her.

A sudden clap of spring thunder released the torrent of rain that had threatened all day. Alan dashed for his car. He had meant to start out for Washington, but the wall of water, the prospect of nine hours, ten with coffee stops, brought home the weariness this whole affair had roused in him. Even if the fickle March rain relented, the gloomy ride was more than he could face right now.

He nosed the car from its spot and turned down Wooster. The inn lay behind the courthouse, on a nice day, a short walk. Now the car crawled, its windshield wipers struggling manfully to give him clear vision.

He struggled to control the unmanful tears that threatened to show themselves. He ached to see her again. Just once, maybe. Even from across the room. If he waited until morning, if he went to Harvey's or back to the Nest, would he see her?

Sure. And maybe a miracle would happen!

Chapter 20

"Him? Marry him?" Sarah asked Alan's back as he turned and walked away. What did he mean?

Had he said that? She must have misunderstood. But the words hung there. He had said them. Marry him. He had not been talking about himself. Liz, of course, but if not Alan, then who? Tom? Liz and Tom?

She called, "Alan, wait," but he was too far away. She tried to stand but gave in to the superior solidity of the table. Feeling like a psychotic crab, she scooted, spilling her coffee as she did. At the door, she did an out-of-sync two-step with an incoming trio of kids. By the time she was outside, Alan was not in sight.

A clap of thunder drove her back into the Nest. She got fresh coffee and went back to the booth to clean up the mess and brood.

Her head told her, "No. It's not possible. Liz wasn't, couldn't marry Tom. She didn't love him. Or did she?" But, yes, Liz could. Anyone would have to love Tom eventually. Her heart sank to the tips of her toenails and lay there panting.

A guy's voice interrupted her furious self-debate. "Hello, Sarah."

She looked up into the face of the last person she ever wanted to see, Rick. Another clap of thunder outside gave new meaning to the phrase, "When it rains . . ." She looked down at her coffee.

"Can I sit?"

"I don't know. Are you able to?"

She could see him bite his tongue. He'd once told her not to be so smart. Guys didn't like smart girls. Well, he at least couldn't afford to, but now he said, politely enough, "May I sit then?"

"Shouldn't you be with Ann? Or do you have another girl hiding somewhere?"

Without protesting further, Sarah watched Rick's tall frame curve into the booth opposite her. She slipped farther into the corner. He reminded her of those rubber snakes. She wanted to say aloud, perfidious, faithless, insidious and a few more of the choicer adjectives.

"Sarah." He sounded reproachful as he tried to take her hand. She pulled back. He said, "Congratulations."

"For what?" Stupidity, maybe. Why had she ever dated this throwback to the Stone Age?

"Haven't you heard? They picked your picture for the yearbook beauty. Gregory Peck, yet. Maybe you'll be discovered. You know, like Lana Turner in the drugstore."

"Don't be an ignoramus. His secretary probably did it." She had heard and the news had not exactly thrilled her. Yes, it was nice to have the honor, but it wasn't the kind of honor she really wanted. Sometimes she thought she'd be a lot happier if she'd been born ugly. Smart and plain, with glasses, the kind men didn't make passes at.

She hadn't wanted to enter the contest in the first place. Back when they'd been going together, Rick had talked her into it, taken her down to the photographer's and even paid for it. She had let him, since he was the one who pushed it.

It was a good picture. Gave her an ethereal look like one she'd seen of that English star, Anna Neagle, in an old *Silver Screen* magazine. Somewhere at home, in one of those boxes of kid memories, she had a fat scrapbook: Clark

Gable in *Gone With the Wind*, a glossy of Cary Grant, pictures of all the big stars. She'd had Charles Boyer, with that lovely accent, and Ronald Colman. What a voice he had!

Rick gave her his best smile, the one she always saw when his fans crowded around after a good score in a basketball game. "I miss you. I wanted to ask if you'd give me another chance." He reached for her hand again, and again she promptly slid it into her lap. He looked a little sheepish for a change as he said, "Ann and I are through. I never liked her as much as I like you."

Men. They were all alike. Except for Tom.

Besides the one on passes and glasses, Parker had another famous quip about the moment two lovers swore fidelity, that ended, "One of you is lying." In the case of Rick and Ann, both.

But not Tom. Damn. Tom. Was he really going to marry Liz? She didn't even love him.

Or did she?

"Sarah. Please. Give me one more chance."

"You never had any chance at all, let alone one more. I never really trusted you. If I were ugly, you'd never look at me twice. To put it in words even you can understand, you're nothing but a conceited beanpole and your mind is as skinny as you are."

She rose, cup in hand.

He held up his hands and tried to lean away. She couldn't help but laugh. There wasn't much room to escape if she meant to throw it.

He protested, "Look. Once was enough. Not again!"

No. Not again. The memory of the punch on him and Ann was one of her best, even though she was a bit ashamed of herself. She'd shocked a lot of people, including herself. The ribbing after that had gotten a bit tiresome.

Still, she was only a little sorry, even though she had ruined Miss Red Fingernails' dress.

She looked at the coffee and back at him, then smiled sweetly, put the cup down and headed for the door. He was so slimy, whatever she said to him would just slide off anyway.

The rain outside had not let up. It lashed the ground as angrily as her own feelings battered her. She slipped her arms out of her jacket, put it over her head and ran. Fatuous, stupid Rick. He wasn't worth thinking about. Alan. Tom. Liz. How could she?

Ten after three. Liz would probably be at the dorm now. With the green monster literally devouring her, Sarah was not in the mood to face her. Why did they call it a green monster anyway? Jealousy was red, angry, and shameful.

She ran for the library. Books were comforting things even in the worst of times. The hard-spined volumes made nice cozy walls where she could hide from the world.

From the stacks, she pulled down a couple of bios, one on Einstein, her hero, and one on Oliver Evans. She put back the Einstein, not in the mood for good thoughts. She'd neither heard of Evans nor cared but the red cover caught her eye. Almost new, certainly not often read, it looked boring enough to put her to sleep and she could forget all this. The intro said he had invented the conveyor belt. It would do.

The bio did nothing to calm the storm within her. The possibility of Liz marrying Tom swirled in her brain like a cyclone. She loved Tom. How she'd come to do that, she didn't know. But she did. Why did he have to like Liz when Liz liked someone else? What was she going to do? In disgust at the general stupidity of people, including herself, she put the book away and headed for Harvey's.

She stopped in the doorway of the restaurant. Even the smell of burgers browning couldn't give her an appetite.

A gust of wind and rain lashed at her and she shivered. If she died of pneumonia, she wouldn't have to worry about it, would she? With no place else to go, she turned back to the dorm.

Her feet were as averse to movement as her brain. The only thing that played there was, Liz does not love Tom. Liz loved Alan. Stupid Alan. Liz couldn't marry Tom. The red monster roared at Sarah, commanding her to say, "Stupid Liz," but she bit her lip. Liz was her best friend, wasn't she?

The room door was closed, well, almost. She hesitated as she put her hand on the knob. It must be past dinner by this time, but no one seemed to be around. The halls had the hollow silence of an empty museum. Slowly she turned the knob. Her roommates wouldn't be sleeping.

Jenny wasn't in. She was never around much anyway. True to her first announcement, she spent most of her time with Ray or at one of the sororities. She did work at Harvey's a couple of days a week.

Liz looked up from her spot in the corner of her paper-strewn bed. Two candy wrappers lay on a pile of crumpled paper. The room looked like she'd left the window open and a storm had come along. Books were strewn on the desk, the bed and one on the floor. Her jacket, once probably draped on the chair, lay in a heap on the floor beside her shoes. Even her hair was tousled and fell in an undisciplined mess. She gave a wistful grin. "Term paper. Yuk. What's up?"

Sarah had to smile in spite of herself. "I'm supposed to be the careless one."

"Oh. Sorry." Liz wrinkled her nose at the almost-empty paper on her lap and moved to put things away. "For all

I've done, I might as well have gone down to eat. Want to get something at the Nest? I'm starved."

"I'm not hungry."

"I just decided if I'm not going to get married, I might as well turn into a brain." She smiled. "I wish I had yours."

"Not get married?" Sarah's desire to fight with her friend evaporated. Was she crazy or were they? "He said you were going to marry him."

"What? Marry who?" Light seemed to dawn. "Who said that? I never told anyone I said it."

Sarah shook her head to clear it. "Whoa! Are you getting married or not?"

"Of course not! That's silly," she snapped back, then flushed. "I did tell Alan I was engaged to Tom, but I didn't mean it." She piled the mess on the bed into one heap. "But how did you know?"

Sarah threw Liz's jacket on her own bed and took the chair. The easy thing to do would be to start at the beginning. "When did you see Alan?"

"Easter vacation. It was a disaster." Liz told her of the encounters. "He looked so smug. I couldn't help it. He doesn't love me at all." She looked like a miserable child caught making mud pies in her Sunday dress. "I got mad and told him I'm engaged to Tom."

Sarah's heart sank.

"But I only said it because he made me mad. It's not true. I never told Tom. He'd probably die laughing."

If there was a storm anywhere in the world, Sarah no longer knew about it. They weren't getting married! Thank you, Lord. He isn't getting married! She made a ball of her fists and clamped her teeth to keep from shouting.

"But how did you know about it?" Liz turned a deeper red. "Tom didn't tell you that, did he? Oh, Lord. I never meant it. How did he find out? He'll think I'm awful."

Sarah cleared the books from Liz's bed and sat beside her. "Not Tom. Alan was here."

Liz jumped up. "Alan, here? Where is he? Why didn't he call me?" She dashed to the mirror and ran her fingers through her hair. "It's a mess. I look terrible. Where is he? Where's my comb?" She desperately rifled the drawer.

"He's gone. Went back to Georgetown."

Liz dropped her comb and went back to flop onto the bed. "Gone? But why did he come?" Tears filled her eyes.

Sarah told her of the phone call and Alan's visit to the Nest, his mission to get her to dissuade Liz from marrying Tom.

The tears that had waited, spilled out. Liz lay back and kicked angrily at the bedsprings overhead. "What am I going to do?"

"What do you want to do?" She knew what she wanted. She wanted Tom. Still, for the moment at least, he was Liz's. But even supposing Liz let him go, Sarah knew it didn't mean he'd turn to her. What a mess!

"If I were you, I'd talk to Alan. Considering that he's a man, I don't think he'll ever change his mind about what he wants from a wife, but then you'll have to decide for yourself what's important to you." Sarah asked herself if she would give up her goals for a man, any man, even Tom. If temptation knocked, she might have to struggle a bit, but she didn't think she'd give up. She thought if Liz was all that driven over a career, she wouldn't dither so much over the decision, play "Should I?" "Could I?" She opened her mouth to say so, but shut it. It wasn't her place.

"I guess you're right. Alan and I will have to talk some more." She brightened a little. "At least now I know he still wants to marry me." She rose and snatched her coat. "I've got to get out of here. I'm going crazy. Want to come to the Nest?"

"But it's raining hard." It was only now Sarah remembered how wet she was.

Liz went to the window, raised it and put her hand out. "Not now it isn't. And look, I see the first star. "Wish I may, wish I might . . ."

Sarah spelled the wish out silently. She wanted Tom. Liz really wanted to marry Alan.

Smiling, they finished the rhyme together, ". . . have the wish I wish tonight!"

Chapter 21

Alan had no problem in keeping his room at the inn in Bowling Green for the night. He unpacked again, laying out his books and paper on the small table. He even sat and took out his pen. But that was useless and he knew it, but somehow, life would have to go on without Liz.

The problem, of course, was that no one else could compare. He'd dated at Georgetown since the split with Liz at Christmas. Beth, then Georgia with her blue eyes. Shelly, brown hair and eyes the color of chestnuts, eyes that had turned black with anger when he wouldn't publicly neck in the balcony. None of them held a match to Liz's flame.

He threw down his pen and grabbed his jacket. He couldn't stand this, rain or not. He wasn't hungry but he had to do something. The Nest was out, and he didn't want all the palaver he'd get at PiKA. What fraternity did that Tom belong to? Running into him was not part of the plan. The plan that wasn't there.

The only other alternatives were driving around in the gloom or Harvey's. Or, he could find Liz and demand . . .

He laughed in spite of himself at the image of his redheaded spitfire's face, if he demanded anything. But what would he demand anyway? That she quit school and marry him? Not likely. All the love he had for her, the love she said she had for him, had not convinced her to quit. His insisting would do little good. And anyway, gentlemen did not demand from ladies.

Blast Sarah. If only she'd have been willing to help.

He parked in front of Harvey's and sat with his hand on the clutch. He needed to talk to Liz himself. He shifted the gear to first, then back into park. Where would he find her? What did she do all day after class? He knew so little of her these days. One of the problems of being so far apart.

A pang of loneliness, of being shut out, crept from his heart to his mind, numbing him, paralyzing his will. After a long moment he turned off the motor and got out. A small voice told him, "Don't give up now. You can get to her somehow." He listened but didn't really believe.

"Perhaps she'll walk in while you're here," the inner voice prompted again. At the thought, his heart did a skip, then a double beat. But, what if she looked happy without him? As much as he wanted to see her, could he face that?

What if she were with *him?* He pushed that thought away. It wasn't likely they'd be out in this rain. If he met them, well, he'd smile and wish them happiness, wouldn't he? Would he? He did, but . . . Thank goodness for the rain.

As though the heavens heard and disagreed, the downpour slowed and turned into a light shower, carrying with it a tiny hint of spring warmth. He paused with his hand on the doorknob. If the rain stopped, she might . . . He shrugged the thought off and went in.

He had Harvey's to himself except for two ladies in tiny hats who might have come from some church committee meeting. They had chocolate cake and tea, but the place smelled of freshly browned beef and onions. Unexpectedly for someone who swore he had no appetite, his stomach growled. True, he hadn't eaten all day, too upset before he talked to Sarah. Perhaps the faint hope, the shadow of resolution gave him an appetite. He ordered a malt and the famous cheeseburger, the one she raved about. He had it before at the homecoming, but his mind had been on Liz, not food.

The waitress, a tall lanky girl not much fatter than her pencil, looked a bit stunned.

She must, after all, know what a cheeseburger and malt were. He was tempted to make a crack about it but let it go. He could not worry about her. The committee women did worry him, though. Like unmanageable children out to play, their presence ringed his mind and pecked at him. They reminded him of his mother. That thought trooped out his differences with Liz, more pesky brats spraying cold water on his hope.

A used newspaper lay on a chair in the corner and he picked it up for a diversion. Last night's *Toledo Blade*, March 23, 1946. For a moment he lost himself in the events of the diplomatic world. His world. A world he would think Liz would die to be part of. Great Britain had signed the treaty giving Jordan independence. What he wouldn't give to be part of events like that. And the UN. What a vision! He pictured himself standing as the U.S. ambassador. His pulse raced and chest swelled just thinking about it. The new organization had set up temporary headquarters at Hunter College in the Bronx. How could she turn down such a life for that Tom? He put the paper down and began to fold and unfold the paper napkins. He didn't even know what Tom did for a living or would do.

He looked around impatiently. Why was it that the fewer diners a restaurant had, the slower the service? The odd girl seemed to be the only waitress. Did they have to call the cook from his nap, or maybe hunt down a cow to kill? He picked the paper up and started on the big spread about Kenny Washington signing with the Rams, the first black in the NFL since 1933.

217

"Sorry it took so long." The waitress put the order in front of him. "I got delayed and your burger got cold. We made a new one."

When the girl continued to look at him, he smiled, not knowing what else to do. She gave him a last curious stare then turned and walked off.

He shrugged and picked up the sandwich. The smell triggered memories of that other visit. Back then. When they were together.

He tried to push the memory from his mind and bit into the burger only to have another memory surface. That Fourth of July barbeque, the one when Liz threatened to throw her plate of half-eaten baked beans at him. For a moment he couldn't remember why. Then he laughed. He'd mentioned another girl. Praised her looks. Live and learn!

"Everything okay?" There she was again with that odd look on her face.

"Yes. Fine. Very good." He cleared his throat. "Is anything wrong? You've—"

"Look, I'm sorry if I'm wrong, but you are Alan, aren't you?"

He blinked. "Yes, but, how . . ."

She gave a quick glance over her shoulder, probably for her boss, then shoved the empty malt glass aside. "Do you need coffee? Mind if I get some and sit with you? It's important."

Confused but curious, he shrugged. "No, thanks. No coffee, I mean."

If a thin girl could be said to plop, this one plopped down across from him. "I only work two days a week; if he fires me, I won't miss much." Her grin softened her thin face. "I don't show up sometimes, anyway. I'd say my employment here is problematical these days. You don't know me but I've seen your picture."

She held out her hand which he shook as though it were a porcupine. How would she have seen his picture? Oh. His heart skipped a beat. Liz. No one else.

"I'm Jenny. Liz's roommate."

The words exploded in Alan's consciousness even though he knew Liz had no roommate by that name. His heart raced as furiously as the possibilities that ran through his mind. Disconnected words surfaced and disappeared. How—could—would . . .

"I'm sorry. I know I haven't any right to interfere but I hate to see two people who obviously love each other be so stupid." She gave a short laugh. "I know where she is. I chased her down."

He almost bridled at the word "stupid," but then the girl was very nearly right, wasn't she? He shook his head to clear it and regarded her.

"I thought Dottie and Sarah were her roommates." But, who cared whose roommate was whose? He wanted to grab this Jenny and kiss her. Not a Liz kiss, a big beautiful bear-hug kiss. A chance. Maybe his last chance. Liz might not go for it, but he had to try. She loved him. She must. She'd said so. She couldn't want to marry that Tom.

Perhaps encouraged by the look on his face, because he knew he had to be grinning—or was he staring, he didn't even care—Jenny went on. "She's not in her room. She and Sarah just went to the Nest. That's really why your burger took so long. I meant, the call is why. Chasing her down took longer than I thought."

She looked over her shoulder at the ladies, and started to rise, then sat again and nodded toward the ladies. "I guess they're okay."

At her mention of Sarah, the hope forming at the back of

his mind vanished. "I talked to Sarah earlier today. That's why I'm here. Thought she might get Liz to listen but she said she was on Liz's side. She thinks I should back off. If Sarah's with Liz, she might talk her out of listening."

Jenny shook her head. "She wouldn't."

He didn't know. He didn't begin to understand women. But damn Sarah. It was Liz's life—and his. He stood, got his wallet, tossed a ten on the table, then leaned over and kissed Jenny on the cheek. So much for bravery and bear hugs. "Thanks."

Her delighted, "Get 'em, Tiger," followed him out the door.

Once out, the night was only marginally warmer than the sudden fear that filled him.

Will she see me? He could not stand to let her walk out of his life again. Should he just leave? No! Just to look at her again would be worth any pain. Maybe they would talk this time. But he had to . . .

The Nest confronted him, dark and oppressive, a dis-approving mama protecting her children.

He saw no Liz, but in a corner booth, Sarah leaned for-ward, talking to someone. He couldn't see who. He walked toward them. His heart didn't beat the whole distance, one surely as long as the great hall of Versailles.

Sarah leaned back. His anesthetized heart sprang to life. She sat there, a dream, red hair glowing like the last warm coal on a chilly night.

His mouth became a desert covered with thick, fuzzy cactus that drained every ounce of moisture. Both his head and his heart drummed in his ears.

He never knew how he got the words out. Perhaps it was his anger with Sarah for her lack of cooperation that finally loosened his tongue. He managed to say, "Hello, Liz." How could the fate of the universe depend upon two words?

She turned white, then as red as her hair. Her voice trembled, "Hello, Alan."

They locked gazes. Alan, too, trembled from an earthquake of emotion.

Sarah cleared her throat. "Excuse me, you two. I believe you have things to discuss!" She was smiling at him!

Why was his enemy smiling? Had she changed her mind somehow?

Picking up her burger and fries, she moved to the only other empty booth, the one next to them. Still grinning she said, "Sorry, I don't mean to eavesdrop, so keep it down, guys!" Alan handed her the malt. Relieved at her tone, he said, "You're fine. Guess you know the whole story anyway."

When he turned back, Liz seemed to have gathered her emotions and lined them up in a row. At least there was no storm on her face. He indicated the seat. "May I?"

She moved one shoulder only slightly but she, too, smiled.

A wonderful, beautiful smile. He slid into the booth beside her. He wanted to grab and kiss her, but his hold on his emotions was too fragile for that.

"Alan, I . . ."

At the same time he said, "Liz."

He took her in his arms and held her close.

She pulled gently away. "Alan. Liz. We sound like that 'Betty and Bob' soap opera, 'Betty—Bob—Betty.' " Between the words she'd made a breathless pause.

Relieved to have something inane to break the ice, he said, "Never listened to those. 'Jack Armstrong, The All American Boy' was more my style."

"How about 'Little Orphan Annie'? I once sent the label

of a jar of Ovaltine in for a secret code ring. Something about Sacajawea, I think."

Disregarding the possible audience, he leaned over and kissed her. A quick kiss, hard enough to say "I love you," yet still testing, wary of being refused.

Her lips were soft but they did not linger and hunt for more.

He drew back and examined her face. No anger. Her brown eyes were soft, startled-looking, like a frightened deer. He reached for her hand and held it in both of his. Now or never. "Liz, you can't marry Tom. You don't love him. I know you don't. You can't . . ." He took a deep breath, winded and even a bit frightened, fearful that she might interrupt and tell him he was wrong. "You've said it so many times. You love me."

"But . . ."

No. He couldn't let her object. Even if he was crazy. Even if it all went against anything he'd ever planned and hoped for. He wanted Liz. "I don't care. You can do anything you like, go to school, take your time, get a doctorate. I love you."

Her eyes glistened and two large tears rolled down her cheeks. "Oh, Alan. I was going to say the same thing. Only the other way around." She snatched a napkin. "I never have a tissue when I need one." When she finally looked up at him, her eyes still glittered, but like a raindrop in sunshine. "I love you, too, and I'll do anything you want. If you need me to go with you, I will. Maybe school can wait. I don't know, but I do know I love you. I've been so miserable."

Had she really said it? He wanted to stand and shout, "She loves me! Not Tom! Me!" He couldn't move. When all he could do was sit there without bursting from the joy of her, he must really be as stuffy as she teased him for being.

She said it again, "I love you. We can work something out."

He squeezed her hand until she made a small yelp.

He reddened and withdrew his hands. "Sorry." They both laughed again. Funny how often love makes you laugh. He leaned over to kiss her.

She moved back a little. Her eyes got the startled look again. "I . . ." She looked away from him, down at the tabletop, then took a deep breath. She spoke almost in a whisper. "I was never going to marry Tom. I'm sorry. I only said it because you looked like you didn't love me. I was mad." She reddened. "I am sorry."

She'd made it up? All of the hurt when he knew he had lost her to Tom? Ever since they'd parted at Christmas, he'd figured somehow they'd get back together. And then she'd said . . . Tom! All of that stewing and she'd made it up?

He gave a short snort of disbelief and drew back, not knowing what to think, or do. How could she? Surprise and pain more than anger made him get up and sit on the other side of the booth to face her. He took a deep breath. He needed time to think.

"But, Alan . . ." She seemed surprised that he should be upset. Her eyes filled with tears.

He shook his head. "I can't believe you did that, Liz. Do you have any idea how miserable I've been?"

"Only you? How about my misery? You just wouldn't be reasonable!" She didn't wipe away the tear that fell.

Sarah interrupted. "Look, you two, let's not be foolish here. Excuse me, stupid." She stood at the end of their table.

Anger made the hair rise on the back of his neck. Why was she butting in? What if Liz listened to her again? Just when he thought they might work it out. Then he remembered again. Liz had made it up. She'd never planned to marry Tom.

Sarah didn't give him time to reply. She slid quickly into the booth beside him. "You, Alan! If you weren't so stubborn and hidebound with what your mother always did, Liz wouldn't have had to tell you a fib." She turned and put her hand over Liz's fist that held the crumpled napkin. "Honey, have you ever thought maybe you can't have the whole pie?"

Liz drew back her hand sharply. "You want the whole pie! Why shouldn't I?"

Sarah shook her head. "I've only realized this since I talked to Alan today. If you want them both, maybe you don't want either badly enough. You know I want a career in math. But with me it is a passion. It isn't something I just think I'd enjoy. I would like to marry. Who wouldn't? But with me, that comes second. 'Le Roi c'est Moi,' or something to that effect. Math is me, Liz. I am math."

Liz sniffed. Alan did not interrupt. "The difference is, you've been miserable without Alan. I'd be miserable without math." She gave Liz a long look that seemed to say, "Understand?" then rose, gave Alan a quick pat on the arm, and left.

Alan went back to sit by and put his arm around Liz. She laid her head against his chest and made his shirt wet one more time that day. It seemed to him rain had been falling too long, inside and out. He lifted her chin and kissed her. The tang of salt on her lips tasted of sea spray. The effect was not one of cool breezes, sand and shore, but of fire and heat. Her lips were a hot sun that consumed everything it touched.

Slowly, the fever burned down and he managed to say, "Marry me?" He kissed her again. This time, softly.

"Mmmm." Then she drew away. "When?"

"It's up to you."

"Will August give you enough time to get things ready for Switzerland?"

"Switzerland? Where's that? I wish I had the ring with me so you won't go away."

"I won't ever go away again. We can work something out."

He reached out and caressed her hair.

She smiled at him and then grinned as she said, "Now is the winter of our discontent made glorious summer . . ."

Alan raised a brow. "Who's the stuffy one now?"

"Proper. Not stuffy."

"Umm. Whatever you say." He kissed her. "I officially amend my statement. Stuffy but apt!"

They both laughed and said it together, "I love you!" He kissed her again. A long sweet moment of glorious summer.

For the first time in his life, he really didn't care who watched him kiss his girl.

Chapter 22

Sarah left the Nest and walked slowly toward Kohl. For want of an oxygen mask or other life-support system, she concentrated on inhaling and exhaling. The calm slipped away as quickly as she found it. Liz and Alan! Tom would be free! Oh, please, God. Let Liz and Alan stay together.

She told herself not to be too delighted. This particular skirmish wasn't over yet. The opposing armies might have moved, but they were still on the field. The battle flag still flew. Perhaps a strategic attack was needed.

With that reflection she picked up her pace and ran toward the dorm, her thoughts keeping time with her flying feet. Tom would be available. Oh, he would!

The crisis came more quickly than she expected. He sat on the steps of Kohl, probably waiting for Liz. Her heart and her feet thudded to a stop. Did he love Liz a lot? Would he be devastated, perhaps even hate all women?

She wanted to feel sorry for him, say "Poor Tom," but her hopes wouldn't let her. Ashamed of her desire to gloat, she told herself he must have known that Liz might, in the end, marry Alan. He must have kept some of himself back.

Holding back wasn't easy, Sarah had to admit. She'd battled to keep her own feelings under control because of Liz, but had only ended up admitting she wanted Tom in the worst way.

She went forward slowly, aching to talk to him, but afraid. He looked toward her and patted the step beside him. "If you're not in a hurry!"

His smile was as serene as ever. If he knew, he didn't look as though he needed comforting. And if he did, what could she say? "I'm sorry but I'm glad? Sad for you, delighted for me?" He couldn't know. He wouldn't be sitting in front of Kohl unless he was waiting for Liz.

He asked, "What's so special that it brings you running?"

Her tongue stuck to the roof of her mouth. Oh, yes, there was something special, him. She looked into those gentle blue eyes that had made a nest in her heart and choked.

She told herself, Speak, Fool! But her mind wouldn't stay in gear. Nor did his hand on her arm calm her.

Luckily, he didn't seem to expect an answer. "I've been trying to find Liz. Missed supper and I'm starved. I know it's late but thought I'd talk her into going to the Nest with me."

The Nest? Oh, no! Sarah had all she could do to keep breathing. He can't go there now! If Liz hasn't come back, she must still be there with Alan, the two of them making goo-goo eyes at each other. How awful for him! "Uh. Well. I, ah." She took a breath. Pull yourself together, girl! "I was just there with her. She and Audrey—was there and Audrey on campus?—were going to stop at the library."

"Oh. Well." He rose and turned to go.

That lovely back when he turned: the strong shoulders, muscles that must ripple like a sail under a perfect wind, the arms that must enfold a girl like an archangel's wings. She couldn't let him just walk away. She gathered her courage or courage came and gathered her. She said quickly, "If you want some company, I don't think Liz would mind if I came along. Actually, I'd rather not go up to my room just now. Jenny ruined one of my sweaters and it would be better if we didn't come face-to-face until I cool down a bit. I'd rather go to Harvey's, though." It wasn't until after she said it that she realized Jenny was probably still working at Harvey's. Who was it—Mark Twain?—who said liars had to have long memories? Maybe that cowboy guy, Will Rogers. Well, couldn't help that now.

He smiled and set her heart spinning. Such an innocent smile. Best of all, he didn't look as though it occurred to him that she was chasing him. He took her by the arm. "Great. I do want company."

"Let's go." He led her to his '42 Plymouth. He let her in and threw the folder of his work from the front seat onto the back window shelf.

She settled herself carefully in the middle of her side of the seat. Not too far, not too close. She liked this little grey coupe better than Alan's big Packard. Even a '39 Packard seemed a bit showy to her. The Plymouth fitted Tom's straight nature and the soft grey interior matched his gentleness. The smell of his Old Spice filled the small space. She closed her eyes and let it surround her. It wasn't an expensive lotion, but it smelled clean and fresh. She bit her lip. He'd probably put it on for her—Liz.

She sat back, grateful for the shadows that deepened as he pulled out from the well-lit curb. In the dimness she could study his profile with impunity. He looked pleased with himself and his world. Her heart lurched once more. Would the news of Liz and Alan break his? Darken that serenity?

From somewhere in her mind, Frank Sinatra opined, "I'll Never Love Again." She wanted to cry. Shut up, Frankie! She ached to move closer to Tom, snuggle against him. No. She mustn't. She was relieved when they pulled up in front of the restaurant.

When they got out, she saw the folder on the window shelf. "Your sketches? I've never seen your work. Can we take them in?"

When they had settled into a booth, Jenny brought water and the menu. She kept a straight face, but curiosity danced in her eyes.

Tom waved away the menu with a questioning look at Sarah.

"Just a Coke." She gave Jenny a quick nod to let her know Liz was all right.

Jenny stepped a little behind him, tipped her head at him, rolled her eyes and, from under the order pad, made a quick motion from him to Sarah.

Sarah looked quickly down, but not before she smiled.

Tom ordered the usual for himself, the cheeseburger.

When Jenny had gone, he said, "I think maybe I shouldn't ask, but I will. I thought you were upset with her over the sweater?"

"I was, but for some reason, whenever I look at her I want to laugh. I can't stay mad at her." Liar, liar, pants on fire! Well, part of it was true anyway. There was something in the tall bony frame of Jenny, the no-baloney air of her, that did make Sarah want to laugh.

"Ray sure is wild about her. They're made for each other."

Glad to have that subject closed so neatly, Sarah pointed at the folder. "May I see them? Do you mind?"

He wiped off the table and opened the drawings. Most seemed to be lessons on perspective. Lines from all over the place zeroed back to a point on the horizon. "It's a bit like math, isn't it? So orderly. I never thought about that before. Maybe architects and mathematicians have the same kind of mind." Yes, minds meant to be together!

Two of the drawings didn't seem to be class work. At least she thought they would be too advanced in design to be part of any freshman program. As he closed the folder, she held on to them. "I want to look at these. They're great. I'll be careful."

She wiped the table again, even though the folder had lain there. The watercolors, of landscaped residences, were too beautiful to let anything happen to them. "These aren't a freshman's work. Too good. But I can tell they're yours. They look like you."

Even his eyes smiled at that. It changed to a grin as he said, "Well, I'm not sure I like that. Am I square or something?"

"Since you mentioned it, see how that roof comes to a point there? Just like your head!"

He touched the top of his head. "Darn! Forgot my hat!" His grin widened. Did his eyes soften?

"They have a look of, not so much serenity, but of being where and how they belong."

"That's high praise. I'm flattered."

"It's not flattery." He smiled, but more than that, she thought he looked at her with new interest, as though he'd discovered something good. She looked quickly down. Mustn't count one's chickens.

"I could say I have a head start. I've hung around Dad's office for years. He always let me do stuff for him. Even listened to my suggestions."

"I think I'd like your father." And, like father, like son. She studied the drawings, wondering what it was about them that shouted, "Tom." "They look so clean yet they aren't cold at all," and held out the one that showed a U shape. "I'd love this. I love courtyards for one thing. They make me feel snug yet they're open."

He glowed. "That's just the reaction I'd hoped for!"

Reluctantly she handed them back. "When I am famous you can design my house for me!" Or when I marry you, you can design our house. That would be even better! She let her fingers linger so that his hand brushed hers as he took the drawings.

"We talked about function versus beauty before. Remember? I just tried to get the best of two worlds there."

Yes, she remembered. She remembered every word of every conversation they'd ever had. But she was surprised, and delighted, that he remembered any of them.

She nodded toward the folder where he had returned the paintings. "I really like them."

As he put the folder aside, she tried to put her enthusiasm aside. The cautious, spoilsport Sarah from the back of her mind hissed at her. "Slow down, girl. Don't forget. He likes Liz."

Jenny saved the day by bringing the order, then went about destroying the mood by filling sugars, wiping the salt shakers, either to overhear any news or to remind them it was near closing.

If Tom noticed, he wasn't impressed. Between leisurely bites, he said to Sarah, "By the way, I haven't seen you since I heard—"

"Heard?" The words startled her. What could he have heard about her? She was pretty certain she wasn't exactly the big topic of conversation at BG. "Have my dark secrets come out?"

Tom tilted his head and smiled.

What a smile you have!

He said, "No dark secret. I heard your photo was first for the yearbook. Did Gregory Peck write a letter or anything?"

Flattery was a whole new commodity when it came from

Tom. She didn't mind it at all. "There was a polite, rather general, well, maybe impersonal, letter."

"If I'd been Gregory Peck I think I'd have proposed to you, but I guess he is married."

Please do. You're not.

"You're awfully quiet. Aren't you pleased?"

"I guess. I mean, it's okay. I really didn't want to enter. Did it to please old Bean Pole. You should have entered."

"Bean Pole equals Rick, right?"

When she nodded, he answered her question, "The fraternity wanted me to enter. You know how they like to look good. It just never seemed important enough to follow through."

"Amen." She sighed inwardly. She wanted this guy— love, lust, who cared? He wasn't drop-dead handsome, but he had rugged good looks: a strong chin, perfect teeth and eyes. And a perfect mind. Best to change the subject. She asked, "How's your family?" Big and close, they ought to keep him talking for a while.

"You know I think everyone ought to have a big family." He held up his hand. "I know. Nothing against 'only' children. Love one myself."

In her fool's paradise Sarah's heart turned over. Did he love Liz so much?

He went on as though he hadn't stabbed her in the heart. "The thing is, big families are a perfect training ground for life. You don't always get a room to yourself, you sometimes get the hand-me-downs, but with all that fighting and loving, you learn what's important."

She hardly heard what he said after "Love one myself." He'd been after Liz ever since school started. What would he do when he found out? In spite of how much Sarah wanted him for herself, she ached for him. It hurt, didn't it? To love someone who loved someone else?

Chapter 23

" 'Night, Tom." Sarah waved from the top of the stairs when he dropped her off after the burger at Harvey's. He waved back and sped off.

She sent him a mental kiss in lieu of the real one she wished she could give. What would he do when he found out about Liz? Catching a man on the rebound wasn't in Sarah's plans but she couldn't still the hope swelling in her heart, "fit to bust" as her southern cousin might have said.

She made it to the room with ten minutes to spare. A grinning Liz sat on her bed, hugging her knees. There was little she needed to say. The grin said it all.

The scolding at the Nest must have worked. "Jenny's not back yet?" She checked the hall then parked herself on the desk chair. Tom pushed his way back into her thoughts. He had been so nice, but then he was always nice to her. She ached for the day when his good night would be a kiss instead of that friendly pat on the shoulder. She closed her eyes and touched the spot where his hand had lain, if innocently. Was there a wish you could make on a touch, like on the first star?

Liz didn't wait for an invitation to talk about Alan. "Oh, Sarah, we made up! I'm going to marry him. This summer."

Sarah rose and hugged her hard. "You can work things out. You've got years to get a degree." She hardly heard the rest of the glowing report on the attractions and virtues of Alan. She was too busy counting her unhatched chickens.

Tom was free. Tom was available. She had a chance. He would get over Liz.

Flying feet in the hallway and an "Ooops! Sorry" sounded as Jenny dashed into the room, the hall monitor at her heels scolding, "You just made that one!"

Unnerved by this whole day of what if's, could be's and oh, no's, Sarah snapped. "She works, for Pete's sake. She's not a magician."

The shocked monitor gave her a weak smile. "I know. It's . . ." She backed out.

Jenny laughed and Liz applauded as she said, "You do have a temper, after all!"

Intending to apologize, Sarah started toward the door, but gave up and sat again at the desk. "You just aren't around at the right time. Don't forget the punch!" As much as that incident still embarrassed her, it pleased her, too.

"Oh, yeah. How could I forget that? You know I used to worry that you were too nice."

"Well, not any longer. I know what I want now and I'm going after it." She crossed her fingers. Tom was first on her list. She added wistfully, "If I could just figure out how."

Liz regarded her, curiosity oozing from her like honey from a graham cracker sandwich. "You mean the degree?"

"I know what Sarah wants!" Jenny grinned smugly, flung herself down beside Liz and hugged her. "And I know you got back together with Alan!"

Liz laughed triumphantly and returned the hug. "How did you know about Alan and me? I know you found me for him, but, but . . ." Jenny couldn't know about the meeting at the Nest, unless . . . "Does the whole dorm know? I didn't tell them yet. Haven't been here that long."

"Sarah and—" Jenny stopped and reddened. "Uh, I saw

Sarah. She gave me the high sign."

A flush started at the base of Sarah's neck, but she quickly told herself Liz had no interest in Tom or the fact anyone had been at Harvey's with him.

Yet she mustn't let Liz think she'd gone after Tom before the reunion with Alan. "Um, well, when I left the Nest, I came back here. Tom was waiting for you and we talked." She examined Liz's face, all the while scolding herself for her cowardice. Liz couldn't have them all, could she? "When I said you weren't here, he said he was going to go to the Nest." Sarah cleared her throat. "I didn't think he ought to run into you and Alan together, so I told him you'd gone to the library. He was hungry so I went to Harvey's with him."

"Oh!" Liz put her hand to her mouth. "How awful! I completely forgot about Tom. Oh, Sarah, whatever am I going to do about him? He is so nice. I hate . . . Oh, my gosh!" She backed up on the bed. Tears glistened.

"Good question!" How much should she say now?

Jenny hugged Liz and winked at Sarah. "What Tom needs is a new love interest."

Sarah choked.

Liz wiped the tear away and sat up. "But who?"

With a sly look at Sarah, Jenny said, "I can't imagine." She rifled her foot locker for goodies, and disappeared. When she returned, she looked like Wellington after Waterloo.

In a few minutes they were all back and in bed, lights out. Sarah, worn out by the stampede of the day's emotions, fell asleep after the third Tom—Tom—Tom . . .

From the single bed, Jenny watched Sarah. When she was sure Sarah was asleep, she hissed at Liz, "Come on. We've got to fix things for Tom."

Liz grunted.

"Shh! Don't wake her. Come on."

Liz, in a big display of drama, mimed her agony at being dragged out, but then smiled and tiptoed to the door where Jenny scouted and motioned her forward. They slipped into Mary Anne's room, next door.

A towel shrouded the lamp but left plenty of light. Giggles greeted the raising of the lid of the locker where the goodies were stored. Jenny, who had the most to lose by collecting demerits, put her finger to her lips. "Shhh! Someone will hear you." She rose, turned the knob quietly and peeked out, then, satisfied, closed it. "Okay. All clear for now but unless you want me grounded forever, keep it down!"

The giggles came again, but quieter. Jenny appointed herself chairman of the meeting. "The 'Help Tom Meeting' is now opened. First of all, we have good news. Liz, tell them."

"Alan and I made up. We're getting married late August."

Mary Anne and her roommate, Alice, clapped softly and hugged Liz. When the hugging was done, Jenny went on, "But we have a problem. Liz has been dating Tom." Jenny paused at the rustle of Mary Anne's silk and Alice's cotton pj's. Had the indrawn breaths been criticisms? Jenny hastened to reassure them. "No. It wasn't Liz's fault. Don't forget she didn't chase Tom. He's tried to get her ever since he first saw her. He knew she was going with Alan."

Cloth rustled again, this time softly. Jenny nodded. "What Tom needs is a new love interest."

Mary Anne waved her hand wildly in the air. "I'll make the sacrifice. He's the cat's meow."

Alice chimed in. "Me, too! I think he's swell. Cute, too."

Jenny cracked, "Big of you both to sacrifice yourself for one of the dreamiest guys on campus. You're all heart!"

She hushed their giggles and shook her head. "I know someone perfect for Tom. And I think he likes her a lot. I've seen them together. Only he doesn't know it yet."

"Who?" "Who?" They sounded like owls gathered for a conference. The hooting set off a new wave of giggles.

Liz neither oohed nor clapped.

Jenny waved at their own room next door. She said, "Tom already has a soft spot for Sarah. Sarah likes Tom. It's easy."

Liz looked stunned. After a long moment she put her hands to her mouth. "I had no idea! I'm so sorry. She never said anything. I only dated him . . . He was so nice and he kept after me. I thought I might learn to love him. But I couldn't." Tears threatened again. "If I'd known . . ."

Jenny leaned over and hugged her. "I can see it in Sarah's eyes every time his name comes up. Every time she's with him." She quickly added, "She never chased him. It just happened and if they met, it wasn't planned. She always worried about you, Liz."

Liz sniffled and shook her head. "I feel so awful."

"Don't worry, we're about to fix it." Jenny hugged her again then turned back to the others. "Okay. You guys all see how it is. What are we going to do?"

"If I can't have him," Mary Anne said with a pout, "I guess I'll have to help. We could keep throwing them together."

Liz shook her head. "He'd be embarrassed and Sarah would die."

"We need something romantic," came from Alice.

"There's the Sweetheart Swing in May," Mary Anne suggested.

"Can't wait that long," Jenny objected. "But the Delta's are having that Daisy Mae–Li'l Abner thing in two weeks. That's made in heaven."

"The Sadie Hawkins dance. Yeah." Liz nodded eagerly.

Liz's look dared Mary Anne and Alice as she warned, "And they can't know we arranged it. So mum's the word. If it gets out, you're dead."

Mary Anne scratched her head. "Okay, but we need more than that."

"He goes to the library a lot." Jenny looked thoughtful. "Then there's always the Nest."

"The bookstore!" Alice turned to Mary Anne. "You do work there on Mondays?" When she nodded, Alice went on, "Tom's in my perspective class. If I asked real sweet, he might stop and deliver a message from me. I could be desperate so he'd be pinned down to a near time frame!"

"Isn't that trapping him?" Mary Anne took the last cracker and slowly slathered it with the remains of the cheese. She had the look of a mouse eyeing the cheddar. Somehow Jenny didn't think it was cheese the girl had in mind.

Jenny recognized the naked envy for what it was—the desire to acquire Tom herself. Over my dead body! She said sweetly, "It's not as though she were kidnaping or blackmailing him. She'd just be conveniently underfoot. We gals have to have some way to get to them without being accused of chasing."

The girl shrugged.

Deciding to end any hope Mary Anne harbored, Jenny pronounced, "We're agreed. Tom and Sarah already like each other. I watched him when he was talking to her tonight. He just doesn't know it yet. Okay?" Mary Anne reluctantly joined in the nods. Jenny stood. She'd done what she came to do. "Okay, guys. We've got to keep in touch. Coordinate our plans. So, let me know if you get any more ideas for getting them together."

"Okay" from Mary Anne. A glowing "Swell" from Alice and a smile from Liz.

With her hand on the knob, Jenny turned for a last, "Okay. We all work on it." She and Liz slipped back to their room.

Liz pulled the blanket over the sleeping Sarah and crawled into her own bed.

Jenny settled in and whispered to herself, "Okay, so I'm a softy. I like happy endings." In the dark she grinned at Sarah. Tomorrow, Cinderella, we drop your slipper!

Chapter 24

Dreading what she had to do, Liz dragged her feet. She'd rather be anywhere else, do anything else than meet Tom at the Nest. "Please, God, don't let him be hurt. He doesn't really love me, does he?"

She stopped when she saw his car.

He opened it and got out. "Hi, Liz." He took her books. "I haven't seen you for so long, I thought you'd left town."

"Come on now, it hasn't been that long." Her voice couldn't even convince her.

"Maybe it's relative." He opened the door for her. They both stopped in the entrance. The booths were full and there was a long line at the counter. "If we ever get food, we'll have to stand or squeeze in with someone else. I'd hoped at least to have you all to myself."

"Me, too." Liz felt like a rat for saying it. She needed to talk to him, but knew her hope wasn't the same as his. She wanted to melt into the floor, disappear. "Let's go to Harvey's. I need to talk to you." She prayed silently, "Jenny, please be there!" She wanted to count on a bit of backup, courage if nothing else, if she got stuck.

He smiled at her but she thought the smile had a forlorn droop hiding in the corner of it. Her heart turned over again. In some ways, she wished it could have worked. He was really sweet and she liked his attitude toward women. At least he didn't expect them to stay in the kitchen.

She'd tried. There were times, like that note with the violets, "A rose is only a rose, but these are Venus's own flower, Tom." She'd thought then maybe they could make it together. But it was Alan, not Tom, who made her heart race. Hearts were strange things when it came to love. You never knew if, how, or why it would beat for one man, sleep for another.

The lunch crowd at Harvey's was only slightly less than that at the Nest. One lone table in the corner stood empty. Fate in waiting.

Liz's heart sank when Jenny hurriedly tossed them menus and went on to serve another table. Jenny as backup would not be much help in a pinch.

When she did come back to take their order, neither Tom nor Liz had bothered to open the folder. "Cheeseburger with a malt, right, Liz?"

She nodded but wasn't at all sure she could eat, in spite of the fact she'd been hungry all morning. Her stomach felt raw and knotted. She envisioned one of those string potato bags, rolled and tied.

To distract herself, she fiddled with the paper napkins. She hoped she wouldn't need them for a hanky. "Tom . . ."

Blue eyes shone softly beneath a frowning brow. "Maybe we should eat first. The tone of your voice sounds a bit ominous. Not sure I want to handle it on an empty stomach."

He knows, or he's guessed, she thought. At least he can eat! Hope I can! This is going to be a long afternoon!

For the lack of anything better to talk about she brought up Sarah's picture in the yearbook. "I saw it before she submitted it. Don't see how she could have lost."

"Mmm!"

I wish he wouldn't look at me like that! It wouldn't hurt to push Sarah a bit. Liz chattered nervously. "Boy, I wish I had her brains. She only needs to hold a book and everything in it makes a dive for her mind."

"I think with a mind like hers, it isn't so much knowledge as an intuitive grasp of the way things work."

He hadn't brightened at Sarah's name, but now at least that contemplative stare had changed to interest. She pushed on. "She was telling me all about some guy who's making this new thing that is supposed to change the world."

He did laugh at that. "You mean Aiken and Harvard. The Mark I. Yeah. She told me all about it. Her favorite topic, I think. She's one dedicated math fiend."

Uncomfortable with the word "fiend," Liz protested, "I think that's great!"

"Oh. I do, too. I told her so. She's a very special person. It's a tough field to crack but if any woman can, she can."

Liz's defenses went up. She'd given up the old ambitious Liz, but maybe not for all time. For a moment the shadow of her came back. "Don't we all have to fight that battle?" Math wasn't the only place that didn't want women.

He regarded her, his blue eyes shining with amusement. "I think that isn't as important to some women as to others."

Liz's heart sank to her knees. She blushed. He did know. He must. But how could she say it?

"You know when I was a kid I was all ready to go out the door to go to the circus. My mom stopped me. She had that kind of look on her face you've had on yours all afternoon. The kind that told me she's sorry I can't have what I want so badly." His mouth turned up in one corner but the frown lines stayed. "That time, my uncle died. It can't be him again."

Liz wiped her eyes with the napkin she'd folded so carefully.

"It's okay." He reached out and touched her arm. "Well,

242

it's not, but I think I've known all along . . ."

She blubbered. "But how did you know that's what I was going to say?"

"Right now the only thing I want is you, but your face tells me I'm not going to get what I want. We've had some special moments." He put his hand on hers. "No use beating a dead horse. There might even be some relief in the dying." He smiled slightly. "Not enough, though."

She fought back her tears. He knew what she wanted to say, but she owed it to him to put it into words. Perhaps owed him that bit of self-flagellation, that bit of pain. But how could she? He'd said, "I'm not going to get what I want."

She took a deep breath, hoping to inhale some courage. She blurted out, "I'm engaged."

As soon as she said it, she regretted her brusqueness. She covered her mouth with her hand then said hastily, "I'm sorry. I didn't mean to say it like that. It's just that Alan was here and we talked."

"Somehow your engagement's not a surprise." It sounded accepting, but he had made a fist.

She wiped away the tears. It was her words, almost babbling words, that flowed. "I'm sorry, Tom. I really am. You are so nice. I never wanted to hurt you. I honestly thought I might . . ." She sniffled and didn't say the rest of it.

He took her hand. "I know. I went after you, remember? Don't feel bad for me. Be happy." After a moment he asked, "Were you able to work anything out with Alan? Are you going ahead to get your degree at all?"

"I don't know. Maybe sometime. He has to go . . ."

"As you said." He kissed her hand. "For old time's sake." He held it for a moment, then gently let go.

She used the paper napkins again.

"When's the big day?"

"Late August. He's got a post in Bern." She laughed a little. "Says it's janitorial."

"I take it you are sure this is what you want?" There was no hope in his eyes, only caring.

She shrugged and gave a tiny smile. "I know I'm miserable without him."

He said again, "Be happy."

She stretched up and over the table to kiss him on the forehead. "Thank you. You really are a sweet guy."

He rolled his eyes toward the ceiling, but when he looked down again he was smiling. "Oh, great! Sweet! And a kiss on the forehead yet!"

Somehow they both managed to eat when Jenny brought the burgers. For her, the worst was over and she hadn't had to call in the Marines. Liz gave her now-unnecessary backup a weak smile.

When they finished lunch, Tom dropped her off at the dorm and watched as she fled up the stairs. Her hair streamed behind her like angry lightning turned to flame. She waved from the top of the stairs, a short motion that signaled "I'm sorry" like his Navy flags might have.

She ran up the two flights of stairs to her room. One foot, light with relief, barely touched the step. The other hammered on her heart at each step. She had hurt Tom. At least there had never been anything dishonest about it. They had both sensed it might not work. Had they both known it wouldn't?

In the car, Tom shook his head at the vagaries of his heart. He had tried but not won. Surprisingly, he was sad but not devastated. Perhaps his heart had been wise and held back a little, knowing all along what his head had refused to accept. At least the romance, or what there had

244

been of it, had been honest. Neither had tried to fool the other.

He closed his eyes and saw the glowing copper that framed her face, the eyes like molten gold when she was angry. He felt her hands in his, hands from a special mold, carved to fit the curve of his palm. Yet, in her embrace, her arms had never seemed to fold him in, make a circle for the two of them.

He put the car in gear. A done thing was a done thing. He drove back to the frat house.

Even though Alice had enrolled in the Catch Tom for Sarah Club, she waited anxiously for the trig class and a chance to see Tom, now that he was free.

He sat there now, dark head bowed over his papers, a slight frown pulling down the corner of his mouth. And such a mouth!

For a moment she lost herself in the contemplation of it, then pulled up short. She had promised. For now, his mouth wasn't her business even though it looked so . . . Well, anyway, no harm in looking and wishing. Maybe, just maybe, this thing with Sarah wouldn't work. Of course Mary Anne was interested, too, but Alice told herself she was prettier than her roommate. This game with Sarah wasn't guaranteed to work. Who knew what luck lay around the corner?

For now, though, her sworn loyalty lay to "The Plan."

She checked her watch. Two minutes until the bell. Get the note. She dug into what she called her traveling bag, a stiff-sided case that would be, for a normal person, large enough for an overnight stay at a vacation resort. She scrabbled past four books, six notebooks, three of those well past any reasonable use, assorted emergency items like tissues, lipstick, old cookies, a candy bar and . . . She yelped, "Uuuuugh!"

Tom leaned over and looked into the case. Laughing, he pulled out a dead frog and dropped it onto the desk. "Been down to the pond?" He could barely get the words out.

She edged nearer and wrinkled her nose. Both from disgust and the formaldehyde preserving the ugly green thing. "Sam, the guy next to me in biology, did that. I'll get him for this!" She tipped it out and stared at it. He'd done it because she'd refused to touch it in class.

Tom, still laughing, took one of the beat-up notebooks and scooted the thing onto it. "I think maybe we ought to return it to the lab." He held it out and when she shrank back, he grinned. "I'm going that way."

"Ugh. It's all yours. Thanks a lot."

He picked up his books and turned toward the door.

She hadn't meant to make two errands for him, only one and the frog was not it. She said quickly, "Tom, you don't happen to be going past the bookstore, too, are you?"

"About three I could. There's some stuff I've been putting off. Why?"

"That would be perfect. The thing is, I've got a class and then I have a makeup test, but I need to get a note to Mary Anne. She'll be working there at three."

He waited while she fished in the case for the note.

He turned it over, sniffed it, said "Perfumed." He held it up to the light. "If you hadn't said Mary Anne, I'd be suspicious."

She blushed. "I just like good-smelling stuff." Actually the note only said, "Done." "I really appreciate your doing this. I told her I'd get the room cleaned up. She gets a bit mad. Thinks I'm not neat." She stuffed her last book back into the jumble in her traveling bag.

"Why would she say a thing like that?"

Alice shrugged. "Well, she doesn't put her stuff away, either." What nice shiny white teeth the man had. The better to eat you with, my dear. She wouldn't mind playing Little Red Riding Hood with him any time at all.

In the bookstore, Tom had to squeeze past more clumps of kids than he had ever seen at one time in here. Mary Anne was behind the register. He'd give her the note on the way out.

That Alice was cute but a bit of a birdbrain. In a way, she looked a little like Sarah, but the likeness ended there. Alice had a lot fewer grey cells. Girls like her were a bit of a bore after fifteen minutes. Unlike Sarah. He could talk to her for hours.

He remembered how excited she'd been when talking of Aiken. He turned to find himself facing the object of his thoughts, at least he faced Sarah's back. He tapped her on the shoulder. "Hi. Talk of the devil, excuse me, angel, I was just thinking about you."

Sarah's books slipped in her arms. "Oh, hi! Didn't expect to run into you!" Blushing, she added, "I had to pick up some stuff for Jenny."

He surveyed the long blond hair, comparing it to Liz's red. Fire and ice. The comparison and reflection surprised yet intrigued him. Liz had evoked a feeling of excitement. Around Sarah, he felt not cold, but calm, perhaps a communion. And a certain sympathy. Not pity, understanding. He thought underneath her reserve was a Sarah who hid from herself and from the world.

Beauty like hers was impressive and the passion for ownership so often passed with a male as the passion of love. It must be awful not to be able to trust.

He said, "Just so you know, I had lunch with Liz." Might as well get it out into the open. Clear the air.

"Oh."

She looked as though she expected him to break down or something. He said quickly, "I hope she'll be happy," then added, "I had to pick up some supplies. As a matter of fact—" He shook the envelope and nodded toward Mary Anne. "From Alice. When you see her, tell her it was delivered in an expeditious and noble fashion, will you?"

"All of that, hmm?"

Her smile brought a big one to his own lips. He motioned at the books in her hand. "All done? We can get in line together. Looks like it may be a while and I can't think of anyone I'd rather pass the time with." He waved toward the register where ten students waited, took her arm and got behind her in the file.

"I can't think of anyone . . ." He'd said that. It took a while for her brain to function again. When it did, she said, "When I first saw you here, you said you were thinking of me. Was that bad or good?" She breathed a silent prayer, Please, Lord, yes!

"I couldn't help but compare you to Alice. Two minutes with her and I'd be asleep. I like a few brains in the girl I talk to."

Did his smile say more than that? Sarah scolded her heart for leaping, and checked to see that her fences were still up. "You have to be the only guy on campus who does like brains in a woman. Maybe in the world!" But in spite of herself, inside that fenced-off place, her head spun with pleasure. She warned herself again not to get her hopes up. It wasn't yet time to open the gate or cut the wires. He was still in love with Liz.

Liz. Darn. Sorely tempted to ask what he thought of

248

Liz's brains, she bit her tongue. It was a stupid question prompted by jealousy. Funny, Liz had often said how she envied her, but Sarah had never really believed it. Often enough, though, she'd wished for Liz's red hair, that acceptance by guys. And it had been hard to watch her with Tom.

"A penny for your thoughts!"

"Oh." She wrinkled her nose at her less than sparkling wit. You're just full of snappy comebacks today!

Tom laughed aloud. "If they make you turn up your nose, perhaps I won't press the question."

She could feel herself turn beet-red. Thankfully he pointed to the cashier. She plunked down her books, paid quickly, gave Tom a weak smile, said "See you," and ran, not walked, to the door. She thought she could hear his laughter every step of the way.

Tom found himself whistling "We'll Meet Again" as he left the store. Funny that song should pop into his head. Hadn't heard it for years now. Tokyo Rose used to play it, the Ink Spots. He tried to imitate the one with the low voice, then the high. Well, so he couldn't sing. It was a beautiful day, wasn't it? How could that be so with Liz gone?

Chapter 25

Sarah leaned out of the dorm room window. Tomorrow would be April Fool's Day but the weather didn't look as though it had any tricks in store. Here and there, frothy tails of clouds scudded across the stars spattering the dusk. The air held the scent and promise of an early spring.

She pulled back. "Maybe I'll walk over to the library."

From her corner on the bed Liz teased, "Tom?"

"No such luck. Funny you should say that, though. Everywhere I go, he's there."

"Bragging or complaining?"

"Certainly not complaining, but it's strange, almost like he's following me."

Liz sang a few bars of "I Can Dream, Can't I?"

Sarah picked it up and danced a few steps.

"You should be a singer."

Sarah shrugged. "Frankie and I. I did think about joining the glee club, only no one I know is in it. You don't suppose Tom can sing, do you?" She went to the closet and reached for a cardigan.

"Believe me, he can barely carry a tune, so you can forget that. He used to kind of whisper the words when we danced. If I were you, I'd find something to talk about or make him believe you are so wrapped in the moment, you don't want a distraction. And, speaking of Tom, when are you going to invite him to the Sadie Hawkins dance?"

Sarah threw the cardigan on her bed and sat on it. She

chewed her lip. "It's probably too late now. He'll already have a date."

"Nope. He doesn't."

Her heart skipped. "Really? How do you know?" She knew exactly what she could wear. Jumping up, she went to the closet again and began pushing hangers back and forth on the rod. "I don't know how this thing gets so full. I'm always taking things home."

"And bringing them back."

"Yeah. Well . . ." She couldn't argue with that. It had been a whole new suitcase last time. She did more shoving, then pulled out a white off-the-shoulder blouse. "Perfect. Just like Daisy Mae."

Liz nodded. "I know he hasn't got a date because Alice said . . ."

"Alice? Why should she know? Did she just ask him? Does she plan to invite him?"

"She has Perspective with him. She keeps me informed, just in case I might be worrying about him and his broken heart. At least that's what she says. But you're right, 'Methinks she doth protest too much.' "

Tom had discounted Alice as a birdbrain, but still thought she was cute. How many other Alice's had their eye on Tom?

"According to Alice, she told him about the guy she was thinking about asking, just to see what he'd say. I don't know what she expected him to do, but he only told her he wasn't going."

Sarah's heart did a little dip. Was that good news or bad? "Do you suppose he doesn't want to go at all?"

Liz threw up her hands and glared at her. "For Pete's sake, girl, go call him. If you don't, someone else will. There's already a line and I think dear Alice would like to be at the head of it. If not her, I know Mary Anne is interested."

"I don't want him to think I'm after him! Especially since I keep running into him all the time. He might think that's on purpose and I really am chasing him."

Liz threw the pillow at her. "Get. He hasn't a date. Yet! You can chase all you want right now. This is the Sadie Hawkins dance. It's the one time we can ask." She drew her knees up and rested her chin on them. "You know, we need to invent a few more days like this. There's only leap year and this thing. It's not fair. We always have to wait for them."

Sarah couldn't help but feel the guy's part wasn't always that easy. What with them being afraid to ask her, she probably hadn't said no too many times, but for them it had to be an unnerving risk. If the tables were turned? "I don't know. It would be terrible to hear someone you liked say no. And it'll be awful if he says it now."

"I just may strangle you if you don't get to that phone!"

Sarah stuck out her tongue and tossed the pillow back. She picked up the blouse, took it to the mirror and held it up. "Maybe I will call him. I can go to the library tomorrow. That history book will still be there. Of course, if I go and he's there again, I won't have to call."

The white lump sailed by her head again. She ducked. "I'm going! I'm going!"

She stood for a moment with her hand on the knob, eyes closed, then opened the door and carefully looked into the hall. No one. Even Mary Anne's door was shut. "Here goes nothing."

She dialed Sigma Chi's number.

"Granny's house. Wolf speaking." Ray's rather high-pitched voice clearly identified him.

252

She tried to sound businesslike. "Tom Butler, please."

"Hi, Sarah."

She heaved a sigh. "How do you know it's me?"

"Sarah, my love, I'd know those mellifluous tones anywhere. If I hadn't met Jenny first I'd make you my very own project. You did say Tom?"

Sarah could hear him laugh and grunt as he tussled with someone. He was a nut. He and Jenny made a good pair. From his end, there was a short silence then more grunts and puffs. Ray came back laughing. He could hardly get the words out. "You can't—talk to him." He wheezed. "He won't pay—my price." His laughter grew fainter. She heard him say, "Pony up!"

Her mind and her pulse raced. Had she embarrassed Tom? She should have waited until class tomorrow. But then someone else might . . .

"Hello, Sarah?"

Tom actually sounded pleased and he was still laughing a bit. She stifled a sigh of relief. "Hi, I hope I haven't interrupted anything."

"No. As a matter of fact, when I heard Ray say 'Sarah,' I crossed my fingers. I rather hope you're calling to invite me to that Sadie Hawkins thing."

She gulped and blushed even though he couldn't see her. "Well, I . . ." His soft laughter traveled the line and brushed her ear with euphoria. "As a matter of . . ."

He didn't wait. "Alice has the room next to yours, right?"

Alice again! What did Miss Nibbynose have to do with anything? Sarah hesitated, took a deep breath and admitted, "Yes."

"She hinted around this afternoon, asking me if I had a date. When I didn't take the bait, she told me whom she planned to ask." He sounded as though he were pleased. "She also said very clearly that she didn't think you had asked anyone."

Sarah gripped the phone hard. That Alice! How could she? I'll choke her!

Tom's laugh came again. He said, "I am waiting. Do I have a date or am I embarrassed?"

She opened her mouth then clamped it quickly shut. She'd almost said, "Oh, Tom, I love you!" She did say, "That's why I called."

"Thank Alice for me!"

"I'll choke her! That's what I'll do."

"Just don't use your own scarf! Too obvious and then you'd miss the dance." He was still laughing when she hung up.

For Sarah, the week lumbered by like an elephant in quicksand. But even that had its advantages. It seemed Tom was constantly there. At noon on Tuesday he asked her to the movie, a rerun of the old *Blood and Sand*. She'd said she liked Tyrone Power. If she hadn't seen it before, she wouldn't have been able to tell the story afterward.

Not that Tom had tried to neck. He'd put his arm about her shoulder and then, in the car, given her a light kiss before he let her out. Better than nothing, but just barely!

Now, Saturday evening in the dorm room, Liz, from her place behind Sarah's chair, gave her hair a gentle yank. "Hold still, girl. I'll never get these braids done."

"Sorry, I was thinking."

Liz laughed. "I can't imagine about whom."

Sarah raised her chin. "What makes you so sure it's him?"

Liz gave her a playful yank again. "Well, if it were anyone but you, the answer would be easy. But you really might be thinking about calculus or that Mark whatever of yours." Liz grinned and chanted, "Tom, Tom, the piper's son . . ." She sighed and looked forlorn. "I envy you. Wish Alan were here."

"You will see him next weekend."

She brightened. "Mom insisted I cut classes Friday and go down. Talk wedding."

"And he'll be there, won't he?"

"Mmmmmmm. Can't wait."

Sarah turned to smile at her, making Liz drop the length of hair.

"Sarah!" She picked up the strands and deftly wove them back. "Not too much damage. There."

"I'm sorry."

Liz put a rubber band around the end and reached for the ribbon. She draped the braids with their bows in front and turned Sarah to face the mirror. "Al Capp should see you. Couldn't have a better model. Here." She stuck one of the daisies Tom had sent into each braid. "That guy always picks out such neat flowers." She stepped back. "Perfect. You're a shoo-in for Daisy Mae. Wouldn't it be great if Tom gets Li'l Abner!"

"You know Alice has been saying that all week to me. It's as though she wants me to think she's pushing me at Tom, but I get the distinct impression she really wants me to keep going right on past so that she'll be next in line!"

Liz brushed at her own shoulders. "Well, if I didn't have Alan . . ." Then she grinned. "I did have my chance, didn't I?"

Sarah turned and hugged her. "I hope you'll be happy. Alan's really nice. Maybe he's not only being old-fashioned.

With him moving around, a career for you would be a big problem."

Liz looked around the room. "I'll miss this. But, hey, I'll be with him. Europe, too. He says he'll teach me to ski!"

"Just don't try the Matterhorn first . . ."

The girl on duty in the lobby stuck her head through the doorway. "Tom's here." She went on down the hall to enlighten others.

Liz hugged her, handed her a sweater and a shove. "You look swell."

Her looks weren't really what Sarah thought about as she went down the two flights of stairs. She wanted a real kiss tonight, not just another peck on the cheek. That was just a warm-up. Now, the one that Tyrone Power had given Linda Darnell, that was a kiss!

Tom's smile, when she reached the last step, pushed Tyrone from her mind. He shook his head at her. "Li'l Abner's a fool. Should have grabbed that gal and carried her off a long time ago."

She touched her braid. "Thanks for the flowers. Do you really like it?" Part of "it" was a skirt she'd cut short in Daisy's uneven hemline.

"Well, Li'l Abner's always been afraid to say, 'I do,' but he just might if he saw you." He reached out, took her hand and led her outside. "Left my mule back in the barn. Thought we might jest amble over them thar hills tonight." He stopped suddenly and gave her another of those quick kisses.

Even that light touch of his lips on hers sent the world spinning backward. The starry night turned sunny. She closed her eyes and tried to hold the glow, but it slipped away. Too quickly.

Tom stopped when they reached the doorway. "It shore

do look lak Dogpatch, Daisy."

"The Alpha Phi's have done a great job, haven't they?" Cardboard had been painted to look like rough wooden shacks. Here and there, fencing off the space for chairs, old wood zigged and zagged as though built by a drunken or short-legged hillbilly. A one-person, three-sided shack with a moon cut into the door took up one corner.

Tom drew her around to the open back of it and ignored the wood box seat with the requisite hole in it.

She tried to ignore it, too, but it wasn't until his lips came firmly down on hers that she managed it. This time, there was no gentle glow. His lips lit a flame that could have set the shack on fire had she not quickly squelched its intensity. She pulled reluctantly away. If so gentle a kiss warmed her, what would happen if he kissed her like Tyrone Power?

From behind them, Ray cleared his throat.

Tom drew back, took her hand to draw her out of the shack. "Jest thought I'd do what Li'l Abner never got around to. Always seemed a shame to let that gal go unkissed." He gave Ray a mock frown. "As for you, you're worse'n that Joe with the rain cloud over his head. Jest spoilin' the fun!"

Jenny pulled Ray away. "C'mon, Joe Beefsteak!" She gave Sarah a wink. "That's as close as I can come to that name."

Tom led Sarah onto the floor. She couldn't help but notice the heads turn, the questions and smiles on the faces, as she passed. For one of the few times since she'd grown up, she didn't mind the attention. She was with Tom. Tom was no trophy hunter.

For a while the orchestra seemed to be stuck in Dogpatch with songs like "Springtime in the Rockies," "A-Feudin', a-Fussin' and a-Fightin' " and even the old "I'll

Be Comin' Round the Mountain."

They finally settled into real dance music, "Stormy Weather." This was one where you could pretend you were gliding while all the time you got to stand almost still and weave in his arms.

As Liz had said he might, Tom tried to hum. Laughing, Sarah drew back. "Maybe we ought to leave this one for Lena Horne."

"My sister used to say I had such a tin ear, I didn't even know how bad I sounded." He drew her close again and went back to the gentle swaying. He rested his cheek against her forehead. "But I forget myself sometimes. Singing and happiness just sort of go together."

She closed her eyes. "I like happiness and silence, myself." She could feel the muscles of his cheek move in a smile. For the next two dances, she had both.

Until an elbow caught her in the ribs. Rick! And Ann! She turned quickly back to Tom. The orchestra played "Dancing Cheek to Cheek." Even Rick could not spoil this.

Sometime in the middle of her glow, the voice of a girl she knew to be an Alpha Phi said, "Good evening, chilluns. On behalf of the Alpha Phi Sorority, welcome to Dogpatch. The leaders of this here town council have picked us a Daisy Mae for 1945–46. So, let's have a hand for a little lady I think every male in Dogpatch would like to claim as a kissin' cousin, Sarah Johnson."

Tom squeezed her hand, whispered, "I knew it would be you," and holding her hand tightly, led her to the bandstand.

With her hand in his, she'd be happy about anything. The crowd smiled and applauded. Someone said, "Yup. A right pretty un." From the back of the crowd a voice said, "Hey, Cousin Daisy, ahl be ryte pleased to come'n greet yer, please ma'am."

When the laughter quieted, the MC said, "She is already spoken for, for this next dance, anyways." She pointed.

Sarah held her breath. Surely it would be no one but Tom.

The MC waved her hand at the kibitzers. "As y'all know, for this next dance, she's spoken for by our own Li'l Abner. Rick Jason, come an' git her!"

Sarah wanted to disappear through the floor. Perhaps she'd heard wrong. Anyone but him. But no, there he was. He even had the gall to look like the rangy cartoon figure.

She tried to smile at the crowd but could not unclench her teeth.

The orchestra leader raised his baton and asked Rick, "Any requests for Daisy here?"

"Since it's for Daisy, how about that old waltz, 'Bicycle Built for Two'?" He added, "If that's not too antediluvian for you," and preened at Sarah as though to say, "See, I know big words, too." Ignoring the glare of the band leader, he offered her his arm. "All for the love of you, Miss Daisy."

She sniffed but took it. "So you do know at least one word with more than four letters. How grown-up can we get!"

"You haven't changed, have you? Always uppity. Let's call a truce. I still think you're the most beautiful girl I've ever seen."

She sighed. If he didn't know by this time why she disliked him so much, he never would. She looked over his shoulder to find Tom.

Tom gave her a thumbs-up, and shook his head slightly. He turned away into the outstretched arms of Ann.

Rick said, "Sarah?"

259

She dug her fingers into his arm and looked back at Tom. Ann smiled at her.

Sarah let go of Rick's arm but he drew her close.

She pulled back and looked for Tom again. Ann's head lay on his shoulder.

Rick tugged at her waist. "I knew they'd pick you for Daisy. That's why I got all rigged out like this."

She sniffed. "They only picked you because you're the bi-i-g basketball star."

"I don't know why you're so mad at me. We made a great couple."

"Oh? That's why you got hooked on Ann's claws then?"

"I have to date someone." He laughed. "She's got a lot going for her."

"I'm sure she has." She added silently, She'd better just keep going with it, too.

The orchestra finished the tune, laid down their instruments and went for a break.

She couldn't see Tom at all. Nor Ann.

Chapter 26

The moment the song was over, Sarah fled from Rick. He would never change and there was nothing she needed or wanted to say.

From the edge of the floor, she searched for Tom. Perhaps he had just stepped out into the hall. But Ann wasn't around, either.

Someone had put a record on to fill in for the orchestra and the words of "Baby, It's Cold Outside" found a roost in the back of Sarah's mind. The sick feeling in the pit of her stomach told her it wasn't the temperature, it was being once more on the outside. She'd have thought she would be used to it, but somehow, being alone never got warmer.

She edged slowly toward the back of the gym where her sweater lay on a chair. Something to do to keep from looking like a wallflower. Where had Tom gone? Where was Ann?

Sarah snatched the sweater and moved toward the door to the fire escape. It would be dark out there. She hated to be seen standing at the edges of things looking on. She scanned the floor again, then eased the door open to go out.

The light, dim as it was, spilled out on to the forms of Tom and Ann. He stood with his back to the door, she facing him with her arms around his neck. Pink-tipped fingernails glinted from Ann's interlocked fingers.

Sarah gasped. She stood, still inside the gym, trying to control the anger that ricocheted within her like the ball in the pinball machine. She let go of the door but could not manage to move away.

The door opened as quickly as it had closed. Ann grabbed her arm. "Sarah. Just the person we were talking about. Come on out and join us." Her smirk begged to be wiped off.

Sarah jerked her arm away. She'd never have thought that Tom, of all people, would be like Rick. She didn't need one Rick, certainly not two. If he was like that, little old Dagger Nails could have him.

She said, "I think I'd like to go back to the dorm," then wished she hadn't. She certainly didn't want him to walk her back.

"Sarah, I . . ." He reached for her but she shrank from him.

Ann interrupted with a laugh. "Don't worry. We weren't making out!" The glint in her eyes could have either denied it or wished it so.

Tom gave Ann a black look. "We were talking."

Ann cooed, "I was just telling him what Alice told me!"

Sarah stepped back. "Please, I . . ." Even in the dark she could see that Tom glared at the girl.

The look didn't stop Ann. "Alice said you all plotted to . . ."

Tom snapped, "Shut up, Ann," and stepped from the fire escape into the gym. This time he didn't let go when she backed off, but gently maneuvered her back outside.

Ann stayed in the open doorway.

Sarah glared at Ann. "What does she mean? What did Alice say?"

He stepped between them. "It's stupid. You don't want to know."

Ann snickered then purred, "Not so stupid. Alice said

the five of you had it fixed up between you. He was supposed to be heartbroken and you were supposed to mend it
by just being around all the time. They spied for you to let
you know his every move so you could follow him." She
tossed her head and smirked, "Could have fooled him," and
flounced off.

Furious with Ann, confused by the accusation and mor-
tified by what he must think of her, if she had been cold before, she shivered now. But I didn't. I wouldn't. How could
he believe it? Her thoughts whirled. Yet, all of those times,
all of those meetings! She'd thought more than once how
odd it was that she so consistently ran into him, but BG was
a small campus. It could have been coincidence.

But it wasn't. Hadn't been. It had been all arranged. For
a moment she thought she might throw up. She fled back
into the gym. She had to get away.

"Sarah! Stop! It's not . . ."

She didn't turn. She knew he followed.

A couple stopped in front of her, and she had to back-
track. From the corner of her eye she saw Ann step in front
of Tom. He sidestepped, but it gave Sarah time to melt into
the crowd in the hall and get away.

Outside she ran around the corner of the gym building.
Trembling with anger, she pressed herself against the cold
wall. How could he believe she would do such a thing? And
who had arranged what? Which five? Alice obviously. Me?
How did I get mixed up in this? Who were the others, and
why? Certainly not Liz. Or was it?

Above the din of her heart, she heard him call again,
"Sar-ah, Sarah!" She flattened herself against the wall. She
couldn't face him. If that's what he thought . . .

All her life she'd been so careful of her reputation. From
the time she was a baby her mother had gone on and on

263

about it. She'd never say what the dark secret was, but there had been some family tragedy that moved her mother's lips to a grim, thin line when anything the least threatening came along.

Anger at the injustice of the accusation brought an unaccustomed flash of pride. As if she needed to go chasing a man! Unconsciously, her hand moved to her face. If she wanted to play games by using her looks, she probably could have her pick of guys, but she could never endure that kind of relationship.

Even as a child she'd hated that kind of attention with people poking each other and whispering, "Isn't she beautiful?" She used to wonder if they thought she was deaf or something. But then, maybe they'd wanted her to hear.

She supposed most people would think she'd be pleased, but when you wanted someone to love you with a torn dress and mud on your face, that other kind of admiration wasn't enough. What would they have done if she'd been born ugly? Ignored her just as they had petted her?

"Sarah, please!" This time Tom's voice was louder. "It's not important . . ."

Not to him, maybe. But he had believed it. How could he think . . . ? Oh! She slipped into the shadow of a doorway. A weak light from the front haloed him as he walked past the corner of the building. He searched the darkness and for a moment he seemed to look directly at her. Her knees turned to rubber.

He scratched his head and went back around the building. She heard his shoes crunch against the cement. Going away.

She let her breath out and eased toward the far corner. She could see him plainly in the glow of the lamps, perhaps headed toward Kohl. Oddly enough, he seemed forlorn.

But that couldn't be true. What had he to be sad about? Except maybe Liz.

She watched, then a shadow among shadows, followed him. Sooner or later he had to go away. Sooner, she hoped. She was cold and wanted to go in, get in bed and never get out again.

The wind had picked up and lapped at her legs, bared to the chill because she had cut up a perfectly good skirt for him! She crossed her arms and hugged herself.

Furious with Ann, worried about Sarah, Tom walked swiftly toward Kohl. She could hardly have reached there yet. She hadn't time. Yet he couldn't see her anywhere. He doubted that she'd still be in the gym. She must have fled to her room. He might have caught her if only that stupid Ann hadn't gotten in his way.

Ann's laughter had followed him across the floor, the peals rising and falling with the click of his heels on the hard wood and down the stairs. Slut! She and Rick deserved each other. Why take it out on Sarah?

He had not yet begun to deal with what Ann had told him. Was it so terrible if it were true? Deceptive. From what he knew of Sarah, she was not that. Funny how guilty she looked, though. But when it came down to it, was it guilt or embarrassment? Or both?

He stopped and turned in a circle. Where could she be? No sign of her. The wind had set the trees and bushes rocking, washing shadows back and forth over the lawn between the buildings. He peered into them, searching, but they were too insubstantial to be Sarah.

He still had no sight of her by the time he reached the dorm. This late, he didn't dare go crashing in, demanding to talk to her. But she couldn't possibly be here already. He would have seen her. He stopped and sat on the top of the stairs, close to the small wall that guarded them. At least it cut down the wind.

When had his life become so complicated? Perhaps he should have stayed in the Navy, never accepted his discharge. A sailor at least could stay away from women or have a girl in every port. Liz, of course, had been his own fault. He'd known the chances were slim that he'd win her. He'd tried because he was a "trier," and he very often got what he wanted. If he had won . . . He couldn't help smiling a little. The chase'd had its moments.

He shifted closer to the wall. Where was Sarah? If she was upstairs already, she moved faster than a bell-bottom with a cigarette when an admiral showed.

Perhaps it had only been the prize out of reach that made Liz so enticing. In his mind he placed Sarah's face beside Liz's. In spite of the promised fire in Liz's copper hair and dark eyes, when it came to sheer beauty, Sarah's face won hands down. Trouble was, such perfection often forged a screen, one that made it hard for a guy to see the person behind it.

She seemed to be gentle, yet he sensed iron, toughness. The gentle Sarah might not be the real Sarah. He pictured her studying his drawings at Harvey's that day he and Liz had split. There had been understanding there, between him and Sarah. He smiled at the memory. She was like a piece of silk, soft but strong.

But, was she tough enough to play the game Ann accused her of? In a way, the whole idea was funny. Five girls out to trap him for her? A soft chuckle escaped him. He thought about his sisters. He'd overheard their chatter often enough, about how to get this fellow or that without letting him know. They thought the guys had the upper hand, but then they didn't understand. How would they like to have to try to read those signals, the smiles, the lack of them, the invitation in the eyes which wasn't after all an invitation, only a trick of light? Tell the difference between the hip that swayed and the one that perhaps only moved naturally in a slow walk?

Sarah was one who would hold her self-respect dearly. Ann's story did not ring true.

If it did, did it matter? If she were, well, Alice, he might have been irritated, felt pushed. With that Ann, downright alarmed. But Sarah?

The idea that she liked him for more than a casual friend, the father figure who only gave her encouragement, winked pleasantly from the tangle of thoughts in his mind. He wasn't quite old enough for daddy yet. That was okay when she was Liz's friend, but now he was free. And so was she. Just like any other girl. If any other girl could be like her.

The clear air and night wind carried the sound of voices from the direction of the gym. Was the dance over? If she was not already upstairs, she would have to come. He would wait.

Sarah could see his head above the stair wall. Wouldn't he ever move? How could she get in? She turned toward the voices from the gym. Two couples. Not even near each other. Please God, send me a big group!

Oh! Anger flared again. How could he believe such a thing? And it did matter that he would think it. If he could believe she was like that, he'd never respect her. She didn't want some guy who thought she was fast.

But how could she get past him without having to talk to him?

She looked again at the second couple walking toward her. Alice and her date, Delbert something! Great! She knew what she could do.

Alice stopped beside her. "Sarah? Where's Tom? What are you doing out here?"

Had there been too much eagerness in that question? Sarah opened her mouth then closed it. In her anxiety to get help, she'd forgotten Alice had been the traitor who . . . She'd take care of dear Alice and her friends later. Now she had to get into the dorm. She nodded toward Tom's figure on the stairs. "Go talk to him, so I can get inside."

Again, did Alice grin? Sarah couldn't be sure but the voice this time definitely struggled to keep from showing pleasure. "Oh. Did you guys have a fight or something?"

Sarah clenched her teeth. Traitor! She wanted badly to tell her she could have him if she wanted him so much, but poor Delbert looked so shy, he'd probably bolt. Sarah stifled a sigh. "It's a long story. I just need you to distract him. Go stand on this side of the stairs where he'll have to look down over the wall at you. Tell him you saw me inside the gym or something, anything. Just keep him talking until I get in the door."

"But he'll see you."

"No. I'll go around back and come up behind him while he's looking at you. Please?" How that please grated.

Alice grinned. "Anything for a friend. C'mon." She grabbed Delbert's hand.

Sarah waited for a moment then circled around Kohl. From the corner, she could hear Tom and barely made out Alice's words. Tom said, "She's still at the gym?" Even to her he sounded doubtful, but it didn't matter. Another couple had just reached the stairs. Perfect.

Almost.

The boy said, "Hi, Tom. Swell dance, wasn't it?"

Sarah quickly ducked below the far wall of the stairs. Darn!

Tom must have turned but Sarah only heard his "Yeah." He went back to talking to Alice and her date.

She took off her shoes and ran quickly up the stairs.

Just before the door closed she heard, "Sarah! Wait!"

Chapter 27

For the next three days, Sarah hung around the dorm except for classes. For once, she wished she'd gone to some major university like Ohio State. BG just wasn't big enough to hide in. On Monday he'd waited at the door of her calculus class. She saw him in time and lurked around the corner until the bell rang, then, using one of the other kids as a shield, dashed past him.

She could easily have touched him.

"Sarah, please . . ."

She ducked her head and scooted to the back of the room. She stood there for a moment, until the prof raised an eyebrow at her. "Miss Johnson, I believe the coast is clear now. You may take your seat."

The class laughed, but it was a gentle laugh.

She blushed furiously, and scooted into her seat in the middle row. She didn't dare look at the doorway. Tom had to be gone. But now the prof knew. The whole class knew whom she'd hidden from.

With a slight smile that said, "We've all been through it," he turned back to the class. "I gave you a special problem for last night's lesson, a tricky one. Did any of you have trouble with it?"

She hadn't but, with a forest of hands waving, Sarah relaxed and tried to lose herself in the order and safety of math.

She'd wanted so much to reach out and touch him as she'd passed. She could have, but hadn't even looked him in the face. Nor, in spite of the ache, did she intend to. Ever. How could she if he thought . . .

She gripped her pen and made herself concentrate on the easier problems on her desk. Gradually the math drew her into its special web and for the rest of the class she forgot him.

On Tuesday she cornered Liz in the dorm with the name of a book written on paper. "I don't want to go out, but I need this at the library. Would you please, please, get it for me?"

Liz had not been helpful about this hiding routine. She kept nagging. Now she said it for the umpteenth time: "You've got to face him sooner or late. Besides, you're being silly. The poor guy is spending all his time trying to get to you. You don't answer his calls or anything. He's going to give up." Liz sniffed, obviously irritated at what she called Sarah's "stupid pride."

Sarah stormed out of the room. Good, let him give up. That was what she wanted, wasn't it? She also wanted to cry.

She went to sit in the lounge at the corner of the hall. Didn't anyone understand how awful she felt? Angry at herself for allowing herself to be set up, she turned the anger on him.

The heavy thump of her heart asserted that Tom was not a trophy hunter and girl chaser. But what was she to think? Had he waited for even one dance to end to reclaim her? No. He'd not only danced with that Ann, but he'd gone out on the balcony with her! Her, of all people! How could he?

Her basic honesty asserted that perhaps things had not been what they seemed. Had he tried to shove Miss Witch with her pink fingernails away? It hadn't looked like it. He'd probably been just revving up to take off! And if he thought she would stoop so low as to chase him, well, he had another think coming. She slapped down every pro-Tom thought that dared show its face. Who did he think he was anyway? Whom? Who cared? Why should she sit here fuming over him?

She looked at her watch. Seven. She had a paper for English and needed the stupid book. If Liz wouldn't help her, she'd have to go herself. Why should she let some guy keep her a prisoner in the dorm? She raised her head. I hate men!

A shadow of a smile, of flashing white teeth, of a quick glimmer in gentle eyes, came to call her a liar.

No. She didn't hate anyone. Well, how about Ann? That was different. Ann was a witch. Sarah wanted to cry for the idiocy of it all. She rose and went to find her library card. She had to go.

It seemed a quarter of the student body congregated on the steps, another quarter inside. Her paper had to be a biography and she'd chosen Copernicus. Trouble was, what kind of angle could make that new? If he'd been a woman, his brains would have been wasted. The men would have laughed and said a woman couldn't possibly understand such things.

She wondered how many events had been delayed or missed because the key lay in a woman's head. That would make an interesting paper if one could prove it. Something besides the same old thing. Well, if there were such things, she hadn't the time to research them.

She'd like to do the paper on Aiken, but then there probably wasn't that much out there. She wondered if *Life* magazine had done anything on him. Probably only some dull articles in technical magazines.

She resigned herself to Copernicus. The church angle always made for controversy if nothing else. She reached for a book on Galileo to see what parallels she could make, if any.

As she closed her hand on the book, a large male hand covered hers. A big arm went around her shoulder and pulled her close. Firm, warm lips covered hers. Sounds of soft laughter and approval surrounded them but he didn't stop.

There was no way she could fight the warmth of his lips, the comfort of the arms now that he held her. The warm, lovely flush of delight chased away her resistance.

After what seemed ages, or only seconds, she wasn't sure, Tom let go and smiled at her. "You can't hide from me forever. I knew you'd have to come here."

She looked quickly down at the floor and had to fumble in her pocket for a tissue.

"Come on. This can wait." He raised her chin and dried the tear that glinted on her cheek. He didn't let go of her hand until they were through the crowd, out of the library and at the verge of grass in front of the cemetery.

For her own part, elation, confusion, a remnant of anger, anger that lessened by the moment—all kept her silent. Would he believe her if she said she hadn't followed him? Hadn't set him up? He certainly didn't seem angry about it.

A small voice inside her admitted that maybe Liz had been right when she'd said, "He must be really serious. Look how hard he's tried to get to you. How long he's waited!"

Lest she give in too easily, another voice snapped, "He deserved it. What about Ann?"

He stopped at the fence and took her in his arms. "You've got it all wrong."

273

The last remnant in the wall of anger crumbled into a dust finer than the sands of the Sahara. She stayed in his arms for a moment, warm and safe and happy. Finally she drew back. He had to understand she hadn't even known about the scheme.

She said, "It's not true. I never did that." She knew that didn't make sense, but she also knew he understood exactly what she meant.

"It wouldn't be so awful if you did. But then, I never really believed it. It's not the kind of thing you'd set up. Besides, Alice finally told me they'd done it behind your back." He leaned toward her and kissed her on the cheek.

She gasped. "Why didn't you tell me?"

His laughter came with a roar. "What do you think I've been trying to do for the last three days?"

She gulped. All that trouble to avoid him and he'd never believed it? That she'd do that? A flood of relief lifted her two feet off the ground, quickly replaced by a flood of embarrassment for her stupidity in not trusting him.

As for Alice and whoever, she'd deal with them later.

She opened her mouth to tell him how sorry she was she had been so difficult but he didn't wait for words. He kissed her again. She knew it wasn't relief this time that lifted her spirits two feet above her head.

His lips didn't search for any answers. His lips told her he loved her.

Hers answered with all the longing and aching that had been building and building since . . . maybe even the first time she saw him, when she'd been with dumb Rick, when Tom had been so sweet to Liz.

The thought of Liz, of Rick, brought Ann in their train, bright fingernails around Tom's neck. She tried to brush it away but the image lingered. He had not even been waiting when the dance had finished. Better to have it out. But she didn't move her head from its nest against his cheek as she asked, "What about Ann?"

She thought his voice smiled as he said, "It wasn't what you thought. I mean, you didn't see what you thought you saw."

"I saw the two of you out on a dark balcony with her arms around you."

"You didn't see how annoyed I was with her. When Rick claimed you, I intended to just stand and wait. Then she came up and grabbed my arm. I didn't want to be rude, so I danced. We were near the door when she said she had a big secret to tell me and pulled me toward the fire escape door. I told her I doubted that anything she had to say would interest me. She said she'd kiss me there in front of everyone if I didn't come with her. By that time, we were practically out the door. I went."

Innocence shone on his face, but laughter in his eyes. "I didn't put her arms around me, you know. I wasn't even touching her. That's when she said I'd been set up. And that's what you saw."

He took Sarah's hands and guided her until they both sat on the grass. "You should have known she's not my type."

In movies they always sing, don't they? Sarah's heart wanted to, but her mind and her lips didn't have time. His lips pressed against hers, warm, soft, so lovingly, persistently. Promising . . .

A girl's laughing voice from a passing bicycle said, "Hey, you two, no necking in public!"

Tom looked up, gave her a wave and turned back to Sarah. "That's her world. This one is only mine and yours." He finished the kiss.

Chapter 28

Sarah waited for the strains of the processional to begin. If this fairy-tale wedding were a promise, Liz and Alan should live happily ever after. She'd been a little surprised at the formality of it, but she shouldn't have been. Liz had done it for Mr. and Mrs. Bannerman, of course. Their guests outnumbered the Chases' about four to one.

Not that Liz minded, but Sarah thought Mrs. Chase seemed a bit sad. It wasn't the formality or the number of guests, though. Liz had said her mother had wanted her to wear the heavy Skinner satin, something Mrs. Chase had not worn. For her own part, Sarah thought the summery peau de soie, with its lacy high-rolled collar and long-waisted, slim skirt, was beautiful.

The late afternoon sun sat directly behind the stained-glass window over the altar and set it afire, drenching the guests and the floor with vibrant blues, reds and greens. From the loft the first notes rolled from the great pipe organ. The music picked up the sunbursts of color, gathered the smiles of the guests and lifted them all to fill the nave with a vibrant joy.

She gave a last glance at Liz who smoothed her skirt again, then flipped her hair to send it cascading behind the high-rolled lace collar. One strand resisted, coiling to lie on her shoulder like a red rose.

"And they lived happily ever after." That was what this day was all about, wasn't it? The movies proclaimed it. Sarah so hoped Liz would be happy.

The first pair of the six bridesmaids, Dottie and Jenny, stepped out. Their lavender blue was the darkest of the bridesmaids' dresses, each of the successive pairs a shade lighter, with the last, Sarah's, a pale blue. The skirts of the gowns wafted down the aisle like so many lilacs washing downstream.

Sarah raised her head, took a deep breath and sought Tom's eyes for courage. Thanks to Liz's insistence for Sarah's sake, and thanks to Alan's good nature, Tom was an usher. He stood now slightly off to one side, a little ahead of her.

He smiled back and for a moment, it could have been their wedding. But they had agreed to wait for their degrees. This one was for Liz.

Time. She gave her skirt a small flip to make sure it was free, then involuntarily sought Tom's eyes once more. He smiled again and she put her foot forward. Dear Lord, don't let me trip and spoil this.

When she reached the head of the aisle, she turned.

The flower girl, Liz's seven-year-old niece, tossed and scattered her petals as though she were a fairy sprite who had never done anything else. The ring bearer, Alan's six-year-old nephew, looked as though he wanted nothing so much as to bolt and run.

Sarah looked at Alan in his striped greys. He had eyes only for Liz. The "Wedding March" vibrated and hummed as she stepped out on the arm of her father. If expressions spoke, Alan's certainly said, "I love you."

"Who gives this bride . . ." Mr. Chase put Liz's hand in Alan's.

Sarah's hand itched for Tom's and she lost herself in her own daydreams until Liz roused her by handing her the bouquet. Yellow, of course. Alan always sent yellow roses.

Sometime in the middle of Sarah's dreaming, Liz spoke a soft, almost hesitant "I do," followed by a firm, yet somehow gentle "I do" from Alan, the rings, the kiss, and they were back down the aisle and out into the sunshine.

The picture-taking, the laughter, jokes and the interminable jockeying for the right spot, the right angle, seemed to take forever, but it did give Sarah a chance to once in a while slip her hand into Tom's. She wondered what he made of all this. Did he only wish it over or did he, too, put himself in the groom's place? The idea seemed to be that men went unwillingly into this foreign land, but she could not imagine that Tom was terrified of much.

Again, at the dinner, she found herself separated by the formalities from him. It wasn't until the dance band wailed the long slow first notes of "Stardust," and Liz was safely dancing in the arms of Alan, that Sarah had Tom all to herself. She pressed her head on his chest and reveled in the golden moments until more formalities, the cake and garter, took him away again.

She found herself standing at last with Dottie, a little aside from the sea of hands waving and signaling "me," "me," for the bridal bouquet.

Dottie quipped, "I don't need to catch that one, but why don't you?"

Sarah shook her head. "Degree first. We've agreed."

Dottie gave a quick soft sigh then grinned as she always had back at BG. "I'm not sorry, you know. Little Bobby is the most beautiful thing that's ever happened to me." She blushed. "Except for Big Bob."

"Your mom have the baby now?"

"She adores him. They're back at the hotel."

"Your dad okay with it?"

"He never said anything about the timing."

"Mothers and fathers surprise us sometimes."

Dottie hugged her, then turned and smiled at Bob. "Every time I lift little Bobby out of the bath and get that fresh soap and water smell right below his ears, I think I'm really lucky. And Bob is so good with him." She beamed. "Changes diapers like a pro. Maybe because he's older, been around. He said the baby and I made up for everything. He doesn't talk about it, but all that bravado he puts on about being a Marine sergeant, it's the only part of that experience he wants to hold on to."

Her dimple showed again. "He has some great funny stories he calls the 'Adventures of a Non-com in Yankee Noodle Land.' I keep telling him he ought to write a book, but then he just grits his teeth."

"You're happy then." It wasn't a question. Aside from the glow on Dottie's face, Sarah had seen them dancing together. There was a whole lot more to Bob than she and Liz had thought. "What about your acting? Will you get a chance?"

"I joined the theater group. You don't get good roles when you're six months' pregnant but I did get to help." She turned again and blew a kiss to Bob. "He says he'll baby-sit and Mom will help, so I will get to do a bit of my thing."

Jenny came and interrupted them. "You guys going to catch the bouquet?" She'd filled out a little, maybe from all the malts at BG, but even in the gathers of the dress, she managed to look like a blue popsicle.

Liz turned her back and raised the flowers above her head. The chorus of "me's" rose in volume.

Jenny said, "C'mon!" and ran toward the waving hands.

The bouquet came sailing straight at Sarah. Automatically she reached for it, then realizing what she was

279

doing, deflected it to Jenny who caught it with a whoop. She waved it triumphantly at Ray and headed toward him. As she passed them, she said, "Thanks, I'm gonna go and pin my little butterfly to the wall."

Liz's mom came up to interrupt their laughter. "Liz wants you two in the dressing room."

Sarah thought again that Mrs. Chase looked sad, but perhaps she was only tired. Sarah gave her a hug. The only thing she could think to say was the old bromide, "You haven't lost a daughter, you've gained a son."

Liz's mother smiled at her but it disappeared quickly. "That's what we raise you girls for, isn't it? So you'll grow up and go away?" She shook her head. "But not so far as Switzerland." She patted Dottie on the shoulder. "At least your mother will get to play with your baby."

She turned and hurried toward her husband.

When Sarah and Dottie got to the dressing room, Liz had tears in her eyes. "Mom's a bit upset."

Sarah handed her a tissue. "She can come visit you all over Europe. I think I could stand that." She bent over and picked up the shoes lying in the middle of the floor.

Dottie hooted. "Look who just did what!"

Sarah looked down at the shoes, laughed and held them out. "See, you thought I'd never change, didn't you?"

Dottie took them with that big grin. "I knew you were made of good stuff." She put them aside then handed Liz a pair of white gloves. "Looking for these?"

Sarah said, "We all have to grow up, don't we?"

The three of them drew together in a communal hug. Sarah hung on to Liz for a moment. "Be happy!" She still worried sometimes that Liz had not made the right decision. For herself, she knew she could not have given up her career. Thank God for Tom and his understanding, his encouragement. She was so lucky to have him.

She hoped that Liz's and Alan's love would be enough for her.

Liz drew on the gloves and gave Sarah a confident smile. "I shall be happy. It's my choice, you know. I intend to make the best of it."

She hugged Dottie. "I'm glad everything worked out for you."

Liz put her arm over Sarah's shoulders. "Darling, I really think this is right. Life is what we make of our choices, isn't it? I've had a lot of time to think now that I'm not running in circles to make up my mind, or trying to change Alan's. I knew it would be hard to practice psychology when he'll probably be all over the map. I just hated to give up. But now, I really think I'd just as soon be a writer. When I was down in Chillicothe that weekend, planning all this, I did a bit of it. I used to, you know."

She handed Sarah a folded piece of paper. "I wrote a poem and I have to say it is a bit corny, but I liked these lines and I wanted you to have them. So you'd understand."

Sarah started to unfold it and Liz covered her hands. "Not now, I've got to go."

They watched as she and Alan ran through the shower of rice and climbed into the Rolls at the curb. The fact that it was a Rolls had done nothing to deter their friends from plastering a "Just Married" sign to the bumper and adding a trail of tin cans.

Dottie laughed. "Hanging stuff on something like that is almost sacrilegious, isn't it?"

Sarah looked at the now-unfolded paper and said, "Mmmm." She read aloud the lines of the poetry written there:

With memories of dances left undone,
and wasted songs, their melodies unsung—
a stardust melody that lingers, bittersweet,
to speak of chances winked at, incomplete . . .

Below it Liz had written, *There are always regrets, no matter what choices we make.*

Sarah did not say her thoughts aloud. Dottie had not willingly chosen. For her there were already dances left undone, but she seemed to have made peace with her dreams.

Liz had chosen. Had she opted for second-best? Perhaps with courage, determination and love, second-best would be first and the song she sang might be more beautiful than those left silent.

For herself? Of the three, she seemed to have it all, didn't she? Tom, a man like no other, and a career, for she would have it despite the claim of some males that brains belonged only to them. For a fleeting moment she wondered what dances for her would be undone, what songs unsung? The thought came, Whatever they are, perhaps I shall never know or miss them. I think Liz is right when she says it is what we do with our choices, that counts.

About the Author

Patricia Abbott, transplanted from her native Southern Ohio, lives in Arlington, Texas, where five of her seven children make their home. She married and raised her family in Perrysburg, Ohio, where she worked for many years as an artist. Many of her paintings still hang in Ohio homes and corporations. The love of color reflected in her paintings shows in her writing, where she likes to weave images and make an emotional contact with the reader.

Her experience as a student, mother, long-distance operator, secretary and artist, is likely to show up in her novels.

If she could have one wish, it would be for another lifetime to do all the things there just is not time for in this one.